Praise for *Girl in Between*

'There's lots to enjoy about *Girl* ~~in~~ offbeat observational humour . . . style really shines.' —*The Sydney*

'Unapologetically populist, home kind of latter-day Bridget Jones.'

'*Girl in Between* is a fast, entertaining read with an endearing cast of characters . . . will have you laughing and maybe shedding a tear.' —*The Weekly Times*

'One of the most striking aspects of Anna Daniels' storytelling is the quintessential Australian flavouring throughout . . . A brilliant debut novel and certainly an author to keep an eye on. —*AusRom Today*

'Never have I laughed out loud so much while reading a book.' —My Books Are Me

'*Girl in Between* was so refreshingly delightful and quintessentially Australian. Often hilarious, but never overdone.' —Theresa Smith Writes

'Filled with great Aussie humour and witty charm.' —Hannah Plus Books

'*Girl in Between* is a love letter to many—to Australia, to Aussie English and to those who find themselves wondering where every-thing is all going. With its easily likeable heroine Lucy, this is a super fun read that crosses several countries but knows that home is where the heart is . . . If you enjoyed *The Castle*, you'll love the Aussie-ness of *Girl in Between*. —Sam Still Reading

'A book that will light up your life . . . the romance gets an A+' —21st Century Once Upon a Time

'A witty, sharp and funny story about what it feels like to be thirty and have no idea what you want to be when you grow up . . . perfect for anyone who's feeling uninspired or unmotivated. —A Girl & Grey

'Light and breezy . . . perfect for those lazy days sitting on the beach or at a café as the world goes by. —*GLAM Adelaide*

Girl IN Between

ANNA DANIELS

ALLEN&UNWIN

SYDNEY • MELBOURNE • AUCKLAND • LONDON

This edition published in 2018
First published in 2017

Allen & Unwin
83 Alexander Street
Crows Nest NSW 2065
Australia
Phone: (61 2) 8425 0100
Email: info@allenandunwin.com
Web: www.allenandunwin.com

A catalogue record for this
book is available from the
National Library of Australia

ISBN 978 1 76052 814 0

Internal design by Romina Panetta
Set in Sabon by Midland Typesetters, Australia
Printed in Australia by McPhersons Printing Group

10 9 8 7 6 5 4 3 2 1

The paper in this book is FSC® certified.
FSC® promotes environmentally responsible,
socially beneficial and economically viable
management of the world's forests.

For Mum and Dad.
And for my friend Ange—
we all love and miss you.

1

Far out, there's nothing like a trip to the family accountant to sober you up. I've just spent the last forty minutes calling out figures on faded receipts to Todd Doherty, who promised to get my tax return done asap so I don't have to exist on two-thirds of bugger-all. What's particularly mortifying is that Todd and I went to high school together, and while he's probably on a six-figure salary he's well aware that I'm flat out finding six bucks.

'Dire' is the word Todd used to describe my financial situation, although he did say it with a kindly smile, which I appreciated. If only I had assets that were appreciating. My trusty old Corolla, which I'm currently driving to my parents' house in Rockhampton, is my sole valuable possession—well, that and my *Anne of Green Gables* collection, and my kelpie, Glenda.

I weave along these wide streets like a dodgem car driver

with the rink to myself, knowing when I recount my morning to my bestie, Rosie, I'll get a great giggle from her.

Ah, Rocky. Our claims to fame are our wide streets, the fact that trains run down the centre of these wide streets, and that the roundabouts within these wide streets are dotted with statues of fibreglass bulls, as befits the Beef Capital of Australia.

Speaking of trains, there's one whizzing beside me now. I think Rocky is the only place on earth where trains just seem to sneak up and share the road with you. It's as if one moment they're all docked at the depot having a cappuccino, and the next they're tailgating you to Wah Hah Chinese.

I feel a sudden wave of nostalgia as I pass Paradise Plaza and get closer to home because nearly every corner holds a familiar story.

There's the Hungry Jack's that used to be a Cash Converters; the laneway beside the cinema where, as teenagers, we'd down West Coast Coolers; and Holy Mackerel the fish and chip shop where we bought dinner on Friday nights. Apparently the new owners of Holy Mackerel recently got done for selling drugs over the counter. Can you imagine? 'I'll have two pieces of battered snapper and five dollars' worth of chips.' Wink, wink.

Still, you'd be hard pressed to find more salt-of-the-earth, give-you-the-shirt-off-their-back, nylon-football-shorts-wearing people than those of Rockhampton. Mum and Dad are a classic case in point, though Dad doesn't wear football shorts, thank God. Forty years ago, the two of them started a combined newsagency and after-five dress shop called All About Town. Surprisingly, the combo worked, and eighteen months ago they sold up to a couple from Newcastle who'd promised to keep the business going but within six weeks had converted it into a waxing parlour called Gone Bush.

As I drive past the old shop building now, a rush of memories comes flooding back. Lenny, Max and I pretty much grew up in All About Town. I was selling Gold Lotto tickets way before I was legally able to do so, and my brothers, with their easy access to certain magazines, were very popular at school. My own weakness wasn't so much capitalising on the magazines as the chocolates. I'd give them to boys I had a crush on. I still remember the day Mum said, 'I don't know, Brian, we just seem to always be running out of Mint Patties!' Looking sideways at me, Dad had replied, 'I can tell you exactly where those Mint Patties are going, Denise, they're going to Paddy Parker, Paddy Wyatt and Paddy Sadler.' My brothers had burst into laughter; I'd burst into tears and run for the refuge of the back office.

He's always been very direct, my dad. In fact, there are times when his frankness borders on the ridiculous. Just last week, for example, I was sitting with Mum and Dad at Bits 'n' Pizzas, Rocky's local coffee shop, when Dad waved at someone coming in. 'There's old bloody Doug McRae—I thought he was dead!'

He's also not backwards in coming forward with advice, even if you haven't asked for it and don't want it. Frustratingly, he's often spot on. Mind you, he doesn't always have a very nuanced take on things. Once, when Mum dragged him along to the ballet, he asked her when the dancers were going to start singing. When Mum explained that didn't happen in ballet he said, 'Well, I can tell you right now that's not going to last.'

And just last week, when I told him how much the new mechanic from Brisbane charged to service my Corolla, he promptly declared, 'Grubs don't always live in the garden, love!'

If Dad's black and white, then Mum's fifty shades of grey, and I suppose that's why they balance each other out. In her own way, Mum's just as eccentric as Dad. I still remember the three of us kids, all squashed into the back of the Commodore, careering around these same streets, with Mum yelling at us to stop fighting. She'd then pull up out the front of St Joseph's Cathedral and we'd troop in after her to Sunday mass, where she'd proceed to read from the lectern in what we liked to call her 'church voice'. After mass we'd all hop back in the Commodore and recommence fighting.

Lenny and Max have both moved away from Rocky but at least Rosie, my crazy best friend from primary school, is still here. In fact, Rosie's the only person keeping me sane at the moment—I always feel lighter in her company and my mood brightens as I remember she said she'd stop by this afternoon. Apparently one of her patients told her that Mum and Dad's new next-door neighbours are moving in this week so she's coming over to check them out. She and I have been trying to get to the bottom of who's bought the place ever since it was sold, but not even my father, the unofficial mayor of Rockhampton, has any idea.

When Rosie and I aren't playing Neighbourhood Watch, I've tried to establish a disciplined writing routine these past ten months. Essentially, I wake up, have breakfast, take Glenda for a run beside the Yeppen Lagoon, shower, then write for three hours, before discussing lunch with Mum.

My regimen appears to be working because I'm almost halfway there with *Diamonds in the Dust*, a sweeping multi-generational family saga set in the pioneering days of the Central Queensland gemfields.

Having set myself the goal of finishing my novel by the end of the year also helps me to justify my decision twelve months ago to leave my semi-glamorous life in Melbourne as a part-time, prime-time TV reporter and move to Port Douglas. At the time I'd rationalised it to my Melbourne friends and colleagues by talking about the weather and the hours I spent commuting.

'It's just too cold down here,' I'd told my bewildered boss after she quizzed me about why I was leaving. 'I'm from Queensland! I can't hack these winters!'

In my heart, though, I knew the real reason I was leaving Melbourne was because I'd decided I was still in love with my ex-boyfriend, Jeremy, who'd got a job in Far North Queensland, and I wanted to rekindle our relationship. Unfortunately, by the time I'd moved north three months after we'd broken up, he'd decided he couldn't see a future for us, and soon after he found the love of his life in Port Douglas.

And so, in a heartbroken daze, I stuck it out up there for about eight weeks picking up shifts reporting for WIN TV, before travelling south on the Bruce Highway and ending up back at Mum and Dad's in Rocky, licking my wounds.

As I pull into my parents' driveway, I'm relieved that the keen sense of my heart being wrung like a chamois every time I think of Jeremy has been replaced by a less intense emotional seesaw of feeling certain that I'm over him one

5

minute, and completely lovelorn, having a Debbie Downer the next. I try to cultivate the former state by steering clear of Facebook, alcohol and anyone who might potentially mention him in passing. Within the comforting confines of Rocky, I feel like the heavy cloud of grief is gradually lifting, and the cloak of sadness to which I've clung is being gently pried away.

As I get out of the car, Glenda runs up to me, tail wagging enthusiastically. 'Hi, little mate!' I say, giving her a hug. Distracted, she breaks away from me and bolts towards the fence, looking around to see if I'm following her. I realise that the source of her excitement is not my arrival but two men who are standing in the driveway next door. In fact, it's all I can do to stop her leaping over the fence to go and give them a lick.

After coaxing a reluctant Glenda inside with promises of liver treats, I shut the front door and call out, 'Hey, Mum, it looks like we've finally got new neighbours.'

There's no reply from Mum, who I find in the lounge room, drumsticks in hand, intently watching an African man's bongo drumming performance on DVD. Since selling All About Town, Mum has gone from one craze to another, and African drumming appears to be the latest. If it's not crystals, it's calligraphy or colouring in. And don't get me started on Cher—Mum's absolutely obsessed with her.

'Ma! You're in your African drumming trance again!' I say.

'No, I'm listening, love,' she replies distractedly, not taking her eyes off the screen.

'Well, what did I say?' I sink down into the couch.

'You said they've moved in next door.'

I nod and pick up a *MiNDFOOD* magazine, but its barrage of articles on how to attract money through mantras leaves me feeling flat, and I sigh heavily.

Mum pauses the DVD and turns to me. 'Are you a bit down, love?'

'No, no,' I say, giving her the brightest smile I can muster.

'Lucy, what's wrong? Have you heard from Jeremy?'

'No,' I reply. 'I don't think I'll ever be in contact with him again.'

'Tell me what it is then,' Mum persists. 'I know something's troubling you.'

'I'm fine, Ma,' I reply. 'Cup of tea?'

'I'd love a cup. Make me one of those Rooibos ones, would you, darl?'

I nod, head to the kitchen and put the kettle on. After I get the milk out of the fridge I pause and stare at the photos of my happy siblings smiling at me from beneath an assortment of magnets. There are pictures of Lenny and Camille's beautiful wedding in Sydney beside similarly joyous snaps of Max and Brooke at the launch of Fancy Pants, their new online business selling bamboo nappies into China. Then there's the pics of all five of my nieces and nephews in various poses. Suddenly the milk I'm holding feels as heavy as my heart.

'Are you making tea, Lucy?' says Dad, interrupting my reverie as he strides into the kitchen.

'Yep. Want one?' I ask, turning around.

'Yeah, thanks,' he says, then hurries off. Dad seems busier in retirement than he's ever been. He's always doing stuff at the Jockey Club, which is weird because I don't remember him ever being that into horseracing. Then again, he worked pretty much six till six in the newsagency before he retired so he didn't have much time for anything else.

'What are you thinking about?' Mum has come to stand beside me as I gaze absently at the whistling kettle.

'Whether I've eaten all those Crabtree & Evelyn choc-chip biscuits.'

Mum laughs but still looks worried.

'Oh, I don't know, Ma,' I say. 'I did my tax with Todd Doherty and it's not pretty. Sometimes I feel like it was a mistake leaving Melbourne, and it's all too late now.'

'Too late for what?' asks Mum.

'Too late to have a career, and to have excelled at just one thing.'

'Lucy, you left Melbourne because producing wasn't what you wanted to be doing, and it was a juggle to combine it with any presenting,' says Mum. 'You were working long hours, and travelling back and forth all that way to even *get* to work. Plus the rent was ridiculous and the weather was miserable. You left because you weren't happy down there.'

I nod, aware that what Mum's saying is completely true.

'It's easy to only remember the good things in hindsight,' Mum continues. 'It's the same with Jeremy. Yes, you had fun times together, but you also had your doubts about the relationship, which I think you're forgetting.'

I nod again, knowing she's right.

'You have to stop fooling yourself that things were perfect in Melbourne.'

'Mmm, I just think—'

'You can think too much,' says Mum, cutting me off. 'Just the other day I read an article by Deepak Chopra, and it was so true what he was saying.'

'What was he saying?'

'How it's a waste to live inside your head, and that we should be more like nature, just existing and breathing, and being open to the universe.'

'Ha! I went to see Deepak Chopra speak when he was in Melbourne,' I say as I jiggle the teabags, 'and he went on and on about how if you followed his advice you could have the perfect body, the perfect mind and perfect health. And he had the most shocking sinus I'd ever heard.'

Mum laughs. 'He didn't!'

'Yeah, he'd be saying how we can command our bodies to overcome anything, and then he'd clear his nose like he had the worst dairy allergy known to man.'

'Oh, Lucy, really?'

'Yes, really. So I'm not sure you should give too much credence to Deepak,' I say, chuckling, as we return to the lounge room with our teas.

'So, they've finally moved in, have they?' says Mum, looking out the window just as the sound of a bike clunking onto our front verandah is followed by the door slamming.

'Who's moved in?' asks Rosie, resplendent in lycra, as she sweeps into the room, unbuckling her bike helmet.

'You, with the amount of time you spend here!' jokes Mum.

I think Rosie would probably be popping in for an afternoon cuppa regardless of whether I was around. Last week she was in the kitchen chatting with Mum for an hour before I emerged from a morning session of writing in my bedroom to find them huddled over the latest HomeHints Direct catalogue, discussing the benefits of extra-long oven mitts. The two of them have delighted each other ever since Rosie first turned up at our house with a sleeping bag, aged six, and said to Mum, 'Turn up this song, Mrs Crighton, I love it!' The song happened to be Mum's favourite—Cher's 'If I Could Turn Back Time'. Rosie also speaks back to Dad with the cheeky familiarity that comes from being one step removed.

For me, Rosie has always been a portal to a different world, a world without rules. I can vividly remember us as children at her parents' house one Saturday night, drinking coffee milkshakes at midnight while we watched *Flowers in the Attic*. We were only in grade three at the time. My parents would have been horrified if they'd known.

Her loud, sunny nature is the perfect antidote to my introspection. When I get lost in my thoughts, she's always there, with a torch, guiding me out of the wilderness of my mind. Unlike me, she doesn't care what people say or think about her. If someone's an arsehole, she'll tell them to fuck off, then forget about it, whereas I'll create a flowchart to understand the sequence of events that led to my mistreatment.

Mum and Rosie are reading their horoscopes to each other and laughing when Dad bustles in with two different ties draped around his neck. 'Denise! Denise! I need you to focus,' he says, clapping his hands and gesturing at two ties.

'Oh, Brian, for heaven's sake, I'm just here,' says Mum.

'Blue or red?'

'Red,' says Mum.

'Rosie?' asks Dad.

'Red.'

'Lucy?'

'Hold the blue up, Dad,' I say, and then pretend to give both options weighty consideration. 'Red.'

'Right. Well, I'm off to the Jockey Club,' he says, putting the red tie on as he marches towards the front door.

'You've got a cup of tea you asked for there, Dad,' I say.

'Too busy!'

'Hey, Brian, leave us your wallet!' Rosie calls after him.

'Get a full-time bloody job, that's the answer for you!' Dad calls back, laughing, as the door bangs shut.

'Yeah, right, as if spending forty hours a week looking into people's mouths and dealing with kids who eat too many bloody lollies freaking out while I do their fillings would improve my life,' says Rosie, chucking a *WHO Magazine* onto the coffee table and picking up a copy of *HELLO!*. 'Fat chance. So, are there any husbands next door for you or what?'

I go over to the window and have a proper look at our two new neighbours—who, I can't help but notice, are pretty hot. I watch as the shorter one opens a bottle of beer, which he offers to a similar-looking but more athletic man who is talking intently on his mobile.

'Hard to tell, Rosie,' I say, gazing across the lawn, and getting a jolt when I lock eyes with the taller, lankier man, who glances up as he finishes his phone call. He looks thirty-something, and has a smile and physique that suggest he'd surely be off the market. I contemplate waving at him, but he walks out of sight before I get the chance.

'She's had her teeth done,' says Rosie, holding up a spread of various starlets in *Woman's Day*. 'So's she. She *needs* her teeth done.'

Mum restarts her bongo drumming DVD, and Rosie is updating me on Brad Pitt's alleged catch-up with Jennifer Aniston, when there's a knock at the door.

Mum stops the DVD again and we all look at each other gormlessly. Hardly anyone we know ever knocks.

We're all still sitting there when the doorbell rings. I jump out of the chair to go and answer the door, only to find the taller of our new neighbours standing on the other side of the screen, smiling.

I grin back at him and for a moment we just stand there, flashing our teeth at each other.

'Hi, I'm Oscar Simpson,' he says eventually.

'Lucy Crighton,' I reply, opening the door and holding out my hand. 'Welcome to Rocky.'

2

I take a step back as I gesture to Oscar to come inside, and bump into Rosie, who clears her throat. 'Oh, this is Rosie,' I say.

Oscar nods at her and says, 'Hi, Rosie.'

She gives him a knockout smile and he starts to say something but most of it gets lost in the awful din of Mum drumming along to the DVD in the lounge room.

'So, I just thought I'd let you know . . . in our . . . this afternoon.'

'Hang on,' says Rosie, before yelling, 'Denise! Denise!'

'Yes, love?' Mum calls.

'Quit it!' shouts Rosie.

I giggle as the drumming suddenly stops. Oscar looks amused, though slightly wary. 'So, as I was saying, we're having drinks in the backyard this afternoon to celebrate finally moving Mum in. We'd love you to come.'

'Drinks sound good,' I say encouragingly.

'Yeah, very good,' Rosie echoes. 'Being Saturday night and all.'

'Can we bring anything?' I ask.

'No, it's fine,' Oscar replies. 'We've got it all covered.'

'We'll bring some sausages,' blurts Rosie.

'Okay, great,' says Oscar. 'And feel free to invite any of your other housemates too.'

'Er, they're not exactly Lucy's housemates—more like her parents,' says Rosie, with a smirk.

'Oh, well, they're very welcome,' says Oscar, sounding a bit bemused. 'See you later, then.'

'See ya,' Rosie and I chorus.

'Thanks for letting him know I'm a major loser who lives with her mum and dad,' I mutter to Rosie as Oscar heads down the front path.

He's barely out the front gate when she wolf-whistles.

I grab her arm. 'There's no way he wouldn't have heard that.'

'He's a good-looking man, Lucy,' says Rosie, smiling and raising an eyebrow at me. 'A very good-looking man.'

'Who's good looking?' Mum calls. 'Besides me,' she adds.

We return to the lounge room, where Mum is now lying on the couch, charging her phone through a nearby salt lamp. Her feet are elevated, pointing towards a signed and framed photo of Cher on the wall.

'The new guy next door. That smile! His teeth are superb! And did you see his eyes? Who has eyes that blue?' gushes Rosie, adding, 'He's asked us over for drinks later, Denise.'

'You should go for him, Rosie,' I say.

'No, *you* should go for him! You're the one who's been moping around for a year,' says Rosie. 'I've got Trent the Tradie, remember?'

'I haven't been moping,' I protest feebly.

Rosie and Mum exchange glances, then simultaneously pull identical hangdog faces at me. I scowl back at them.

'Go and get changed, Lucy,' says Mum. 'And for God's sake, wear something a bit flattering and put some makeup on . . .'

'Yeah, for God's sake!' agrees Rosie, laughing.

'You two are out of control,' I huff, walking to the hallway and lingering there, knowing I'll hear them talking about me.

'Rosie,' Mum whispers, 'make sure you help her out when you go next door, okay?'

'Aren't you coming?'

'I'll pop over later, darl. I need to align my chakras or they'll get away from me.'

'Fair enough, Denise. Anyway, what can I do?' says Rosie.

'Get her chatting with those young men or something—anything!' Mum says, then pauses before asking, 'Has she mentioned Jeremy recently?'

'No, not lately,' Rosie says with a sigh. 'But that doesn't mean she isn't thinking about him.'

'I know, just the other day I saw her on that Facebook . . .'

I continue to my bedroom. Though I know they both have my best interests at heart, a sense of despair looms when you hear your loved ones talking about you in hushed, urgent tones. And when the despair cloaks you, its favourite playmates—hopelessness and frustration—are never far

15

behind. I try to shake my sudden gloom off, and replace it with positive thoughts like all those self-help books and Lululemon carry bags advise, but the reality of my present situation sinks into my bones until I'm sitting on my bed, cursing myself for lacking the strength to change my perspective and take charge of my life.

I stay there a while, listening to Mum recap the latest episode of *The Crown* before Rosie starts talking about an article titled 'Sixteen Ways with Leftover Bolognese'.

'Look, Denise,' I hear her say, 'you can do chilli con carne, fajitas—oh, and here's an exotic one: toasted sandwiches!'

I smile as the two of them burst into laughter. When they're not discussing me, I find Mum and Rosie's banter very reassuring. There's no need to feel anxious when your best friend and Mum are only metres away, listing the advantages of leftover bolognese.

Looking across at my laptop I zone out, thinking about when I'll have the heroine from *Diamonds in the Dust* dig up a 64-carat green sapphire. Probably in the next chapter. After a while Rosie calls out, 'Are you sewing an outfit or what?', bringing me back to reality. I sigh and start rifling through some drawers before finally settling on my favourite comfy jeans and a floral t-shirt.

As I walk down the hall I hear Mum and Rosie resume their quiet, conspiratorial chat and when I enter the lounge room they look up guiltily.

'You two have been talking about me, haven't you?' I say.

'No,' they chime back in unison, unconvincingly.

'Yes you were.'

'Nah we weren't,' says Rosie, looking me up and down. 'Maybe pop another top on?'

'You don't like this one?' I ask.

'It's a bit Noni B,' she replies. 'Why don't you wear that sparkly top I got you?'

'And put on some lippy,' says Mum.

I go and change into the silver Country Road top Rosie gave me for my last birthday, which I usually avoid because I worry it's too revealing. Then, ducking into the bathroom, I put on a dash of makeup to please Mum. When I return to the lounge room Rosie and Mum look up from the latest HomeHints catalogue and nod their approval.

Peering out the window into next door's yard I see a woman who must be Oscar's mum along with the bloke he was with before and feel quite excited at the prospect of socialising with new people. I chuckle as a familiar figure appears carrying a carton of Dark 'n' Stormy. 'They've invited Ruth,' I say, knowing this will get a rise from Mum.

Mum grimaces. 'Oh well, they'll learn.'

Even though forty odd years have passed since Ruth and Dad were sprung skinny dipping in the pool at TAFE, Mum still holds a real set against her. Which seems weird, considering Mum and Dad weren't even dating at the time. I mean, sure, Ruth's personality is abrasive, and she has a way of throwing her considerable weight around, but underneath her gruff, man-eating, take-no-prisoners exterior, she means well. Rosie always says she wouldn't trust Ruth as far as she could throw her, invariably adding that it wouldn't be far. Rosie thinks I put too much faith in people but I still think Ruth's pretty harmless. Anyway, I've given up asking Mum what her issue is with Ruth, and accepted that not everyone likes everyone.

I'm watching Ruth knocking back a tinnie when I hear the sounds of glass chinking and look over to see Rosie crouched in front of the liquor cabinet carefully placing bottles into a Woolies bag.

Mum, meanwhile, is horizontal on the couch again, highlighting sections from *Ask and It Is Given*. She's always been a modern-day hippie with lippy, but since she and Dad sold the business she's become more attuned to messages from the metaphysical. I suspect she's still struggling to fill the void of losing her daily work routine selling frocks. She loved chatting with all the shoppers. Sometimes you'd even find her in the change rooms trying on the same outfit as a potential customer, convinced that if they saw her in the clothes they were considering they'd appreciate how smashing they too could look.

'So I'll see you there later, Mum?' I ask.

'You sure will,' she says, closing the book and reaching for her phone. 'I just want to revisit this podcast about the five people you meet in heaven.'

'As you were, Denise,' says Rosie, loaded up with her heavy stash of spirits. 'Let's go for a drive and get some ice, Luce. Then I'll need to duck in home and get changed, if that's okay?'

'Yeah, no worries.'

'Have fun, girls!' calls Mum as we head to the front door. 'And remember what Cher says!'

'"These suspenders are too tight and I've got a massive friggin' wedgie!"' shouts Rosie. 'Ha ha!' she grins as we hop in my Corolla. 'That's what I'd say if I was Cher.'

With Rosie beside me, Triple J on the radio and the wide blue skies overhead, I feel happier. We whiz past the schools on the range and down the hill, spotting familiar faces queued up at Bernie's pie van in Allenstown, and a few girls we knew from high school pushing prams along the wide streets.

'Hey, Susie!' I yell out to a brunette with a Bugaboo.

'Hey, Lucy!' she yells back.

We've barely gone a block further when Rosie rolls down her window.

'Hey, Katie!'

'Hey, Rosie!'

I turn the corner onto the Bruce Highway and spot another old friend. 'Gina!' I call out and get a wave in return.

Rosie peers intently into the rear-view mirror. 'That wasn't Gina,' she says.

'Wasn't it?' I say.

'Nuh.'

We're giggling again as I pull into the bottle-o, where a middle-aged woman I've seen around heaps ambles over to our car. According to the name badge pinned to her dark green polo top, she is Colleen.

'Hi, just a bag of ice, please,' says Rosie.

'That's all?' the woman asks.

'I think so,' replies Rosie. 'You don't want anything else do you?' she says to me.

I shrug my shoulders. 'Doritos?'

'And a packet of Doritos,' says Rosie, handing over ten dollars.

Colleen sighs and shuffles off.

'They don't work on commission here, do they?' I say to Rosie.

'I don't think so,' she replies.

Eventually Colleen returns with the chips and ice. 'Chuck 'em in the back?' she asks.

'Yeah, thank you,' says Rosie.

We jolt in alarm at the almighty crack that sounds as the ice hits the floor.

'Here's your change,' says Colleen, leaning on Rosie's window sill. 'So, what have you girls got planned?'

'Just drinks with people who've moved here,' says Rosie.

'Two cartons of Tooheys New, a magnum of champagne and a few wine coolers?'

'Sorry?' says Rosie, clearly bewildered.

'Couple of blokes came through earlier and got that. I think they're brothers. Could that be them?'

Rosie nods. 'Could be.'

Colleen steps away from the car and taps the roof twice, like she's just serviced us at a Formula One pit stop.

'I see her everywhere, that woman,' I remark as she walks away.

We drive the three blocks to Rosie's apartment complex at the top of hilly Denham Street.

'Hey, Luce, have you seen this?' Rosie says, pointing as we cross the lawn.

'Uh, it looks like a sprinkler,' I say, not sure why that would be of interest.

Rosie shakes her head. 'Nup, it's a fake! It's a sprinkler head hide-a-key.' She flips over the fake plastic sprinkler to reveal her house key.

I laugh. 'What's the point of that? You've got a sprinkler head that doesn't work, and a key that could just as easily be hidden under a rock!'

'Oh, where's your sense of fun, Luce?' Rosie retorts. 'I ordered it from Denise's last HomeHints Direct catalogue. It's got some fucking useful things.'

I roll my eyes. Mum and Rosie are always buying useless contraptions from that ridiculous magazine.

'How's Trent the Tradie going?' I ask as we walk up to her unit on the second floor.

'He's good,' she says, opening her door. 'Handy when he's around. He can fix things.'

'How often is he around?' I ask as I sit on the couch.

'I know what you're getting at,' she replies, 'and yes, I'm still limiting it to Monday, Wednesday and Saturday nights. If I find that I like him more, then I'll add in a Tuesday or Thursday. Maybe a Friday.'

I smile wryly. 'Well, it's only been three months—I think he's lucky to be getting three days a week at this stage.'

'He's fucking lucky alright,' says Rosie, admiring her reflection in the microwave. 'Anyway, sometimes you just need to have sex,' she adds before heading into her bedroom.

'But tonight's Saturday, Rosie! It's a Tradie Trent night!' I call out to her.

'No it's not!' she yells back. 'He's up fishing with some friends in Arnhem Land.'

'Oh, righto,' I reply, secretly glad that she's unlikely to bail early on the drinks.

I go out onto the balcony and admire the view. Soaring into the air about a kilometre away are the iconic sandstone spires of St Joseph's Cathedral. The Fitzroy River glistens in the distance, and traffic streams across the two bridges separating the north and south sides of town. Beyond the bridges, in the north, lie the lofty blue mountains of the Berserker Range.

Wandering back into the kitchen I pour myself a glass of water. Cookbooks are stacked up in a pile beside the sink, and a tall glass vase bursting with pink bougainvillea sits to one side of the stovetop. Rosie's fluorescent orange kettle and toaster happily clash with the fridge, which she painted yellow. When it comes to Rosie, whether it's her shoes, her handbag or her language, you can always count on it being colourful.

I examine an unopened plastic box on the bench, emblazoned with the title Universal Can Colander, and look up to see her walking into the kitchen looking stunning in a summery blue dress.

'It's a little tiny colander that fits over the top of your can when it needs to be drained,' she says, smiling.

'It's going to be a bloody godsend, Rosie!'

'I know,' she says, ignoring my sarcasm. 'We'd better get that ice in an esky, hey?'

3

As we walk over to our new neighbours' house, my heart races like I'm a sixteen-year-old at her first co-ed dance and it strikes me that it's been an age since I last went to a party. Looking at Rosie, I can tell she feels the same.

'If we need to leave, at least we don't have far to go,' I whisper.

'You're absolutely right,' Rosie says, swinging open the creaky gate. 'By the way, what *does* Cher say again?'

'What?'

'Your mum said . . .'

'Oh, yeah—Cher.' I shake my head. 'Cher says, "Are you strong enough?"'

Rosie looks at me. 'I just hope my drinks are strong enough,' she says, deadpan.

I grab her shoulder. 'Shit. We forgot to get sausages.'

'It doesn't matter, you just say you'll take stuff,' she reassures me as we head around to the backyard, where we find Ruth, Oscar, and the others I'd spotted earlier, lounging in a semi-circle of collapsible chairs beneath a sprawling poinciana tree. A large esky is in front of them, and a clothesline to their right. Triple J plays in the background, which I take as a good sign. Oscar smiles and we exchange greetings before he introduces us to his kindly-looking mother, Helen, who has a mumsy-style haircut.

'Nice to meet you, Lucy,' she says, smiling brightly and extending her hand.

'Nice to meet you too,' I reply. 'I live next door with Mum and Dad at the moment. And Rosie practically lives there.'

I smile across at Rosie, who is pouring herself a generous amount of rum.

'So, did work or family bring you to Rocky?' I begin.

'Neither,' says Helen. 'My husband passed away in Sydney earlier this year, and I decided a complete change could be good, so the boys helped me move up and are staying for a few days to help me unpack and settle in.'

'Oh, I'm sorry to hear about your husband,' I say, surprised to find myself also feeling slightly sorry that Oscar and his brother won't be here for long.

'He was in pain, so it was a blessing in the end. But both the boys are taking it really hard, particularly Ben.'

I follow her gaze towards Oscar's brother, who's just downed a shot of Sambuca.

'Lucy!' Rosie calls out, having already finished her rum. 'Can you get me a beer?'

'I don't think we brought any, did we?' I say, knowing full well we didn't and suspicious of the glint in her eye.

'That's alright,' says Oscar, flipping open the esky. 'Help yourself.'

I glare at Rosie and bend over, feeling my top gape as I rummage around in the ice. I sense Ben and Oscar's eyes on me, and abruptly stand, clutching a Tooheys New with one hand and trying to hold my top up with the other.

Rosie winks and takes the beer from me.

'So, what do you do, Lucy?' Oscar asks as I return to my seat.

'Oh, I used to work in the media but I've taken a break to try to write a novel.'

'Much sex in it?' asks Ben.

'Ben!' Oscar scowls at him.

'Well, sex sells,' says Ben with a cheeky grin.

'Yeah, don't I know it,' agrees Ruth, shifting her hefty frame in the plastic chair. 'I decided to wear my bikini for my latest flyer for the car wash, and now I'm that busy I don't have time to scratch myself.'

Helen nods politely as Ben almost chokes on his beer. 'So, are you in a franchise, Ruth, or . . .?' asks Helen.

'Christ, no! I do it all myself. Ruth's Wax 'n' Shine on the unused corner of Fitzroy and Albert streets,' Ruth replies, crushing a Dark 'n' Stormy can in her hand and chucking it over her shoulder.

'Right,' says Helen slowly.

'How about you, Ben?' I ask as he battles to stifle his giggles and Rosie walks over to the clothesline gasping with laughter, unable to show any control at all.

'Real estate . . . in Sydney . . .' he says, taking a deep breath. 'North Shore, the high-end stuff. But I'm taking a break for a week or so.'

'That's good,' I say, smiling.

'Is it? I don't know,' he replies, his expression suddenly serious.

Before I can say anything, the front gate creaks open and we all turn to see Mum walking towards us wearing a tropical muu-muu and carrying a fruit basket under one arm and gifts under the other. 'Hello, hello, hello! I'm Denise Crighton. Welcome to the street,' she says, handing the basket to Helen.

'Oh, how lovely! Thank you. I'm Helen Simpson, and these are my boys, Ben and Oscar. And do you know . . .'

'Ruth,' says Mum evenly. 'Yes, I know Ruth.'

'Terrific! Well, take a seat, Denise,' says Helen cheerily.

'Oh, I also have these for the boys,' says Mum, smiling and holding up two parcels.

'Thanks! Chuck 'em here so I can have first pick,' says Ben, his hands at the ready, like he's at the end of a tunnel ball line.

'Ben!' says Helen as Mum walks over to Ben and hands him the gifts.

Grinning, he unwraps both presents to reveal two very large Hawaiian shirts. 'Thanks, Denise,' he says as he holds them up, before whispering, 'Random,' to Oscar.

'What beautiful colours, Denise,' says Helen. 'Just lovely.'

'Mmm.' Mum nods. 'They were Brian's before he started walking again.'

'Oh,' says Helen, looking stricken. 'Was he in an accident?'

'No, he just stopped going for his morning walk and really porked up, so they've been sitting in the cupboard for ages.'

'Oh,' repeats Helen, shifting in her seat.

'Yes, he watched an awful lot of television after we sold the business and retired,' Mum rattles on. 'I tried to get him interested in tandem bike-riding and clogging and such, but he wouldn't have a bar of it. Even bought him his own set of bongos, which just gathered dust.'

Rosie looks across at me and I shrug my shoulders.

'But anyway,' continues Mum, sitting up straighter, 'like Cher says, "You don't take your toys inside just because it's raining", and thank goodness Brian found the Jockey Club—and his waistline again.'

A crow caws loudly from the fence, startling me, and I realise I've been holding my breath and exhale deeply. Ruth noisily crunches another can in her fist and carries on as if Mum isn't even there. 'Toss 'em my way,' she says to Ben. 'They'll be too big for you runts. I could do with some more tops down at the car wash.'

Ben throws the shirts to Ruth, who tugs one on over her black lycra singlet. It fits perfectly. 'Cheers, Denise,' she says, raising a Passionfruit UDL in salute.

'Alright,' says Rosie, clapping her hands together, 'we're not here for a haircut, let's get this party started. Whenever anyone says the word "drink" or "Sydney" or "Rocky" they have to do a shot of Sambuca.'

'Oh not Sambuca, Rosie,' I plead, 'you know that's my kryptonite.'

'I know, Luce, but you've got to be in it to win it,' she replies with a not-so-subtle jerk of her head towards Oscar.

'I could show you how I've arranged my furniture inside, Denise,' says Helen half hovering out of her chair. 'Would you . . .?'

'I'd love to, Helen,' says Mum, leaping from her seat.

As they walk into the house the rest of us drag our chairs closer together.

Ruth clears her throat loudly and proclaims. 'Well, if I didn't live in Rocky, I'd love to have a drink in Sydney.'

'Good on ya, Ruth,' I say and slap my thigh.

Ben pours her three shots and Oscar looks on in awe as Ruth unflinchingly downs them, one after the other.

'What was that movie where Sylvester Stallone played a boxer, Luce?' asks Rosie.

'Never heard of it, my friend,' I say with a grin.

'*Rocky*, *Rocky II*, *Rocky III*, *Rocky IV*, *Rocky V* and *Rocky Balboa*,' says Ruth, counting the Rocky mentions on her fingers. 'That's six shots, Ben.'

'Ruth, you're not playing fair,' says Rosie crossly.

'Well, there's nothing stopping you from saying "Rocky", "Sydney" or "drink", is there?' retorts Ruth. 'By the way, Ben, that's another three shots. A total of nine. Actually, just give me the bottle, would you?'

Ben tightens his grip on the Sambuca and Oscar stares down at his shoes.

'Look, don't worry,' I say quickly, 'there's plenty for everyone to drink.'

Rosie and the boys suddenly yell like they've just caught me out in cricket.

I realise my mistake and put my head in my hands. Ruth and Rosie are chuckling now. I may be as sick as a dog later on, but at least I've dispelled the tension. I reluctantly accept the shot from Ben's outstretched hand and grimace as the warm liquid rushes down my throat. There's no turning back now, and I decide that if I'm going to get off my trolley I may as well do it on my terms. 'Right,' I say, standing up, 'let's play Wheel of Goon.'

'Wheel of Goon?' exclaims Oscar. 'What the hell's that?'

'You've never played Wheel of Goon?' I reply, smiling. 'That's crazy. Oh, hang on, maybe you know it as Goon of Fortune?'

He laughs. 'Nup. I don't know what that is either!'

Rosie bends over the esky and rips the wine bladder out of a Coolabah box.

'Now, if you'll just follow me,' I say, walking over to the clothesline, where Ruth has already positioned herself under one of the steel spokes. The boys follow our lead and the five of us fan out under the crossbars. Rosie ceremoniously pegs the silver wine bag up to the wire, then stands directly beneath it, opens her mouth, and twists the nozzle. After an alarming amount of amber liquid has gushed down her throat she twists the nozzle closed and solemnly declares, 'Welcome to Wheel of Goon.'

Then, with an almighty shove, she sends the clothesline spinning, and we watch the silver wine bladder whir around and around until she abruptly puts her hand in the air, stopping the metal bar. 'Oh, not again!' she exclaims in mock disbelief, opening the nozzle. The wine cascades down her throat and she swallows several times before declaring, 'Right, someone else better have a go now.' She weakly pushes the clothesline, and the wine bag comes to a stop above Ben. He turns the nozzle and yelps in pain when the liquid enters his mouth. 'Oh shit, that stuff's sweet!' he exclaims, clutching at his jaw. 'Think I've got a dodgy tooth.'

'Here, let me have a look,' says Rosie, walking across to him. 'I'm a dentist.'

'Yeah, and I'm a Supreme Court judge,' jokes Ben.

'No, she really is!' I say. 'She's the best dentist Rocky's ever had.'

'Not sure about that,' scoffs Ruth. 'I go to Justin Adams on the northside and he's very good.'

'Whatever, Ruth,' says Rosie. 'Open up, Ben.'

I look over at Oscar and we laugh as Rosie peers into Ben's mouth.

'You'll have to lie down,' she instructs. 'I can't get a good look from here.'

Ben immediately obeys and Rosie leans over him until their faces are so close she may as well be doing mouth-to-mouth. I'm laughing so hard I have to steady myself against the poinciana.

Suddenly she sits back and declares, 'You've got receding gums. Get yourself some Sensodyne and a soft head tooth-brush. That'll sort you out.' Then she unpegs the shrivelled goon bag from the clothesline and swallows the last of the liquid before blowing into the nozzle and inflating the bag like a balloon. 'Here,' she says, handing it down to Ben, 'it's a silver pillow now. You won't fucking know yourself after a nap on that.'

We return to our circle of chairs around the esky and Oscar angles his body towards me and asks about my novel and how long it takes to write a book. I explain that I've been writing for six months and have set myself a goal of seventy thousand words by the end of the year, and when I indicate how many typed A4 pages that would equate to, he shakes his head in wonder and with a lovely smile says, 'Wow, I could never do that.'

I worry that I might be boring him when he insists that I tell him the plot for my story, but he listens intently as I take him into the colourful world of the Foster family and the fossicking fields around Rubyvale.

'Sounds very interesting,' he says. 'I'd like to say I know more about that history, but the closest I come is having "Gold Digger" on Spotify.'

We both laugh. Who knew this man with eyes like a Siberian husky would be so warm and funny? And as our easy chatter moves from authors we both admire to our shared secret love of Bruce Springsteen, I find myself desperately hoping that no-one will interrupt our conversation, and that I can continue to keep his laugh just for me. To be honest, though, I don't think I have much competition. Ruth's flared up a durry by the front gate and Rosie is asking Ben if he mightn't need a root canal treatment, to which he replies that he's certain to need three.

As the cans stack up and the afternoon drifts into dusk, Oscar continues to ask me questions about myself and my life in Rocky, and I'm so taken by his genuine curiosity that it's only when Dad walks through the gate at eight o'clock, after returning from the Jockey Club, I realise that in all the time we've been talking I've hardly learnt anything about Oscar. He'd vaguely mentioned earlier that he worked in hospitality and I'm about to ask him more when I spot

Rosie stumbling towards Mum and Helen under the moonlit poinciana.

I struggle up from my chair—I'm not that sober myself as it turns out—and go after her.

'Denise, Brian, thanks for your hospiltality,' Rosie slurs, then reels around and mock whispers to me, 'Pash him.'

'He's probably married, Rosie,' I whisper back.

'No, I heard him telling Ruth earlier about some on-again/off-again thing with a bird in Sydney.'

'Well, that doesn't mean I should make a move on him.'

'Don't try and tell me you're not a slut.'

'Rosie! Go home!'

'Oi, Oscar!' she yells. 'Pash Lucy!'

'Sorry!' I call to him, mortified. 'She's off her chops.'

'No dramas,' he says with a laugh.

Meanwhile, Ben, who is now swinging from the clothes-line, appears delighted by the exchange. 'You country chicks are awesome!' he yells, letting go of the line with one hand to high-five Ruth.

'I think I might head off too,' I say, sensing there's no salvaging my chat with Oscar after Rosie's outburst. 'Nice to meet you guys. No doubt we'll see you around.'

'For sure.' Oscar smiles. 'See ya.'

I thank Helen and welcome her to the street again, then walk to the footpath and find Rosie attempting, and failing, to hop on her bike.

She looks at me sheepishly. 'I know, I know—sorry, mate.'

'That was the worst! Rosie, how could you do that to me? We're thirty-two!'

'It's not my fault!' Rosie protests. 'There was Wheel

of Goon, there were nachos! I felt like I was twenty-five again!'

'Yeah, me too,' I concede. 'Oh well, I'll just have to lie low. How about that brother of Oscar's?'

'Oh! Wrong! When I fell over, he grabbed my arse while he was helping me up.'

She rides off, wobbling all over the road. 'See ya, Luce!'

'See ya.'

'Love ya, Luce,' she calls, her voice growing fainter as she rides away.

'Love ya,' I call back.

'I still think you should pash . . .' she shouts, her voice fading as she disappears around the corner.

⌒ᥱ᧧ᥲ

Inside, I collapse on my bed and take a photo out of my bedside dresser. It's of Jeremy and me, when we first met in Perth on a scuba diving course. I put it back and stare at the ceiling. Sometimes I wish Jeremy would just get engaged. Maybe then I would finally recognise that enough's enough and sort of dust myself off to keep trekking on.

I try to look at my situation rationally. I've got two thousand dollars in savings. I'm almost halfway there with my book. I've got my kelpie, Glenda. My life is not over, but somehow it feels like it's lost that shimmering gloss of possibility it had when I was in my twenties.

Apart from Rosie, most of my friends are married and have kids—and absolutely none of them live with their parents. I know I need to get out of this house, and get out of Rocky, but where would I go? I could head back to

Melbourne and try to get an agent and crack the television presenting circuit, hoping to end up on *Getaway*, but how realistic is that? Or if I see myself bringing up a family in a regional town like Fremantle or Newcastle, shouldn't I be moving there, meeting someone, and getting a job?

Anyway, what if I nail it with this novel and become a published author? When I was little, I dreamt of either being a writer like Anne from *Anne of Green Gables* or operating a show bag stand; perhaps I just need to have faith in my childhood aspiration. I can write anywhere. I don't have to be in Melbourne or Sydney. I can write in Rocky, and Rosie's happy here, so why shouldn't I be? Do I put up these barriers in my own head? Is it only myself I have to overcome?

I shuffle the playlist on my iPhone and put it in the stereo dock. The first song is Radiohead's 'Fake Plastic Trees'. The drunken tears roll down my cheeks and onto the pillow.

Moments later, there's a knock on my bedroom door and Dad yells, 'Turn it down, Lucy!'

I lower the volume and hear him trudge along the hallway, muttering, 'Awful bloody mournful music.'

Soon after, I fall asleep to the lullaby-like lilt of Thom Yorke.

4

I'm woken up the next morning by a horrendous whirring noise. I turn over and sandwich my head in a pillow, trying to block out the sound, but it cuts through and I sit up suddenly. Too suddenly. I feel rougher than a pair of hessian undies.

As I lie down again, flashbacks from the night before hit me like a ton of bricks. Oh God, how embarrassing, I think, remembering Rosie yelling at Oscar to pash me. Ah well, who cares? I ask myself. He's not available anyway. No-one that lovely and good looking is available. I hope we can be friends, though. I get up and change into some shorts and a t-shirt, then open my door to discover the source of the shocking racket is a silver disc whizzing around the hallway floor.

I stride into the lounge room and find Mum doing Qi-Gong to Cher's 'Just Like Jesse James'. 'Mum!' I say, raising my voice above the din, 'what's the thing on the floor making all that noise?'

'It's Roomba!' replies Mum, her arms outstretched and her left leg extended. 'I ordered her from the HomeHints catalogue and I think she's going to be the best thing that's ever happened to me.'

'She woke me up!' I exclaim, making a mental note to burn the bloody HomeHints catalogue the next time it arrives.

'Well, it's about time you got up, isn't it?' says Mum. 'It's midday! And don't you go bad-mouthing Roomba—she's vacuuming up all of Glenda's white dog hairs!'

'Oh, righto,' I say, keen to avoid an argument. 'What's Dad doing?'

'He's in the TV room watching a rerun of *Meals in Wheels*. I have to admit she does a good job, that Tiffany Bloxsom.'

'Mm,' I grunt. Tiffany Bloxsom and I started out presenting on television at the same time in Perth. She now hosts *Meals in Wheels*—a reality TV cooking show where contestants prepare dishes in a van and compete for the title of Australia's best food truck. Unbelievably, it rates through the roof.

'Do you ever hear from Tiffany?' asks Mum, adjusting her sweatbands.

'Mum, why would I ever hear from Tiffany? I haven't spoken to her in four years.'

'Well, forgive me for trying to make conversation,' says Mum, reaching for her water bottle. 'Someone's a bit touchy today, aren't they?'

My phone pings and I read the text message, which is from Rosie and says: *You up? If so go and get us a DVD! I'll be over in 15.*

Okay, see you soon, I type, and head for the car.

⁊℮☯

Fading fast, I stand at the Video Ezy counter waiting for the cashier, who I immediately recognise as Colleen from the bottle-o yesterday. She flips over the case of season five of *Girls* and reads the blurb, eventually saying, '*Girls*, hey? What's this season like?'

'I don't know—I haven't seen it yet,' I reply wearily, looking at the chicken Twisties longingly before realising I've still got the pack of Doritos from yesterday in the car.

Colleen scans the barcode, removes the DVD, and slowly inserts it into a cleaning machine. 'Maybe one not to watch in front of the kids?' she says.

'Yeah,' I agree. 'Definitely not in front of the kids.'

She hands me the case. 'Alright, love, have a good afternoon.'

⁊℮☯

When I arrive home I hear Mum and Rosie laughing in the lounge room but I go straight to the kitchen, shovelling Doritos into my mouth. After a couple of Panadols and a few glasses of water I join them. Rosie is sitting on the couch with her feet on the coffee table, burger wrappers strewn across its surface.

'Oh, mate,' I say.

'Don't even start,' she says. 'I've already spewed twice this morning.'

Mum says she'll make us both a nice cup of globe arti-
choke tea, claiming it's good for hangovers, and bustles off.
Then I pop on the DVD and within minutes a very vocal sex
scene fills the room.

As if on cue, Dad walks in and stands in front of the TV.
'Doesn't sound very good!' he says gruffly.

'Brian!' yells Rosie, trying to shoo him out of her way.
But Dad just stands there glaring at us, so Rosie pauses the
DVD and says, 'Oh, by the way, did you know he started
Bev's Buffet?'

'Who started Bev's Buffet?' I ask.

'Oscar,' she replies.

God, I think, he certainly downplayed that when he said
he 'worked in hospitality'.

'Who's Oscar?' asks Dad loudly.

Rosie massages her temples. 'Oh, painful. Can you turn
your voice down a notch, please, Brian?'

'Oscar's the guy next door, Dad,' I explain. 'The taller one.'

'Shit! He started Bev's Buffet, did he?' says Dad. 'Well,
there's a very sensible young man. Combining a buffet with
unlimited beverages.' He claps his hands together. 'Goldmine!'

Rosie suddenly perks up. 'He'd be loaded.'

'Oh, he would be,' says Dad. 'There's already a franchise
in Yeppoon . . .'

'And one just opened in Gladstone,' I say.

'Right, that's two in Central Queensland,' says Dad
happily, loving this type of talk.

Hearing the conversation, Mum hurries in and hands us
our teas. She's wearing a one-piece bathing suit. I avert my
eyes as she begins lathering sun cream onto her upper thighs.

'I saw four Bev's Buffets when I was in Mackay,' she says breathlessly.

'And there's one at the Townsville airport,' I add.

'I think there's a couple in Cairns too,' says Rosie.

'Wow,' says Dad enthusiastically. 'And that's not taking into account the south-east corner.'

'God!' exclaims Mum, lowering her leg. 'There's probably hundreds down there!'

'No, he hasn't reached Brissie yet. Still expanding, he told me.' Rosie takes a large swig of the tea and almost gags. 'Holy Moses, Denise, what *is* this?' she exclaims.

Before Mum can answer, Dad says, 'Regardless, he'd be doing well. He'd be doing *very* well. Good on him.'

'While we're at the farm, you should ask him about all that public liability stuff for when the Jockey Club runs the gymkhanas,' says Mum.

Dad nods slowly. 'Yeah, I could. That's a good idea.'

'Farm? Why would he be going to the farm?' I ask Dad.

'Shit, I thought you girls were ready!' exclaims Dad. 'I organised last night to take Heather—'

'Helen,' corrects Mum.

'—Helen and her sons down to the farm with us this afternoon! Come on, I just saw them all sitting around outside . . . poor bastards.'

I go over to the window and peer out. Helen's perched on the front step of the house next door reading *The Happiest Refugee*, and Oscar's pacing up and down the yard, engaged in intense conversation on his mobile. Meanwhile, Ben is lying on the grass, wearing sunglasses, looking a bit ragged.

'Can't you and Mum go alone?' I plead.

'No, I told Henrietta we'd all go,' says Dad. 'Besides, fresh air is just what you girls need.'

'I might choof off home . . .' Rosie rises from the couch.

I pull her back down. 'No! You owe me,' I say, half begging, half demanding.

'Oh, righto,' she says with a wince. 'But I don't have togs or anything.'

'I've got spares, darl,' says Mum.

ℴℯℴ

We bounce along the sand dunes in the tray of Dad's ute, Oscar and Ben clinging to the sides with white-knuckle grips, while Helen, Rosie and I grasp the bar at the back of the cab. Dad is careering around the farm like a cowboy, oblivious— or not—to our delicate hungover states. I can just picture Mum inside, telling him to slow down in between spraying Rescue Remedy into her mouth.

He finally reaches the farm's seafront and pulls up with a start.

'Well, here we are,' he says, hopping out of the car and gesturing with his hand to the wide grassy savannahs running down to a deserted beach and sparkling sea. 'Welcome to paradise.'

'This is just incredible, Brian,' says Helen, lowering her sunglasses.

'It is a lovely spot,' Dad replies, crossing his arms. 'So peaceful. No mobile coverage, either, so even better,' he adds.

'That's a jolly good thing. You can finally have a break from that phone, Oscar,' says Helen, smiling across at her son before turning to Dad. 'Brian, the cattle we saw on the way in look tremendously healthy.'

'The cows are that fat Jenny Craig'd shoot herself if she saw them,' replies Dad.

'So, would you ever subdivide and create a new suburb?' asks Ben.

'No,' replies Dad.

'You must be pretty rich, hey?' says Ben.

'Oh, I don't know about that, Ben, just worked hard all my life,' says Dad, giving Rosie and me a sidelong glance.

'What are you looking at us for?' protests Rosie. 'I'm a dentist!'

'Part-time,' mutters Dad as he goes to retrieve some collapsible chairs from the tray of the ute.

We unfold them under the ironbark trees and sit down as he carries over a picnic basket.

'Who wants a cup of tea?' I ask, taking Dad's thermos out of the basket.

'Oh, that'd be lovely, thanks, Lucy,' says Helen, smiling.

'As long as it's not that horrible stuff from earlier,' says Rosie, looking a bit green.

'Two with moo for me, darl,' says Mum.

'I can tell you've worked hard for this, Brian,' says Oscar. 'It all comes back to hard work and taking risks, doesn't it?'

'Totally, Oscar. I mean in your case too . . . a buffet with unlimited beverages,' says Dad, shaking his head in wonder. 'Cha-ching! How'd you think to start it all off?'

'Well,' says Oscar, looking animated, 'I've always been a fan of the Sizzler model . . .'

'I could be a Sizzler model,' says Rosie under her breath, patting her stomach.

'. . . and about ten years ago I was having dinner one night at Sizzler on the Gold Coast with my girlfriend at the time,' continues Oscar, 'and I said to her, "Laura, why haven't I seen a Sizzler in Sydney?" And she said, "Because it's too bogan."'

'That's a bit rough,' I object. 'I love the cheese toast at Sizzler.'

'So do I!' says Rosie. 'Sizzler's unreal.'

'I always like the cheese toast too,' says Oscar quickly, 'but Sydneysiders—for good or bad—want something a bit classier. And that's when I came up with the idea for Bev's Buffet.'

Dad nods in admiration.

'We're picking up real momentum in regional Queensland, and I've got my sights set on Brisbane next,' continues Oscar.

'Bev's Buffet's not really the classiest name, though, is it?' says Rosie.

'No it's not, but it's all clever marketing, you see? We had to give the chain a bogan exterior, to appeal to the bogans, but once you get inside, you can see it's top shelf.'

'Bit like Lucy,' says Rosie, elbowing me, but I couldn't care less. It's just dawned on me that maybe I was wrong about Oscar and he's actually a bit of a business-type bore.

'Well, Lucy, I admire what *you're* doing,' Helen says kindly. 'Writing a novel is a risk too, but I'm sure it will pay off.'

'We'd like to hope so, Hel . . . thie,' mutters Dad. 'She hasn't got two bob to rub together.'

'Even one Bob for her to rub'd be fine,' says Rosie, and we both collapse in a fit of giggles.

Dad shakes his head in dismay. 'They just don't take anything seriously, Oscar. I mean, Rosie did graduate with honours in dentistry at UQ and she does work three days a week—max—but Lucy . . .' He sucks in air through his front teeth.

'Brian, it's *fine*!' says Mum emphatically. 'Lucy worked hard in Melbourne and she knows about the line in the sand.'

'I know about lines in sand,' snickers Ben under his breath.

'Mum and Dad think I should have a line in the sand,' I explain to Helen. 'A point at which I say enough's enough and sort of give up on writing, I suppose.'

'Oh, you can't give up,' says Oscar earnestly, and I suddenly remember going on and on to him about my book last night. 'You should never give up.'

'But there has to come a point, I think . . .' Mum begins hesitantly.

'I mean, Lucy's thirty-two and flat out affording a flat white let alone a flat,' says Dad. 'Mind you, she'll be right,' he continues. 'I've told Lenny and Max that when we're gone they have to look after her.'

'Dad!' I protest. 'I'm not an invalid! And I've been putting the feelers out for freelance work. I've pitched articles to *National Geographic*, the *New York Times* and *Vogue*,' I explain to Helen.

'Have you heard back from anyone, love?' enquires Mum brightly.

'No.'

'You were on that TV show, *The Headline Act*, weren't you?' asks Ben.

I nod, smiling. 'Yeah, I was presenting stories with them in Melbourne for about three years.'

'I thought it was you!' says Ben. 'Oscar and I googled you last night and a few of your stories came up. They were great—very funny.'

I smile, wondering if I should be pleased or alarmed that they googled me.

'Oh, thanks, yeah, I enjoyed doing them,' I say.

'So, why did you leave?' asks Ben.

I swallow hard.

'I think Jason from Adelaide in that "Roll With It" food truck is going to take out *Meals in Wheels*,' says Dad, leaning forward in his chair.

I'd shoot him a grateful smile but I know his interruption is more to do with not paying attention than saving me from awkwardness.

'His hot and peppery Texan brioche, or whatever you call it, had me salivating.'

'I tell you what had me salivating,' chimes in Ben. 'Tiffany Bloxsom. She's stunning!'

'Well, who's keen for a game of touch footy?' asks Rosie, glancing at me and hopping up.

'Touch?' says Ben. 'Nah, if we're playing at all it's got to be tackle.'

'Alright,' says Rosie, looking around. 'Chuck us your cup, Brian.'

We make our way across the dunes and onto the beach, with Rosie and Ben walking ahead of Oscar and me.

'I know I only just met you yesterday,' says Oscar, 'but I think you're doing the right thing by writing your book and going for something.'

I smile. 'I hope so.'

'There were so many times I felt like giving up when I was trying to get Bev's Buffet off the ground. The number of banks that knocked me back—jeez, I had more rejections than a Vinnies bin.'

'Alright, so Oscar and I are on one team and you and Ben are on the other,' says Rosie, taking charge. 'We're Queensland and you guys are New South Wales.'

'Well, give us a ten-point start then!' I say at the same time as Ben says to Rosie, 'I can't believe you're a dentist.'

'Okay, so Queensland will tap off,' she says, ignoring him.

Rosie throws the cup to Oscar, who runs towards me. I motion to tackle him and he half falls down, making it easier. We're both laughing as Rosie whispers in my ear, 'Rip his pants off.'

'A quick game's a good game!' yells Ben.

Oscar throws the cup to Rosie and she sprints down the beach with Ben in close pursuit. He catches up and ankle taps her and she lurches forward, hitting the sand like a sack of potatoes. In the process, the oversized togs she's borrowed from Mum slip off her shoulders and Ben looks away, horrified. 'Oh shit, I didn't mean for that . . .'

His words trail off as Oscar runs over. 'Are you okay, Rosie?' he says, giving Ben a dirty look.

Sprawled face down, Rosie adjusts her straps before flipping over, spitting out sand and spluttering, 'I'm fine.' She glares at Ben. 'And you're a typical cockroach cheat.' She gets up and taps the cup to her foot, before running directly at him. He raises his arms in surrender but she barrels into him with all her weight. He collapses, winded.

'Rosie!' I yell, appalled, before running over to check on Ben. Meanwhile, Oscar is falling about on the sand, laughing.

'Piss off, Oscar,' says Ben, rolling over gingerly and staggering to his feet. 'Might just get myself a drink. My fitness isn't what it used to be.' He heads up to where our parents are sitting.

'Shit,' mutters Rosie, 'Maybe I shouldn't have done that.'

'Don't worry,' Oscar tells her. 'He's okay. Probably a bit embarrassed.'

'Still, that was pretty ordinary,' I admonish Rosie. 'Swim time anyone?' I start stripping off my shorts and top.

'Yeah, suppose I'd better give these gorgeous togs an outing,' says Rosie, looking down at the padded breast cups and faded pattern of coral seahorses.

I laugh and shake my head. 'Rosie, they're ridiculous,' I whisper as we wade into the water. 'Mum couldn't even sell them when they were reduced to five bucks in the bargain bin at their Everything Must Go sale!'

'Yeah, she's clearly trying to give you a head start over me with the bros,' Rosie says, laughing.

'Is it safe?' Oscar calls from the beach.

'Yep!' I yell back.

'No jellies?' he calls.

'No jellies,' I assure him.

'No crocs?'

'None that we can see,' teases Rosie. 'Oh, hang on, what's that?'

'It's beautiful!' I shout. 'I've been swimming here since I was little and there's never been anything to cause alarm.'

'Apart from when Brian wore those see-through purple Speedos,' mutters Rosie. 'And that bloody jet ski he used to have.'

Oscar tears off his t-shirt and dives in. Bore or no bore, there's no denying those broad shoulders, I think, as he surfaces.

'Oh, how good is this?' he exclaims.

'Took you a while—I thought you Sydney boys were meant to be tough?' jokes Rosie.

'Only when you compare us to Melbourne boys!'

'True.' She nods.

'Yeah, true,' I agree. 'Speaking of which, the Broncos are playing the Rabbitohs tomorrow night, if you want to come around. Dad's got a TV on the back deck and a barbecue. Ray Warren'll be in a frenzy!'

'Sorry,' replies Oscar. 'That sounds great, but my girl-friend Kate's flying in tonight.'

'Sure, no worries,' I say, looking at Rosie with told-you-so eyes.

'Do you two have partners?' Oscar asks, oblivious to the silent exchange between Rosie and me.

'Yeah, sort of,' says Rosie. 'I'm seeing a tradie, Trent, part-time.'

'Do you do everything part-time?' asks Oscar, smiling.

'Pretty much. Except look shit-hot.'

I laugh into the water.

'That's a full-time job,' she explains.

Oscar looks at me questioningly.

'Well, I was sort of in something on and off with a guy for five years in Melbourne,' I begin, 'but—'

'Blah, blah, blah,' says Rosie, cutting me off. 'Lucy couldn't see the wood for the trees and kept trying to make something work that had died about six months before. His name's Jeremy, he now lives in Port Douglas, he's got a new girlfriend and good luck to him.'

'Yep, that's about it,' I say. 'So, what does Kate do?'

'She's at uni, studying hotel management. She'd love it here.' Oscar looks around us.

I nod and begin wading out of the water towards the beach. 'It's hard not to love. I'm going to sit in the sun for a while.'

I look up to see Ben jump down from the dune onto the beach. We smile at each other as our paths cross. He joins Rosie and Oscar in the sea. I lie down and place my arm over my eyes, and drift off to sleep. Ten minutes later, the intensity of the sun wakes me with a start, and I spot Oscar walking out of the water. Ben and Rosie are splashing about in the waves and, oddly enough, appear to be playing Marco Polo.

'So, do you enjoy being a journalist?' asks Oscar, sitting down beside me. 'Is it a good industry?'

'It's good and bad,' I reply. 'Good in that you can be creative, and shine a light on issues you care about, but bad because it can sometimes be a bit fickle, and churning out material for a daily deadline can wear you down.'

'So you're enjoying the break from it?' he asks.

'Mmm. To be honest, I don't know if I want to go back to journalism.'

For several minutes we watch Ben and Rosie attempt underwater handstands.

'Well, they seem to have sorted things out,' I say.

'Yeah, Ben's a sucker for feisty, attractive girls.'

I smile, knowing Rosie will love to hear me recount this later.

'Maybe you should consider a complete career change after you finish your book,' he says.

'It's funny you say that because it's been on my mind,' I reply, then pause and look at him. 'I think I might start a franchise, called Kev's Buffet.'

Oscar chuckles. 'Yeah, a change can be as good as a holiday, they say. My girlfriend Kate used to be a teacher but she got sick of it, so she went back to uni and now she feels like she's following a path she loves.'

'Oh, that's good,' I say. 'It's important to enjoy what you do.'

He lies down and drapes a beach towel across his eyes and I realise I was being unfair earlier, labelling him a business-type bore. He's just as nice as he was last night. I lean back on my elbows and look up at the sky. It's only one o'clock in the afternoon and yet there's the silvery-white shape of the half-moon stark against a blaze of blue, rudely reminding me that my days are numbered. The audacity of the moon!

'Sorry I'm not being very social. My hangover's really kicking in now,' I say rolling over to face Oscar and finding I'm unable to tear my gaze away from the gentle rise and fall of his chest. Thank God he's asleep!

I close my eyes too, and replace any inappropriate thoughts about this dozing Adonis with the squawk of swirling seagulls, and the laughter of Rosie and Ben drifting from the sea to our bodies on the beach.

5

The sound of Roomba whirring down the hallway wakes me up at eight the next morning. I suspect Mum's setting her off near my room on purpose. And it's working; I get out of bed and dress.

Sitting at the kitchen table after breakfast I take a deep breath and search on my mobile for Henry Billing's practice, Pets and Vets. One of my pitches for a story on country vets has been picked up by R.M. Williams' *Outback* magazine, and I've also decided it's time to seriously consider alternative career paths. I'd tossed up doing vet science after finishing school, and if Oscar's girlfriend Kate went back to uni, why couldn't I?

I dial the number for the practice and Henry picks up immediately.

'Pets and Vets, Henry Billing speaking,' he says brusquely, sounding like my dad.

'Hi, Henry, it's Lucy Crighton here. How are you going?'

'Good.'

'Um, I'm Brian Crighton's daughter. We met a while back when Ruth was holding that disco at the—'

'At the car wash! That's right. Gee, that was a wild bloody night!'

'Yeah, I never saw that slip 'n' slide coming,' I say. 'Anyway, I'm actually in Rocky for a bit and I wondered if you'd mind—'

'Well, we're booked out for today, but it's a kelpie you've got, isn't it? What's wrong with him?'

'Her—but there's nothing wrong with Glenda. Um, there's actually something wrong with me.'

'With you? Well, you need a doctor, mate. You called the wrong surgery. Your dad'd have the number for Ken Saunders.'

'Sorry, Henry,' I say. 'I'm not explaining myself very well. I want to write a feel-good story about country vets for a magazine, and I also wouldn't mind doing some work experience.'

'Work experience?' he asks, incredulous. 'Why?'

This is suddenly becoming excruciating. 'Um, well, in the back of my mind, I've always thought that I'd be a good vet, and I figure there's only one way to find out for sure.'

He sighs down the phone. 'Okay, Lucy. Come down this morning then. We've got a fair bit going on, so it'll be good for you to have a gander.'

'Okay, great! Thanks, Henry.'

I end the call, chuckling to myself.

'What are you giggling away at, Lucy?' asks Mum, walking into the kitchen and repositioning Roomba under the table.

'Oh, I just had the silliest conversation with Henry Billing,' I say, raising my voice over the cacophonous vacuum cleaner.

'Henry Billing?' Mum shouts. 'From Pets and Vets?' Her forehead creases in concern. 'Is something wrong with Glenda?'

'No, Mum! I'm just going there to research a story and see what a vet does. I just want to have a look!'

'You think she could be crook?' she asks.

I crawl under the table and turn off Roomba. As I glance around, I'm struck by a powerful sense of nostalgia. I remember Rosie and I sitting under this table with my brothers when we were little, eating Le Snacks by torchlight, thinking we were super cool to be hanging out with the big boys. Even now, being under the kitchen table feels like I'm in a cosy cubbyhouse, and so I decide to sit back on my heels, and stay there.

Mum has turned on the taps and is clanging some dishes around. 'What did you say's wrong with Glenda?' she asks.

'Nothing, Ma. I'm going to Pets and Vets to do a story and I thought I'd combine it with some work experience.'

The silence is deafening.

Finally, Mum says, 'Work experience? Lucy, I think it's real work that you need. Just money coming in.'

I look down at the floor.

'Don't you want to stand on your own two feet?' she asks, exasperated.

'My feet are tired!' I yell.

I hear Dad's heavy boots on the lino.

'What's going on here?'

'Nothing, Brian, nothing,' says Mum furiously, splashing water about.

'Where's Lucy?'

'Under the table.'

'Under the table?!' exclaims Dad.

I crawl out from my refuge, then stand and walk quickly out of the kitchen, grabbing my keys on the way.

'I'll see youse later!' I yell, closing the door.

❧

'You're Brian's daughter?' says Karen, one of the senior vets at Pets and Vets, squinting at me through her glasses as she scrubs in to operate on a German shepherd.

'Yep.' I smile at her.

'You were on that show, weren't you? *The . . .*'

'*The Headline Act*. Yeah, I was.'

Karen raises her eyebrows. 'What on earth are you doing here then?' she laughs.

'Well,' I reply sheepishly, 'I'm thinking about a career change and thought I'd see what being a vet's all about.'

'How old are you?' asks Karen, making an incision in the dog's stomach.

'Thirty-two.'

'Mmm.' She glances at me quickly. 'Don't do vet science now—not at your age. It's too long a haul. Five plus years of intense study.'

I feel my heart sink—not because Karen's extinguished my overnight flame of becoming a vet, but because the reality hits me again that at thirty-two I mightn't have many options.

After watching the shepherd have her tubes tied and a boxer have his spleen removed, I jot down a few notes for my story, thank Karen and walk from the surgery into reception, where I almost butt heads with Henry.

'Hello, hello,' he says. He's carrying a kitten in one hand. 'How did it go with Karen? Get everything you needed for your article?'

'Yeah, Karen's amazing. She was brilliant to watch.'

Henry nods. 'Very experienced,' he says.

'It's been fascinating.'

'Well, it's a good job. Particularly if you've got young kids at home. The hours are flexible and the pay's pretty decent.'

'Yeah, I think it'd be a great job,' I say.

'Well, feel free to come down again. Sorry, I'm flat out today. Got to get this one desexed.' He holds up the kitten, then walks past me into the surgery.

⌀℮⌀

On the drive home, I contemplate my morning.

Why did I just do that, really? I ask myself. Why am I continually looking for something else? Why do I think the grass will always be greener? Why can't I just commit to one path and stick to it?

As I near my old high school, I spot Mr Banks, my English teacher from grade twelve, crossing the road. I remember how he used to stand proudly at the back of the halls and classrooms when I competed in the interschool debating and public speaking competitions, and how cutting his words could be when he'd hand back a written assessment piece and tell me that, even though I'd topped the class, I could have done better.

He always pushed me to try harder and knew what I was capable of achieving. I remember him telling me, before I graduated, that I would go far. I wonder what he'd say to me now. I wonder if he'd tell me that I was coasting, and that I could do better. I wonder if I've let him and that seventeen-year-old Lucy down. I watch him until the car behind me beeps and I move off.

As I drive along, I think about how I'll structure the article about the vet practice. Maybe I could write an article for one of the newspaper careers sections about people in their thirties who feel stuck and the value of work experience, I muse. Maybe it's not too late to show Mr Banks that I haven't given up on myself.

Without being consciously aware that I was heading there, I find myself outside the unit where my grandma used to live. She had such a wicked sense of humour. She was my hero. I stare across at the windows of her old bedroom, now home to a new resident. In my memory, I walk slowly behind her as she shuffles on her wheelie walker from her front door into her living room. We both sit on the couch and I remove her glasses and wipe the lenses clean on my t-shirt. She declares, 'That's much better,' and I rest my head on her shoulder as the Sunday afternoon sun shines softly through the curtains. She always told me there was nothing so lonely as a Sunday afternoon.

I blink the tears from my eyes and start the car. I'd give anything to be sitting back on that sunlit couch beside my grandma.

When I nose into Mum and Dad's driveway, Glenda paws at the gate in excitement.

'Hello to you too! Aren't you a good girl? Oh, you're the best girl, Glenda!' I scratch under her jaw as she stares up at me. She doesn't care if she becomes a vet, or stays in journalism, or lives in Rocky, or writes a book; she's just happy to be with me and eat chicken necks. I lower my face to her snout and kiss her between the eyes.

At that moment, Dad walks through the gate, returning from the Jockey Club, no doubt. 'You shouldn't have your face that close to the dog, love,' he says. 'It's unhealthy.'

I kiss Glenda again. 'We don't care what he says. We're good friends, you and me.'

I follow Dad inside and find Rosie on the couch, nursing a bucket of KFC.

'Rosie!' I smile. 'What are you—?'

She shakes her head. 'First of all, where have you been?'

'At the vet's, doing work experience.'

'Oh, that's right,' says Dad, walking backwards from the kitchen. 'Are they very busy there, Lucy?'

'Really busy. I saw a German shepherd get her tubes tied.'

'Did you have a chat to Henry? How did he seem to you?'

'Yeah, I had a quick chat to Henry. He was good.'

'So, what do you think about it all?'

'Nah,' I say, sitting down next to Rosie. 'Probably not for me.'

Dad sighs heavily and walks back into the kitchen.

Rosie crosses her arms. 'Trent the Tradie called it off!'

'Oh shit, why?'

'He said he wants something long term. He wants to be in a committed relationship.'

'I thought he was just as keen as you were for part-time!'

'I know, so I said, "Well, how about I add in a Tuesday?" and he said, "This isn't how it's meant to happen, it should just happen organically. It shouldn't be a structured thing, and if it was going to happen, it would have happened by now, and we're just fooling ourselves."'

'Oh shit,' I repeat. 'Well, that sucks. It sounds like he wasn't giving you a chance, that he didn't really want something bigger with you.' I look down at the coffee table. 'But did you want something bigger with him, Rosie?'

'I don't know. I don't think so. Chook?' She holds the bucket out.

'No, I couldn't eat a thing after seeing that dog opened up.'

She nods her head and chews on a wing.

Doing her rounds with the Aura Cleaner spray, Mum finds us grim and silent on the couch. 'Oh, for heaven's sake, girls! What's wrong now?'

She sits down between us and I relay Rosie's news. Mum quietly takes it in.

'Oh well,' she says eventually, 'it sounds like it just wasn't meant to be. It wasn't anyone's fault; it just wasn't right.'

'Yeah, but he could have told her earlier,' I say defensively.

'That's true, Lucy, but who knows what anyone's thinking? Whenever I talked to you about it, Rosie, you told me how it was all a bit of fun and you didn't know if you could see a future with him. He obviously wanted more.'

'But maybe I wanted more as well, and now it's too late. I should have added in the Tuesdays and Thursdays. He's probably got someone else in mind now. I'm going to be sitting on this couch when I'm eighty-five.'

'Well, it is a comfy couch,' I point out, smiling weakly.

'You girls,' sighs Mum. 'You're as bad as each other. What are you both looking for? What do you expect? Why do you have these unrealistic fairy tales of the dream man and the dream job and the dream life? They don't exist!'

Now my eyes are welling.

'They just don't,' says Mum, looking from Rosie to me. 'But you have to choose something and make it work, or you'll end up choosing nothing—or, worse, you'll end up choosing this!' She gestures to the lounge room. 'Do you girls want to be sitting here, with old farty Brian coming and going from the Jockey Club, and me doing jazz aerobics, when you both could be out there, enjoying life and meeting people?'

We examine our laps in silence.

'It's times like these,' continues Mum, 'that I ask myself, "What would Cher say?"'

I begin to smile. As soon as Mum mentions Cher I can't take her seriously anymore, and I know if I look at Rosie I'll laugh.

'"Are you strong enough?" That's what Cher says,' Mum tells us.

'I thought it was, "Are you brave enough?"' says Rosie.

'I thought it was, "Do you shave enough?"' I giggle.

'Oh, you two are impossible,' says Mum crossly, getting up. 'That's the last time I try to talk any sense to you. You're incorrigible.'

We're both giggling now, and Rosie stretches her arms above her head. 'I feel a lot better actually,' she says brightly.

'Me too,' I agree. 'Ah, don't worry about Trent, you always had doubts about him.'

'Yeah,' says Rosie, 'he wasn't the one. I think deep down I knew that, but I just couldn't face the effort of meeting someone new.' She pauses. 'And I'll miss him as a handyman.'

'I know.'

'I think he just hit on a few raw commitment nerves.'

We sit in silence until Rosie pushes the bucket of chicken across the coffee table. 'There's a reason I only get KFC when I'm a bit down . . . it's disgusting. Luce, how long do people feel like this for?'

'If you're a guy, six months. If you're a girl, six years.'

'Six years!' she exclaims. 'Fuck, I can't eat that much fried chicken.'

'Do you think we should get some hobbies, Rosie?'

'What, like play chess or something?'

'Maybe—or gardening, or learning a language or the ukulele?'

'What's got into you?'

'I don't know . . . I just wonder if I'm boring.'

'You read too much, that's your problem, Lucy. You read those *Monthly* magazines, and *MiNDFOOD*, and 'Body and Soul' lift-outs, and you see all those fabulous people doing amazing things and it makes you feel inadequate.'

'Well, I'm not entirely sure that's it. I do read a lot, but—'

I'm interrupted by a knock at the door.

'I'm not getting that,' says Rosie.

I smile at her and walk to the front door, where I find myself face to face with Oscar. He grins at me just as his mobile begins to ring. 'Sorry,' he says, looking down at the screen. 'I have to get this.'

'No worries,' I reply, opening the door. 'Just come on through when you want.'

As I walk back inside I hear him say, 'Hi, Cynthia. What's the latest on the pasta salad?'

'Who was it?' asks Rosie as I flop down beside her.

'Oscar.' I'm careful not to catch her eye.

'Wonder why he'd be coming round,' she says breezily.

'Don't know,' I reply, picking up the TV guide. 'He probably wants to talk shop with Dad.' I flick through the pages uninterestedly before a glossy photo causes me to stop and stare.

'Check it out, Rosie.' I flip the magazine around to reveal a double-page spread of Tiffany Bloxsom leaning from a food truck, spilling out of her low-cut apron as she ladles sauerkraut onto a German sausage. MEALS IN WHEELS DELIVERS SWEET RATINGS FOR TIFFANY BLOXSOM! hollers the headline.

Rosie glances at it. 'No respect.'

'Hi, Rosie,' Oscar says, walking into the lounge room. 'How are you going?'

'Good. Hey, I wondered if you both might like to come fishing this afternoon? Kate has a group assignment due so she had to cancel her trip. I'm flying back to Sydney tomorrow and thought I at least needed to chuck a line in before I left.'

'Oh cool, where are you thinking of going?' I ask.

'Well, I thought I might just head to the Fitzroy; I heard there's barra.'

'True, but you might need a boat. Sometimes there's crocs on the banks of the Fitzroy.'

'Really?!'

'Uh-huh, but we could go to the farm, if you like. You know the beach we went to yesterday? You can just stand in the sea and catch decent whiting and bream.'

'Well, that sounds a lot better than my plan. Does your dad want to come?'

'I'll ask him,' I say. I stand up and go to the door of the lounge room. 'Dad!' I yell.

'What?' he bellows from the back of the house.

'Do you want to come fishing at the farm?'

'No, I've got a board meeting with the Jockey Club—but if you do go, make sure you shut all the gates.'

'Alright.' I sit down. 'He's not coming. What about Ben?'

'Ah, Ben's gone back to Sydney early. Left this morning.'

I glance at Rosie. She crosses her arms. 'Look, I apologised to him for yesterday. I don't know what came over me, but I thought we made peace playing Marco Polo.'

'Oh, I think you did, don't worry about that, Rosie,' Oscar assures her. 'He had to go back for work.'

'Do you want some chicken, Oscar?' Rosie asks.

'No, I'm right, thanks.' He smiles curiously at the remnants of the bucket before picking up the TV guide. 'Tiffany Bloxsom is pretty hot,' he observes.

Surprisingly, I rejoice at his comment. I have zero interest in anyone who finds Tiffany attractive, and I can now happily hang out with Oscar as a friend, secure in the knowledge that our relationship will never be anything but platonic.

'Do you want to come fishing too?' he asks Rosie.

'No, I've got to go home and watch *One Day*.'

Oscar nods as if he understands.

'It's the ritual whenever I go through a breakup: KFC bucket and *One Day*.'

'I'm sorry to hear about your breakup. You must be feeling pretty ordinary.'

'I was, but now I'm over it,' she says, standing up. 'Basically I just love the occasional fucking piece of fried chicken and *One Day* is a top flick. Anyway, you'll love reeling in Lucy.'

Oscar looks confused. I stare hard at Rosie.

'Reeling them in *with* Lucy . . . *with* Lucy,' she mutters, picking up her bike helmet.

'Oh, mate,' she says, turning around as she walks to the front door, 'can you make a note of the time I was here?'

'Why?' I ask.

'I've been watching that series *Making a Murderer* and I'm terrified I'm going to get framed for a crime I didn't commit. So I'm just trying to make sure I always have an airtight alibi.'

I walk over and wrap my arms around her. 'I will always swear you were with me.'

'Thanks, Luce,' she says, stepping out the door. 'Appreciate it.'

6

Oscar and I drive along Emu Park Road, the windows down, the sun on our arms, Nick Murphy's album playing, the conversation easy.

'So, what else is there to do around Rocky?' he asks.

'Well, you can go abseiling at the caves, diving over at Great Keppel, swimming at the Byfield waterholes, walk up Mount Archer, go to the Wild West Saloon for a steak and see the rodeo built inside the pub . . .'

'I've heard about that rodeo in the pub.' He smiles. 'Sounds like I've still got a bit to see.'

'Yeah.' I nod. 'It's got a lot to offer, this region. People talk it down, but look, here we are, driving past these beautiful valleys and kilometres of eucalypts, and there's no-one else on the road.'

'It's great,' he agrees, looking out the window. 'I think I'd miss the energy and action of a city, though. I don't know how I'd go in a country town.'

'I know what you're saying. I mean, I don't see myself here forever, but I could potentially have kids here, if I come back.'

'Where are you going?'

I suddenly feel foolish. 'I don't know.'

He laughs. 'You sound a bit like Ben. He's been all at sea since Dad died, not sure whether he's coming or going. Doesn't think real estate's too crash hot anymore.'

'Does he know what he'd like to do instead?'

'He talks about architecture, and I think he'd be great at it, but he talks about a lot of things. He just needs to make the leap.'

I nod. 'Making leaps is hard. There's too much that screams, "Don't do it!" as you get older. Or maybe that's just inside my head. It sounds like your business is pretty full-on, though. Your mobile doesn't stop.'

'I know—it gets a bit much, doesn't it?' He smiles across at me. 'But while I'm expanding the franchise that's just the way it's got to be.'

'Oh well,' I say, 'lucky for you we just went out of range.'

'Nice. Anyway, Bev's Buffet can't compare to your high-flying TV adventures.'

'Oh, I don't know if you'd call them that,' I say. 'These days my adventures are to Woolies and the dog park. I'd be lost without Glenda. She's my best friend.'

'What about Rosie?'

'She's my best human friend.'

We laugh and I reluctantly admire his good looks. That

curly brown hair, gentle gaze and ready smile would win over many women. But not me, I tell myself, remembering that he thinks Tiffany Bloxsom is hot.

Our vehicle traverses the sand dunes until we eventually reach the gate that leads onto the beach.

'It really is incredible here,' says Oscar, looking from one end of the deserted beach to the other. 'You'd never find a spot like this in Sydney.'

We stand in the waves and bait our lines as the seagulls squawk and dive for baitfish. It's so peaceful, I wonder why I don't come down with Dad more often, and as I'm pondering this, my rod bends dramatically.

'Wow! Impressive!' says Oscar, as I wheel in a twenty-five-centimetre whiting.

'Yep, your turn now.'

'The pressure's on.' He casts out again. 'Do you have a secret?'

'Not telling.'

His line quivers slightly at first, then becomes taut. 'I think I've got one,' he says, grinning at me like a six-year-old boy with a new Xbox game. He reels in a large whiting and dangles it in front of my nose.

'Good one!' I say. 'Whose is bigger?'

We move closer together to measure our fish.

I win by half a centimetre.

'Best of five,' he challenges me. 'Come on, best of five!'

We fish for another hour, and wind up with nine whiting.

'That was awesome,' he says on the return journey. 'It's a shame I'm leaving soon. I'd love to hang out there and go fishing every day.'

'Oh well, it's not going anywhere,' I say with a smile.

'I'm less convinced that you aren't.' He glances at me. 'You want to leave Rocky?'

'Yeah, I do. I'm in the process of elimination now.'

'What do you mean?'

'Well, after our conversation yesterday about careers, I went and did work experience this morning at the vet's.'

He raises his eyebrows. 'You want to be a vet?'

'No, I don't want to be a vet, so now I can rule it out. But I know I want to have a change. It's just where to go next and what to do that I struggle with.'

'What about writing your book?'

'I'm enjoying the writing, I just don't know if I'm using it to avoid figuring out what I should actually do with my life.'

'Would you go back to Melbourne and work on *The Headline Act* again? From the clips I saw, you're a natural!'

'Thanks. It was a great experience, but I don't really see myself having a family in a big city, and now that I'm thirty-two, I suppose I'm considering that side of things more.'

'But you've got ages yet. You're still young, Lucy. Man, I'm thirty-six and I consider myself young. You're talking as if you're about ninety-five and nearing the end of your life.'

I grin. 'I know. My problem is that I feel I've been out of the TV loop for a while now, and so my perception of what it was actually like is a little hazy. And I think my confidence was a bit shot from the last relationship not working out.'

He nods, and then I remember one of those 'Body and Soul' experts advising that you should never bring up past relationships when you're hanging out with new people; apparently it puts a dampener on things.

'But that was over a year ago now,' I add quickly, 'and I am feeling a lot better.'

He looks at me sympathetically. 'Relationship breakups are the worst. Just so hard. So much of your identity and your plans and your dreams can be tied up with one person, and when all of a sudden it ends, it can be shattering. It's a real grieving process. You can't rush it.'

I nod, recognising the truth of what he's saying. 'I seem to have developed this bad habit of second-guessing myself, and when it comes to making big decisions, I'm almost paralysed by indecision. I find that hard.'

'What do you think you're scared of?'

'Making the wrong choice.'

'Regret,' he says.

'Yeah. I know it's silly, but what if you choose to herd camels in the Sahara because it's adventurous and pays the bills, and then on your deathbed realise all along you should have been a diesel fitter?'

He laughs. 'Give me another example.'

'Alright; well, what if you choose to live in Melbourne because you can go to the theatre and the big comedy shows and the fancy cafés, and then one weekend when you're in your eighties you visit Port Douglas and are forced to acknowledge that really your bliss lies with the sun and the tropical downpours? What then? At least I suppose you haven't got long to live with your decision. You just die and regret that you got something so fundamental so wrong.'

'Wow.' He smiles and shakes his head. 'Your mind sounds exhausting.'

'It is,' I concede.

'That last example was more about you, wasn't it?'

'Yep.'

'This guy that broke up with you, he lives in Port Douglas, doesn't he?'

'Yes—Jeremy.'

'Do you think, subconsciously, you want to move up there? Just in case there's hope?'

'No. I know it's over. But I think Far North Queensland is so beautiful. Those cloud-covered mountains falling into the sea and the lush green of the rainforest. It takes your breath away.'

We drive along in silence for a while.

'I just don't think I can rule out an entire region because of one person,' I say eventually.

'No, you can't. But you also don't want to go backwards—if you're moving forward with everything, I mean. You can't fool yourself if you still care a bit about that guy.'

'I know.'

'Sorry, I don't mean to intrude.'

I turn up Triple J and we continue along the deserted coastal road without speaking until the first set of traffic lights on the edge of town signals our arrival back into Rocky.

'So, have you and Kate been together long?' I ask.

'About six months.' He smiles. 'She's really nice. Full of energy and fun. Gets into everything, open to new experiences. We get along well.'

I nod. 'That's good, that's what you want.'

'Yeah, it started out as a really casual thing but it's sort of grown from there, and I think it could have potential. We'll see, it's early days yet. We're still getting to know each other.'

'That's the fun part, though,' I reply.

'Yeah,' he says, looking across at me, 'that's the fun part.'

As we cross over the Fitzroy River, the sun glinting off the masts of sailboats moored in the muddy water, I find myself yearning for cattle trucks and trains, anything that might allow us to continue hanging out a little longer.

'Tea in a cup,' I say awkwardly as we near my street. 'Would you like some?'

He grins. 'You mean a cup of tea?'

'That's right. Sometimes I can't talk properly.'

'Same here,' he says. 'Particularly after a few wines.'

⁓

At home, I lead Oscar into our quiet lounge room and flick on the lights. 'Mum and Dad must be out,' I say, hardly able to believe my luck. 'Would you like to see the rest of the place?'

'Sure,' he replies, and I guide him into the kitchen and out onto the back deck, then inside and down the hallway to my bedroom.

Bloody hell, I think, turning crimson as he scans the books along my shelf. I hadn't thought this through!

'You can tell you're a writer because you're obviously a great reader,' he says warmly.

'Couple of self-helps up there,' I say, figuring that it's better I beat him to it.

'Ha!' he says, looking at me. 'I did notice that but I didn't want to say anything.'

I laugh with him. 'Oh dear,' I say, and glance at my feet.

'Wow, look at you,' he says, picking up a framed picture of me from my uni graduation. He smiles down at the photo for a few moments and I'm wondering what he's thinking when he suddenly turns to me and says, 'I know you're a bit between worlds at the moment, Lucy, but from an outsider's point of view, I don't know why you'd lack confidence.' He glances at the photo again. 'There's nothing at all for you to be insecure about.'

Holy shit Luce, I think, looking at him, maybe you should just treat your bedroom like a crab pot and lock the door and he won't be able to escape? No, no you can't! Come on, get a grip. Repeat after me, he finds Tiffany Bloxsom hot, he finds Tiffany Bloxsom hot, he finds—

My mental incantation works a charm because Oscar's mobile starts ringing, slicing like a knife through any tension between us. He takes the phone from his pocket, looks down at the screen, then smiles at me.

'Thanks for a great arvy, Luce,' he says, and I slightly raise my hand to wave goodbye as he leaves the room. I hear his phone continue to ring as he walks along the hallway before I faintly perceive him say, 'Hello! Did you get your group assignment in?'

7

The next week passes pretty uneventfully, for which I'm grateful. I'd been feeling restless with all the recent interruptions to my writing routine, and I happily chip away at my novel every morning, and spend a couple of after-noons composing my article on country vets and another piece on what it's like to do work experience in your thirties. Glenda and I catch up with our old gang at the dog park, and I go with Rosie to the markets while she does her weekly shop. By Sunday night I feel like I'm on top of things again, and on Monday I awake refreshed and resolved with two intentions: to buy a coffee and to write the next chapter of *Diamonds in the Dust*.

With not a skerrick of shrapnel in my wallet, I creep into Mum and Dad's bedroom, where they are still sleeping, and head directly to Dad's bedside table. Spotting a bounty of gold coins lying atop his latest *Queensland Country Life* newspaper, I quietly scoop it up; there must be about six dollars' worth.

Dad opens one eye. 'You can have whatever's there, Lucy. That's for you. Go on, you can have all that.'

'Thanks, Dad—just want to get a coffee.'

'You're right, love,' he says before rolling over.

I walk back into the lounge room, grab my keys and head onto the verandah. I kick the door shut behind me, and when I look up, my heart drops and my hand falls open, unleashing a cascade of coins onto the ground. I can feel all the colour drain from my face as I look at him, this ghost from my past.

'What?' I shake my head in confusion. 'What are you doing here, Jeremy?'

He scuffles his feet. 'Sorry, I just wanted to say hello and see that you're going okay.' He glances at the coins, then back at me. 'Maybe I shouldn't have come.'

My heart thuds ferociously, and I can feel myself getting sucked into a familiar storm of anxiety and hope. I'd imagined this scene a thousand times; I'd never thought it would happen.

Glenda barks from inside, and glancing behind me I see the curtain slide across the window of Mum and Dad's bedroom. Mum peers at us through the flyscreen.

'Everything alright, love?'

'Everything's fine, Mum,' I say impatiently.

'Hi, Denise.' Jeremy waves.

'Is that you, Jeremy?' asks Mum hesitantly. 'Okay; well, I'll leave you to it.' She pulls the curtains closed and I know she'll be standing with her ear to the window, straining to hear what we say.

72

'Do you want to get a coffee at Bits 'n' Pizzas?' I ask.

'Yeah, sure.' Then, as I scrabble around for the coins, he adds with a slight smile, 'Don't worry, I'll shout you.'

We get into my car and I lurch forward instead of reversing, then put on the windscreen wipers instead of the blinker. He looks amused and I briefly hate him for it.

'I like this song,' he says, turning up Vance Joy's 'Play With Fire'.

'Me too.'

We drive along listening to the music, like we used to, and for a moment it feels as if nothing's happened, as if all the torture and sadness I've been going through for so long were pointless. In the next instant, I feel angry and upset, and want to turn off the radio, pull over, and tell him to go back to Port Douglas or wherever the hell he came from. But the part of me that likes him being beside me in the car again, that has so desperately missed his quiet company, that has longed to drive around with him just like this wins, and I arrive at Bits 'n' Pizzas with tears in my eyes. As we walk inside, I tell myself to pull it together, that I know everyone in this town, and that it just wouldn't do for them to see me crying into a coffee at Rocky's most popular meeting spot.

We sit down and order, and I look at him like you would an apparition that you dearly love, yet at the same time dread seeing.

'So, how's the fam?' he asks.

'Good,' I reply. 'Dad's trying to keep the Jockey Club afloat, and Mum's taken up African drumming.'

'What?' He laughs. 'African drumming?! Ah, Denise . . . I don't remember Brian being into horseracing, though.'

'Yeah, who knew?' I say with a smile. 'Lenny and Max are going well; Max and the kids are coming up from Brissie for a visit soon. Jack and Isla are gorgeous . . . here, look at this picture.'

'Oh, so cute,' he agrees, smiling at the photo on my iPhone. 'And Glenda?'

'Glenda's beautiful. How are your family?' I ask.

'Mum and Dad are good and Luke's great—he's engaged.'

'Oh wow, Luke's finally going to tie the knot!'

I realise with another pang that I'm now so removed from these people that I wouldn't know if their house was flattened in a cyclone. But isn't that how it's meant to be when you break up with someone? Aren't you meant to act as if they and all their kin have suddenly died?

'That's great news. Your mum must be excited.'

'Yeah.' He shrugs. 'I think she'd be more excited if *I* was getting married. She reckons I'm going to be an old man soon.'

'Going to be?' I jibe. 'But what about Claire?'

'Claire's good,' he replies, averting his eyes.

I look at him, at that face, which has been at the forefront of so many of my thoughts, which has caused me so many sleepless nights. 'Why are you here, Jeremy?' I ask.

He gazes at the coffee in his cup. 'To be honest, Lucy, I don't know why I'm here. I don't know about anything.'

My shoulders slump in defeat, and my heart sinks again. He's not here to reconnect with me. He's confused, that's all.

'So, what's going on with Claire? What's happening?' I ask, attempting to play the supportive-friend card, rather than the sad-as-hell hand.

'Well, she doesn't know if she wants anything long term, and I think I do, so . . .' He looks up at me. 'I know this really doesn't concern you, but I suppose I've done a bit of thinking, and I know you had a tough time in Port Douglas with everything last year.'

'I chose to go to Port Douglas. I had to do it. I had to break my own heart, I suppose. But it has been hard, leaving Melbourne and my job there—all that stuff was hard . . .' I take a deep breath and continue. 'Maybe you should just tell her straight out that you want to commit. Maybe that's the answer for you.'

He reaches across and puts his hand on mine. 'You're a good person, Luce.'

I look away and see Oscar walk into the café. I withdraw my hand quickly and wave.

There's a quizzical look in his eye as he walks over.

'Hello,' he says to Jeremy. 'I'm Oscar.'

'Hey, mate. Jeremy.'

Jeremy gets up and they shake hands. They're about the same height. I can feel myself blushing.

'I'd better jump in this queue before it gets any longer,' says Oscar, giving me a smile as he leaves.

Jeremy looks at me. 'You're blushing.'

'No, I'm not,' I say, my face burning.

'Ah well,' he says, finishing his coffee, 'I'd better get back on the road, I suppose.'

'So soon?' I ask.

'Yeah. I sort of think it might have been a mistake to come here.'

'Well,' I say, exasperated, 'what were you expecting? We're not together, so what was the point?'

I slide my chair back from the table and he does the same. We walk outside and I resist the urge to throw my arms around him and beg him to love me, to promise that I'll change the aspects of myself he found frustrating, tell him that I'll follow him anywhere or prove to him that I can set my own agenda, that I'll become tougher and less introspective. But I do none of this, and we get back in the car and drive towards Mum and Dad's.

'You know what I wish?' he says as we pass the Irish pub on William Street. 'I wish you'd been more assertive.'

'But you never knew what you wanted either!' I counter. 'You used to say how you just needed to get away from Melbourne and figure things out, but it wasn't that at all—it was just that I wasn't right for you.'

'Yeah,' he says quietly. 'I suppose I felt a bit restless with you.'

'Mmm.'

We pull up in the driveway, and I turn off the engine.

'Lucy,' he says. 'You're awesome. You'll find someone.'

'Mmm.' I stare at the steering wheel.

'I'd better get going.'

'Okay, well, I don't even know where you're going . . .'

'Back up to Port Douglas,' he says and then pauses. 'I'm off to Berlin in a few weeks to see my cousins.'

His words rattle in my heart and I look across at him. 'All I ever wanted to do was to walk arm in arm with you around Berlin.'

'You know,' he says whimsically, 'I always hoped I'd end up with someone like you.'

'That makes no sense, because I am me, and you could have ended up with me, but you didn't want to.'

He reaches over and gives me a hug, and I sense that we will never be like this again, hugging, in my Corolla.

I watch as he gets out, walks to his car and drives away, knowing he's not looking back, not even for an instant. I put my head on the steering wheel and sob like I'm going for gold in the sob Olympics.

It's not long before there's a tap on the window, and Mum's concerned face is pressed against the glass. Then the car door opens and I look over to see Rosie clambering into the front passenger seat.

'Oh, mate,' I say.

'Lucy, what the fuck? What the hell was he doing here?'

I'm vaguely aware of Mum opening the back door and hopping in.

'Well, what was all that about?' she asks, doing up her seatbelt.

'Mum, you've just done up your seatbelt.'

'Oh, it's an automatic thing,' she says, unbuckling it. 'I hope he hasn't set you back, Lucy. By God, if you're thinking of chasing after that man, I'll throttle you both.'

'What did it all mean, Luce?' asks Rosie, her eyes searching mine.

'Nothing,' I say, looking at her. 'It meant nothing, Rosie, and the worst part is that I wanted it to mean something.'

'Then why did he come at all?' asks Mum, with a sigh. 'What was the point?'

'I think he just wanted to make sure I was okay and didn't want me to see him as the bad guy.'

'So, it was a guilty conscience thing,' says Rosie. 'That's rough. It just makes him feel better, not you.'

I want to put an end to this tedious and unproductive talk. I don't want to become emotionally engaged in the Jeremy saga again; it does my head in too much. And yet I know full well I will spend hours mulling over his visit, going back over every word of our conversation and analysing it for deeper meanings or glimmers of hope.

I turn to Rosie. 'I don't know what to do.'

'Often when I don't know what to do, I—'

'Mum, I don't care what Cher would say or what Cher would do. I don't care about Cher.'

We sit in silence.

'Do you want me to get you a KFC bucket?' asks Rosie.

'No.' I stare straight ahead.

'Well,' says Mum, 'you just have to dust yourself off. Completely move on now, and not give Jeremy one more thought.'

'But why would he have come if it meant nothing?' I say weakly, knowing Mum's answer as I ask the question.

'Because he's had time to reflect and wants to hear that you're alright.' She pauses. 'Obviously he cares about you, but not in a meaningful way, or you'd be together.'

Rosie nods. 'You have to completely cut each other. It's the only way.' She speaks with the authority of someone who's been there.

'But I had! I hadn't spoken to him for nearly nine months, but it didn't mean I hadn't thought about him. I could have contacted him a thousand times, but I didn't, because this is how I thought it was meant to be. You just carry on like the other person never existed. You don't expect to see them out of the blue, talking about where their relationship's at with their new girlfriend.'

'So they're still together?' asks Mum.

'Yes, he said he thinks he might be keener than she is, so I ended up giving him advice.' I chew my fingernails.

'It's not your role to give him advice and support, particularly about his new relationship. You're too nice, always letting him back in and being understanding. You have to respect yourself more. I bet this new girlfriend doesn't let him walk all over her, and that's probably why he's with her. You have to be tougher or people will take advantage of you. It's not being unkind; it's protecting yourself.'

I feel sick in the stomach, because I know Mum's right.

'He's looking at you to boost him up when he feels a bit flat, but where does that leave you?' says Mum, who's on a roll now. 'You'll probably get a message from him in a few months saying, "Thanks, Lucy, for the chat, everything's rosy with my girlfriend again now. Good luck!"'

I look at her in the rear-view mirror. 'They'll get married. I know it. He loves her.'

'Oh well,' says Rosie, 'who cares who or what he loves anymore? He's of no concern to you, Luce. Yes, you care about him, but your heart's so big you'll be able to care about someone else—someone who loves you back.'

'I couldn't agree more, Rosie,' says Mum, winding down the window. 'Look, I'm going to have to get out of this car—the perspiration's just rolling down my back.'

'Yeah, me too, Denise,' says Rosie.

'Alright, I'll come up in a sec.'

'A sec!' exclaims Mum. 'What are you going to do? Not gas yourself, I hope!'

'No, Mum, I don't even know how I'd do that. I'm going for a drive. I need to be by myself, even if it's just twenty minutes. I'll take Glenda.'

'Good idea, I'll go get her,' says Rosie.

'Lucy,' says Mum, after Rosie has left, 'I want you to know how beautiful you are. You're going to meet a lovely young man, I have no doubt about that, so please don't give Jeremy any more of your energy, because I can guarantee he's not wasting one second thinking or worrying about you. Not one second.'

Rosie opens the car door and Glenda leaps up onto the passenger seat and licks my tear-streaked face.

⁓

We drive to the Yeppen Lagoon, one of our favourite spots, and after a long walk we sit on the grass, watching the pelicans glide by. Glenda's getting older now, so isn't as keen on chasing the birds, but she still cocks her head to one side when they stray close. I take a deep breath as the sun winks at me through the swaying eucalyptus leaves. Kookaburras cackle from the ghost gums along the lagoon edge and a couple of cattle stray further up the cracked bitumen path where a fence has broken. I relax my shoulders and try to let go of all the tension. This sadness I've been carrying seems so futile now, particularly when I know with gut-wrenching clarity how considerably Jeremy has moved on.

Glenda rests her head in my lap and looks up at me.

'Yes,' I say to her, 'I know I've been silly. I know, Glenda. But how do I regain my trust and confidence?' The tears slide down my face. 'How do I do it, Glenda?'

She licks my hand, closes her eyes and sighs heavily. I smile. She knows how to let go.

8

It's been a month since Jeremy visited and, just like I knew it would, his visit has hit me for six. Our conversation from that day has gone round and round in my mind like dirty laundry on a heavy-duty cycle. It all leads back to one cold, hard fact: he's still with Claire. Even though he's not sure if Claire's on the same page, it still hasn't made him think I was actually the right one for him all along, so there it is.

I've stopped writing, stopped test-running careers and making plans, and adopted Mum's daily routine. In the morning, we put on any washing, go for a coffee with Dad at Bits 'n' Pizzas, then I do yoga with Mum and her friends, and hang out the washing on our return. We have lunch and a cup of tea, and she leaves for the drumming circle, or to have her hair cut or blow-dried or coloured, and I sleep. In the afternoon, Dad goes to the Jockey Club and I walk Glenda, then help Mum prepare dinner. Dad returns from the Jockey

Club. We watch *New Tricks* or *Inspector George Gently* or *Midsomer Murders*, then I head to bed, read a self-help book and sleep on and off for about three hours. I wake the next morning to Mum drawing my curtains open, and the new day is a repeat of the last.

Mum, poor thing, is clearly worried. Right now, she is standing outside my bedroom, hitting what sounds like a gong. It's horrifically loud.

'Mum!' I yell above Glenda's frantic barks. 'What are you doing?'

'Sorry to wake you, love, but it's nine o'clock and I tried to hold out as long as I could.'

'What? What do you mean?'

She opens my door clutching a huge cymbal and wearing a full-length, bright pink embroidered robe and matching headpiece.

'It's part of Qi-Gong, darl. You bang this healing symbol ten times in the morning around a person who's hurting, and gradually the sound brings about peace and harmony.'

'Well, right now it's bringing about a headache and Glenda's not a fan,' I say.

Mum perches on the edge of my bed and peers down at me.

'That outfit is ridiculous,' I say. 'You look like you're about to audition for *The Mikado*.'

'I know!' She laughs. 'I got the set over the internet. Lucy, I hate to see you like this. Look at the bags under your eyes. Talk to me.'

'I can't talk to you while you're wearing that thing on your head.'

'Alright, it's gone,' she says, taking it off.

'I'm just tired, Mum.'

'No, it's more than that, and it's gone on too long. You're still thinking about Jeremy, aren't you?'

'A bit.'

'Lucy, only you can decide you're better than all this. Only you can move on. I can't do any more.'

Mum leaves and I stare at the ceiling. What *is it* that I'm waiting for? If I'm giving myself a three-year window before I hope to have children, then shouldn't I be heading back to a capital city and steamrolling ahead with my career? Or even going overseas for a last hurrah? Who knows who I could meet on a train in Vienna? I'm certainly not meeting anyone lying on this bed at Mum and Dad's. Maybe I'm giving off the wrong vibe. A girl who's scrounging around her parents' car for spare change is not going to be eligible for *WHO Magazine*'s annual list of Sexiest People.

My bedroom door opens and I brace myself for another pep talk from Mum, but it's Rosie, in her bicycle lycra.

'Lucy,' she says sternly, sitting down exactly where Mum had sat, 'I don't like to say this, but you're turning into a bit of a dickhead.'

'Man, are you and Mum working in good cop/bad cop shifts or something?'

'You can't do this anymore, Luce. You can't lie here and mope around all day and only go out to do yoga with your mum. You're acting like you're fucking retired and you're thirty-two! You're wasting away!'

'Mmm.'

'Even Ruth is worried about you. She stopped me when I rode past the car wash today and asked how you were going and said to wish you all the best. *Ruth* is wishing you all the best! Mate! Come on!'

I give a half-hearted chuckle. 'Has she ever wished you all the best?'

'She's wished me dead and buried, but that's not the point. Come on, Luce. Get out of bed. We'll go to Bits 'n' Pizzas for a coffee. I've got a plan.'

'A plan?' I sit up straighter.

'Yeah, a plan. A definite plan.'

'Okay, but I'm not going speed dating, or joining RSVP, or hanging out at that pub opposite the meatworks.'

'Well, neither am I, so that's good. Come on, get up and get dressed. I'll see you in the lounge room.'

'Rosie,' I say, 'I love y–'

'I know, mate, I know you love me, just get up.'

'I love yoga—I was going to say I love yoga,' I reply, laughing properly this time.

✑

Colleen from the bottle-o and Video Ezy slams down our cappuccinos. Rosie and I look at each other and grin as the froth splashes onto the saucer. Colleen walks away, sighing.

'Right, so, today is the twenty-fifth of June,' says Rosie. 'We've got exactly six months until Christmas.'

'Yep.'

'So, here's two sheets of paper. We have to write down the top five attributes we're looking for in a guy.'

'I didn't think you were into this stuff?'

'I'm not, but let's face facts: we're thirty-two, time's not slowing down, and some of our friends are having their

84

second children. The aim is to find this man by Christmas Day. We've got to try this.'

'Okay,' I say, nodding.

'Right, so all the best.' She scribbles furiously and hands her page to me within seconds.

'Oh, Rosie, you've thought about this already!' I laugh. 'You've cheated!'

'No, I haven't cheated! I've just had a bit of time to reflect while on the bike recently. What do you reckon?'

I look at her list, which reads:

1) Hardworking
2) Honest
3) Fit
4) Wears decent pants and shoes
5) Has good dental hygiene

I almost choke. 'Hardworking?'

'Yeah, I know I'm not, that's why he has to be.'

'Okay, but what about four and five: wears decent pants and shoes, and has good dental hygiene. Aren't they the same thing? Don't you think if someone wore decent pants and shoes, they'd also take care of their teeth?'

'You've got a point, but I can't be arsed thinking of an alternative.'

'Fair enough.'

I hand back her list and she studies it.

'Rosie?'

'Yeah.'

'Do you think we're too old to get married and have kids now?'

She puts her paper down.

'We keep hearing from all these friends of ours who are going back to work after sorting out childcare, you know, and it's made me wonder,' I say.

'Lucy, we've got to cross that bridge when we come to it. We've still got at least five years, don't you think? And surely we'd have met someone by then? And I don't think you're ever too old to get married and have a big fucking party if that's what you want. Don't you reckon?'

'Yeah, you're right,' I say.

'I generally am,' she replies, ever modest.

I'm silent for a while, then say, 'I think I might want to be a doctor.'

'What?' says Rosie, surprised. 'Really?'

'Yep.'

'Really?!'

'Yep.'

'Why?'

'Because you're helping people,' I say. 'It's a worthwhile job. And I could live in a big city *or* a small town.'

She runs her hand through her hair. 'Lucy, can I just say this . . . nothing that you do, or say, or achieve, will make Jeremy come back to you. It's over for you guys, Luce. He wouldn't care if you won the Nobel bloody Prize for literature or became the first woman in space. He's not coming back.'

'I wouldn't be doing it for Jeremy; I'd be doing it for me,' I reply. 'And anyway, I think I've missed the boat on being the first woman in space.'

Rosie laughs half-heartedly. 'I'm not so sure you'd be

doing it for you, Luce. You always said he wished you were tougher, or more assertive, or driven, or whatever it was. But you don't have to prove anything to him. Do medicine if that's what you really want to do, but *is it* what you really want to do? Is it?'

'I don't know,' I say, starting to feel upset.

Rosie reaches over and puts her hand on my wrist. 'Sorry. Sorry, I just want this all to be over for you.'

I look into my lap as my eyes fill with tears. 'So do I.'

She moves to sit beside me and puts her hand on my shoulder.

'I just . . . want . . . to run away . . . with Glenda,' I sob.

The café door slides open. 'Oh shit! Here, pop these on,' Rosie whispers, handing me her massive Jackie Onassis sunglasses. 'Hi, Oscar,' she says, waving cheerily.

'Hey, Rosie, hey, Lucy, how are you going?' He walks over to our table with a petite woman with strawberry blonde hair close behind. She's wearing the same navy-and-white-striped dress I admired recently—but couldn't afford—in Witchery.

'This is Kate, my girlfriend,' says Oscar, placing his hand on the small of her back.

'Hello,' she says, and smiles at us. 'Oscar said we might run into you around town somewhere. Nice watch,' she adds, gesturing to Rosie's wrist and raising her arm to reveal they both have the same blush pink and rose gold-coloured watch. We smile back at her. She seems lovely.

Oscar looks at me. 'You okay?'

'Yeah,' says Rosie firmly, 'she's okay.'

I smile and nod. 'Yeah, I'm okay.'

'I might see you around. Katie and I are up for the next ten days, so . . .'

'Sounds great,' enthuses Rosie. 'Well, we're about to take off.'

'Oh, sure,' says Oscar, moving aside. 'Well, see ya.'

∽

'That was fairly embarrassing,' I say to Rosie as we drive along Gladstone Road, passing the double-decker cattle trucks and bull statues.

'No, what's embarrassing is that I just realised I left that bloody top five list there,' she says.

'You didn't!'

'Yes, I fucking did. And they sat down at our table when we left—I saw them.'

'Oh shit—Rosie, that's gold. But they don't know which one of us wrote that list.'

'I'll just have to pretend I know nothing about it, or that it was there before we sat down,' she says.

'Oscar won't make a fuss about it. He's too nice for that. God, I hope he doesn't think *I* wrote it.'

'Yeah, now your mind's on something else, isn't it?'

'Rosie, wind your window up! These cattle trucks stink.'

She laughs. 'You're not in Melbourne anymore, Luce!'

9

A week later, when I get back from taking Glenda for her morning walk, my heart soars at the sight of Max's new black Subaru Outback in the driveway. He'd been vague on exactly which day he and the kids would arrive, and as I bound up the front steps to the sounds of little people playing in the front yard, I realise his visit couldn't have come at a better time.

'Lucy! Lucy!' call Jack and Isla, my seven- and five-year-old niece and nephew, who race towards me and run into my arms.

I swing them around. 'Oh, you two! It's so good to see you!'

'Can you take us dinosaur hunting?' asks Jack, wide-eyed, latching onto my leg as I lower him down.

'Please!' pleads Isla, jumping on the spot.

'Alright! Go and get your hats and put some shoes on.'

Max walks out onto the verandah and the kids scoot past him as he envelops me in a bear hug. 'Come on in, mate, we've just boiled the kettle!'

In that moment, all seems right with the world. Mum is in the kitchen, making tea, two little sandy brown curly heads are tugging on their shoes, and Max is standing at the open fridge door, scanning for chocolate, like he always did.

When we were growing up, I idolised Max. He's only fifteen months older than me, but when you're seven, fifteen months is a lifetime of cool, and I used to shamelessly copy his every move. If Mum and Dad took us to a restaurant, for example, I'd wait to see what drink Max would order before ordering mine. He soon cottoned on, and I remember how devastated I was one time when he ordered a lemonade, which I duly requested too, and then as the waiter walked away he called out, 'Can I please change that to an orange juice?'

As we got older, I copied him less and less, and now, in our early thirties, our lives couldn't be more different.

'I won't have tea yet, Ma,' I say as Jack and Isla take my hands. 'We've got a date with the dinosaurs.'

'We're going dinosaur hunting,' Isla whispers to Mum.

'Dinosaur hunting? How lucky are you!' exclaims Mum, looking down at them. 'You be good for Aunty Luce.'

They nod earnestly and then we all walk hand in hand out the back of Mum and Dad's house and down the gently sloping green fields of the outer botanic gardens, which lead to patches of rainforest, hoop-pine-lined pathways and—our ultimate destination—a playground shaded under a canopy of weeping figs.

'What would you do if you saw a dinosaur?' asks Jack as we walk along.

'I'd stand very, very still,' I reply solemnly.

'But what would you do if the dinosaur still saw you?' persists Jack.

'I'd run very, very fast,' I reply.

'I would run *so* fast that the dinosaur would be like, "Hey! Was that even a person?"' says Isla.

'Yeah,' I agree, 'that would be really fast.'

'Did you know I'm the fastest boy in grade two?' says Jack.

'Really?' I say, looking down at him.

'Yeah, Mum said so.'

'Cool,' I reply. 'I was pretty fast when I was little, you know.'

'How many years are you?' asks Isla.

'Thirty-two.'

'*Thirty-two!*' exclaims Jack. 'Gee, mate, that's even older than Mum!'

I chuckle; he sounds like a mini-Max.

'Are you really that old?' he asks.

'Yep, I'm really that old. But I'm still totally awesome!'

'You're thirty-two and not married! You don't even have a boyfriend! Are you going to have babies?' he asks, and I can almost hear his little mind ticking over.

'I hope so one day,' I say.

'Well, you'd better hurry up and get married, mate, because then you could have babies, or else you get older and soon you could be dead!'

We walk in silence through the grass, listening for dinosaurs, then Isla asks, 'Do you want to get married?' She peers up at me intently, her tiny voice piercing my heart.

'Yeah, I do, Isla,' I say, squeezing her hand and smiling to myself. I can't believe I'm being held accountable by a five-and seven-year-old. The crazy thing is, their interrogation is so devastatingly, touchingly effective. As I let go of their hands and watch them run into the playground, I sit on the grass, and realise they've made me acknowledge two things out loud that I rarely admit to anyone. Yes, I want to get married and yes, I want to have children. I watch as they wave to me from the top of the climbing castle. The little buggers.

ɔєѳ

'Hey, Luce,' says Max, handing me a cup of tea on our return and settling into the couch, 'tell us your news.'

'I don't really have much news.'

'Finished your book?'

'No, still going.'

'She's broken-hearted, Max,' says Mum frankly.

'I thought you looked a bit sad. Who is it this time?'

I don't reply.

Max looks to Mum. 'Not Jeremy still?'

Mum nods.

'No! Luce, I thought you were over that. What happened?'

'She was doing so well,' says Mum. 'And then he suddenly turns up on the doorstep about a month ago.'

'He didn't!' exclaims Max.

'He did,' says Mum. 'He came here and they had a chat and he told her he's still with his new girlfriend. Then he left again.'

'Shit, he could have just texted you that.'

'That's what I said,' says Mum, sighing. 'So of course now Lucy's dropped her bundle again.'

'Oh shit, Luce.' Max looks at me sympathetically. 'Well, you've just got to dust yourself off again, don't you? There's no alternative, is there?'

'No.'

'How are you going for money?' he asks.

'Not great,' replies Mum.

'Mum! I can answer questions for myself,' I say. 'I've still got a grand left.'

'You'll be right, Luce,' Max assures me. 'You've always landed on your feet. You'll land on them again.'

I take a deep breath. 'I think I want to do medicine.'

'Ha-ha!' Max laughs and claps his hands in delight, as if it's the funniest thing he's ever heard. 'Now there's a good one,' he says, grinning.

'No, I'm serious—I want to be a doctor.'

'Medicine! At thirty-two! You've got to be crazy!' cries Mum, looking over to Max for support. 'Say you did get in, you wouldn't start until the following year, which would make you thirty-four! Thirty-four, studying without an income for at least five years! Well, you could forget having a family. There's no way you could have kids.'

Dad walks into the lounge room, having overheard the tail end of the conversation. 'Lovey, you're as much a GP as I am a ballerina,' he comments before leaving again.

'What sort of medicine interests you, Luce?' asks Max, causing Mum to shoot him a dark look.

'I wouldn't mind being a geriatrician.'

'A doctor for old people?'

'Yeah, we'd probably all be the same age by the time I graduated, so I'd relate well to my patients.' Max and I laugh, though Mum doesn't see the funny side.

'Why not do teaching, Lucy?' says Max. 'You've already got a BA, so you'd only need to do a DipEd for nine months and then you'd be on eighty grand a year, have heaps of holidays to travel. You'd make a great English and drama teacher.'

And though I think I would be an okay teacher, I don't want to be. I don't want to listen to commonsense advice when I still think I have options.

Before I can say anything, Jack and Isla run into the room and jump on my lap.

'Can we sit on your back and you walk like a dog?' asks Jack, his eager blue eyes anticipating a positive response.

'Okay,' I reply, getting down on the floor. They clamber onto my back and I crawl around the furniture.

Max watches us. 'See, look how much fun you're having! Don't you want to have a few tin lids of your own, Lucy?'

'Woof woof,' I reply.

'Or at least think of us, mate; Jack and Isla need some cousins.' He sips his tea. 'You know what I've learnt?'

'What, love?' asks Mum.

'I've learnt there's no right time to do the big things in life. There's no right time to get married or to have kids, you just have to do it or you never will.'

We hear a knock at the door.

'Come in!' yells Mum.

The weight of Isla on my neck makes it impossible for me to see our visitor.

'Oh, hello, Oscar,' says Mum, beaming. 'Let me get you a cup of tea.'

'Sorry, you've already got a big gang here, I didn't mean to interrupt,' says Oscar. 'I can come back later.'

I wiggle my back until the kids slide off. 'No, no, you're right, Oscar. This is my brother Max, and his kids Jack and Isla.'

Isla scurries behind my legs and Jack eyes him curiously.

'Hello, Jack, I like your *Star Wars* t-shirt,' says Oscar.

I smile, and wonder why he's here and not with Kate.

Mum bustles back in, determined not to miss a second of the lounge room banter, and hands Oscar his tea. He sits beside me on the couch, and Isla settles herself in my lap.

'Hello, Oscar,' says Dad, striding into the lounge again and shaking Oscar's outstretched hand. 'Isn't it lovely to have both Max and Oscar in the same room, Denise?'

Max looks across at me and I feel my stomach churn, knowing there'll be twenty questions from him when Oscar leaves.

At Dad's insistence, Oscar explains the Bev's Buffet business model to Max, and I busy myself with Isla and a colouring book on the floor. It's actually quite meditative, shading between the lines of Peppa Pig, and as conversations about State of Origin referees, house prices in Brisbane and Sydney, and the lucrativeness of selling bamboo-based nappies to China swirl around me, I feel more relaxed.

Mum chortles with delight at Oscar's every second comment; if I didn't know better, I'd say she was flirting. Despite Oscar being a cockroach and a Manly supporter, I can tell Max likes him.

Hearing the theme song for *Teen Titans Go!* Isla races into the TV room to join Jack, and Oscar stands, saying he promised he'd fix his mum's clothesline after Ben broke a few spokes swinging on it at their housewarming, and that he'd better set off to Bunnings. He nods at Dad and Max and lightly hugs Mum when she insists he 'give her a squeeze'. I follow him onto the verandah and down the path to the front gate, where he pauses with his hand on the latch.

'You going okay, Luce? You looked a bit upset at Bits 'n' Pizzas the other day.'

'Oh, that.' I laugh. 'No, I'm right. I'd just dropped my bundle. Needed to get back on the horse.'

'Ha! You sound like my grandma.' He grins and pushes the gate open.

'Have fun at Bunnings.'

'Do you need anything?' He turns to look back at me.

'Nah, I'm right for ladders and chainsaws.'

We wave goodbye and I am walking back along the verandah when I hear Mum, Dad and Max discussing me in conspiratorial tones.

'He wouldn't come around if he wasn't keen,' Max says, to which Mum replies, 'You're right, Max, there's definitely something there. I just hope she pulls herself out of this rut . . .'

'Well, I think Oscar's a very capable young man,' says Dad. 'And if Lucy had any sense she'd—'

I walk inside and their round table discussion about me immediately ceases.

'You know he's got a girlfriend,' I say, annoyed by their presumptuous matchmaking. 'I met her and she's nice.' I drop onto the couch.

Dad crosses his hands behind his head and says, 'Did you see Tiffany Bloxsom's been nominated for a Logie?'

'Has she?' asks Mum. 'You know, it doesn't surprise me.'

'No, it doesn't surprise me either,' says Dad. 'Remember that first night she presented Sportsbet all those years ago at half-time between Canterbury and Cronulla and I said to you, "That girl's got talent."' Dad looks across at Max. 'You know, they asked Lucy to present Sportsbet.'

I feel my heart thumping hard and fast against my chest as Dad turns to me and says, 'That could have been you, Lucy.'

I stand up and stare him down. 'Dad!' I exclaim. 'I would rather shoot myself in the head than present Sportsbet!'

'Well, maybe you should!' he retorts.

I storm out of the house, slamming the screen door behind me like a ten-year-old. I search for Glenda, and when I can't find her I march back into the lounge room, my body trembling, my blood boiling, my heart racing, and Mum, Dad and Max swivel their heads to stare up at me.

'You can all get fucked!' I yell.

Their jaws drop.

'I didn't really mean that, but fuck you all!'

They look at me like I might be about to fit.

'Okay, what I'm trying to say is, enough's enough. I've had it. I've fucking had it! I'm going to Broome on a holiday!' I then burst into tears.

Max starts clapping. 'Well,' he says, 'I think this is just wonderful. Lucy's finally snapped! I've been waiting over a year to hear you say that, and you're finally there. Congratulations, Lucy!'

'Yes!' agrees Mum. 'This is a day to celebrate! I'm so glad you've officially cracked!'

'I hoped to push you over the edge with my Tiffany Bloxsom comment, love,' says Dad. 'I didn't really mean to tell you to shoot yourself in the head, that was a step too far and I apologise for that, but regardless, you got there in the end.'

I look at them in disbelief. 'What are you talking about?' I gasp through sobs.

'Today's the beginning of a new chapter,' says Max. 'Finally, you're going to get off this couch, and get out of this house, and go on an adventure, and figure out what you really want to do.'

'This is a real breakthrough,' says Mum, dabbing at her eyes. 'A real breakthrough.'

I stagger back to the couch, bewildered yet smiling. Bloody hell, I think, all I'm doing is booking some flights to Broome.

10

There's nothing like the sound of monks running on floorboards to jolt you out of a Zen-like state. I'm sipping green tea and admiring the beautiful gardens outside my room, when their heavy footsteps remind me I'm in a Buddhist temple, atop a forested tableland, in the sacred monastic village of Koya-san. The temple, Eko-In, sits high on a mountain on the Kansai region's rugged Kii-Hanto peninsula, south of Osaka.

A fortnight ago, Mum and Dad decided to shout me three weeks in Japan. They said they were sick of the sight of me, and Broome was still too close. Besides which, Mum had asked Rosie where I'd go if I could choose anywhere, and Rosie had immediately replied, 'Japan.' Mum had then taped a copy of the ticket to the top of Roomba, and set her off outside my room at 5.30 am. I flew from Rockhampton to Brisbane and on to Tokyo the very next day.

I'd hugged Mum at the Rockhampton terminal, and she'd cried into my neck, telling me all she wanted was for me to feel brighter. She then blessed me with oil, which she claimed to be holy but I think was canola.

The temple I'm staying in now, Eko-In, is a beautiful wooden building of several levels and with staircases that twist and turn around a delightful central garden. The rooms are simple yet elegant, with cane chairs, a glass table, and floor-to-ceiling windows with garden views.

For tourists, the village provides a peaceful escape from the crowds of Kyoto and the opportunity to stay in a working Buddhist temple. For followers of Buddhism, Koya-san—along with its incredibly atmospheric cemetery, Okunoin—is one of the most spiritually significant sites in Japan.

Though I'm clearly no Buddhist, getting here felt a lot like a pilgrimage. I caught a series of trains heading south of Kyoto, travelling on gravity-defying tracks that wound between soaring mountains, before a final cable car ride that grazed the treetops. I felt so alive, it was like I was reconnecting with my fearless twenty-five-year-old self: the Lucy who existed before Jeremy, before *The Headline Act*, and before the various missteps and wrong turns I'd taken. I was rediscovering the Lucy who'd travelled around Portugal on her own, who had made the decision to move to Perth after living with Rosie in London, who had danced on a table at the Oktoberfest beer halls—the Lucy who had fun!

Heavy footsteps stop outside my door and one of the monks knocks and then walks briskly into my room, carrying a tray laden with several dishes. He arranges them on the tatami mat with precision, each dish more colourful and exotic than the last.

After he leaves I feast on sesame-seasoned tofu, plum-flavoured miso and soba noodles with pickled ginger root and white radish. It's easily the best meal I've eaten so far during my fortnight in Japan, and I savour every bite. Soon after I've slurped the last of my miso, the monk returns to unroll my futon.

I lie down and listen to the rain falling lightly outside. This holiday is exactly what I needed. Walking through the ancient forests of Okunoin, gazing out at the changing landscapes from the train and doing some meditation classes, I've been gradually letting go of all the turmoil in my heart and mind over Jeremy, and finally seeing our former relationship for what it was.

He and I had both harboured misgivings about each other. From our first meeting in Perth to breaking up in Melbourne, one of us was always more into the relationship than the other. We never seemed to dance to the same tune for very long. I'm the one who hasn't been letting go and has been clinging to the sadness, and acknowledging that, and forgiving myself for remaining captive to it, has been a revelation.

Some people seem to be masters of letting things go, to the point where you wonder if they ever hold on to anything in the first place. Perhaps therein lies the secret; to be detached yet engaged; to not hold on too tightly to an emotion or an outcome. Finally, it's sunk in that nothing is really holding me back and, to be honest, there probably never has been.

It's both exciting and confronting, though, for me to realise that the world might again be my oyster, because then I feel compelled to do something amazing with the opportunity. I think one of the greatest gifts for me would be to know myself more: to understand what makes me happy and what makes me sad, and to cultivate the former. I wonder why something that sounds so simple can be so complicated. Is it because your ego is too quick to join the conversation, convincing you that you can do better than what you think makes you happy?

This past fortnight, I've resolved not to dwell on what I'll do next and just focus my efforts on finishing *Diamonds in the Dust*, while continuing to earn money writing freelance articles. If I'm ever going to have a shot at becoming a published author, I need to back myself and be disciplined and diligent.

I've also been thinking about Oscar. He's messaged a couple of times, asking how much sushi I'm eating, marvelling at the speed and efficiency of the bullet trains, enthusing about some of the chain eateries he visited when he was here last, and enquiring whether I've mastered chopsticks and basic Japanese. I think he kind of likes me, and I definitely like him, but I'm well aware that he has a girlfriend, and I don't want to make grand plans in my mind built on false hopes.

Right now, lying on the futon, listening to the rain, I feel content. I want for nothing, and so I say to my mind: Let's, from this day on, travel down different pathways. No more default-mode self-defeating thoughts about indecision or low self-esteem dictating your life. No more beating yourself up about Jeremy. No more of any of that.

◦ℰℴ

By the time I leave Koya-san to meet up with Rosie in Tokyo I am feeling extremely Zen. Miraculously, I manage to spot her at the pedestrian crossing outside Shibuya Station, which is one of the busiest intersections in the world. Then again, with Rosie wheeling along her bright pink Samsonite and causing havoc by photo-bombing every second tourist's snapshot, the task of finding her was relatively easy.

'Fancy meeting you here!' I say, hugging her as she spins around to face me.

'She's a bit busier than the corner of Fitzroy and Albert streets, Luce!' she declares, taking my arm as we join the throng of humanity crossing from one corner to the other.

'How about it, Rosie!' I yell, craning my neck to take in the dizzying spectacle of towering video screens and flashing neon lights. We grin at each other, energised by the electrifying streetscapes.

'Wow!' she exclaims, patting my shoulder as we finally reach the footpath. 'How fucking good is it to be in Tokyo?!'

I lead her into a brightly lit, fairly crowded sushi train café and we squeeze ourselves and her suitcase into contention for the passing plates.

'Can I buy you a beer as big as your head?' I ask.

'Only if you're buying yourself one too,' she replies, smiling.

I order our drinks and we high-five each other as they arrive.

'Gee, I haven't seen you looking so happy and well in ages,' she observes. 'Japanese air done you a world of good, has it?'

'Well, I don't know about the Tokyo air,' I say, 'but the time I spent meditating up at the Buddhist monastery on the top of a mountain in Koya-san was absolutely magic.'

'Oh, she was right!' says Rosie, resting her chin in her hands. 'Sounds like I got here just in the nick of bloody time. But she's always right, isn't she?'

'What are you talking about?' I ask, though I know the answer.

'Your mum. She said that after two weeks alone with only your thoughts and the self-help books you no doubt snuck into your bag, you'd be barmy.'

I smile at the thought of Mum, still scheming from seven thousand kilometres away.

'She told me I couldn't delay one more hour in getting over here,' Rosie says, taking a large swig of her beer. 'She even bought me some packing cells from Kathmandu!'

'They're actually very useful, Rose!' I say in my mother's voice.

'Oh, Lucy,' she says, patting my back. 'Staying in a monastery on top of a mountain with fucking Buddhists. Well, I can tell you right now, I'm cutting all that crap out. For the next week, I'm in charge. I've got it all planned.'

'Ha!' I say, laughing. 'It's so good to see you! I don't know what I would have done without you in Rocky.'

'Neither do I,' says Rosie. 'Anyway, *kanpai*!' She raises her glass.

As we clink beers as big as our heads, I feel the happiest I've been in twelve months.

ⴄⴄⴄ

True to form, Rosie's plans consist of little more than a desire to follow the fun. Hence, the next day we find ourselves heading to the 'hot spa capital' resort city of Beppu, our destination a place we can only decipher as 'Mudworld Onsen'.

'Thirteen-yen admission, cheap as chips!' says Rosie, handing over some crumpled currency to the attendant as we stroll under the entry flags into a large building of labyrinthine corridors and follow the signs to the ladies' section, which consists of a bathroom lined with naked women sitting on stools, scrubbing themselves and shampooing their hair, using showerheads connected to washbasins. The onsen bathing rituals are a significant part of Japanese culture, and I'm determined to approach the experience with maturity.

'Oh shit, Rosie!' I exclaim, turning around to find her stark naked. 'You could have given me some warning!'

'Get your gear off, Luce, we have to wash ourselves before we get in the mud,' she says, sitting down on one of the stools. 'It makes no sense to me, but they're not my rules to break, are they?'

I should have known Rosie would take us to a city that has more than two thousand onsen. I can tell she's absolutely loving this, and delighting in my awkwardness.

'The water temperature is just divine!' she gushes.

I turn away and strip off my jeans and unfasten my bra, then sit beside her and twist on the showerhead.

'So, how have you been, Luce?' she asks casually, soaping up her chest, and I start giggling under my breath. It's too much for me.

'Alright, enough washing, Rosie,' I say, turning off the showerhead and getting myself together. 'Let's hit the mud.'

'After you, Luce,' she says, looking across at me.

'No! After you!' I say, finally meeting her eye.

'Oh!' she exclaims, 'you may have been school captain but you've got no initiative! Follow me!' she orders.

We walk quickly across the tiles and down a dimly lit corridor. At the end of the corridor we walk into a brightly lit bathroom full of naked men washing themselves.

'Fuck me!' exclaims Rosie as some of the men glance up. 'Quick, turn around,' she sputters between gasps of laughter. 'We've taken a wrong turn!'

I run back along the corridor feeling ridiculous with Rosie trailing after me, breathless from laughing.

'Here!' I say, pointing to a sign that looks similar to the one printed on our entry ticket. 'I think if we go along here, we'll . . .'

'Bingo!' says Rosie as we emerge from the tunnel into a vast, open field of mud.

We walk across the muddy expanse, joining dozens of other naked bodies in the centre, all wading around with mud up to their necks. A flimsy rope, strewn across the surface, divides the field into male and female zones. We lounge about by the rope.

'Rosie, I haven't been able to stop looking at men's crotches,' I say, to which she almost doubles over laughing. 'And not just today,' I continue. 'I'm talking guys on trains, guys walking down the street, young guys, old guys, it's like a disease.

'No, I'm serious! It's not funny,' I say as she continues laughing. I add, 'Oh, and guess what? I pitched two articles to *Travel and Leisure* magazine about the Buddhist monastery and cemetery, and they've accepted them both.'

'That's great, Luce!' Rosie says. 'Well done!'

'Yeah, I think they'll be published in a few months, so I've been getting my notes together, and it just feels so good to be writing again.'

'How about your book?' she asks. 'What's the Foster family up to?'

'Yeah, they're back on track. Trying to make a go of it on the gemfields.'

Rosie rubs mud into her cheeks, like it's an exfoliator.

I take a deep breath. 'So, there's something I've been meaning to tell you.'

She looks across at me. 'You're moving back to Melbourne?'

'No.'

'You've got a job?'

'No.'

'You're getting back with Jeremy?'

'No, no, no.' I shake my head. 'Oscar.'

'Oh, hello.' She grins, ceasing her exfoliation.

'No, Rosie, I don't know if it's an "Oh, hello" or not.'

'Continue, please.'

'The thing is, I've been thinking about him, but I don't want to play games anymore, if you know what I mean. I've already wasted too much time. I just want to meet someone who loves me and knows they love me, and that's that.'

'You've got to love them too, though.'

'Oh, of course.'

'Mmm,' says Rosie, 'I know what you're saying, but realistically, anyone we meet now, unless they're twelve years old, is going to have a past. They'll have been with other people, and there's going to be some people that really got under their skin and that they'll always love, and we just have to accept that, so I think we have to be okay with finding someone who may still love someone else, but is not so in love with them that they can't make a happy future with us.'

I stare at her. 'Bloody hell, that was philosophical!'

She smiles and flings mud at me. 'Well, I've had a lot of time to think, haven't I?'

I gaze around at the sea of bathing bodies. 'Maybe you're right, Rosie. Actually, I think you are right, but it's a bit depressing.'

'Depressing but realistic,' she replies.

'God, you sound like my dad!' I begin to apply a mud mask to my neck. 'I think I'd prefer to meet a twelve-year-old.'

She laughs. 'So let's get back to Oscar. Shame you didn't pash him at Helen's housewarming when I told you to. He's very good looking.'

'Ha! Yeah, well, it can't go anywhere as long as he's with Kate. But he has messaged a couple of times since I've been over here.'

'What, nude pictures?'

'No, just trivial stuff about bullet trains and the best karaoke bars.'

Rosie nods approvingly. 'Useful information. I wonder if he went to the one we were at last night.'

'Anyway, you'll be pleased to know Jeremy is out of my head and I feel a lot better about life generally.'

'Good, mate.' She smiles. 'I'm very pleased to hear that.'

'What about Tradie Trent?' I ask.

'What about him?' she replies. 'I saw on Facebook that he's got a new girlfriend.'

'You don't care, though,' I say, knowing that she does, if only a little.

'Yeah, I don't care.'

'He got under your skin, didn't he?' I ask.

'I just can't understand why he wouldn't want to be with me. I mean, I'm me!' She breaststrokes through the mud. 'I've had far too much time on my hands since you left Rocky, Luce. I was round eating dinner with your mum and dad most nights, and taking Glenda for walks. I started feeling like you, God help me!'

As we both laugh, we notice a man slip under the rope. He grins widely in our direction, and ever so slowly inches towards us. Rosie and I exchange a glance but pretend not to notice him and splash about on our backs. When we stand up we're startled to see that he's almost on top of us.

'Hey, Luce,' Rosie says, her voice an octave higher, 'did you just touch my thigh?'

Between convulsions of laughter, I manage to say, 'No!'

'Might pop out, hey?' she says, giving the interloper a dirty look.

'Yeah.' I nod. 'This mud stinks a bit.'

'I know!' she says. 'I didn't want to say anything, because it was my idea, but this mud's fucking feral!'

We clamber out of Mudworld Onsen and in stitches of laughter, but without a stitch on, we run back along the corridors to our clothes.

⁓

After shouting ourselves a stiff drink to recover from Mudworld, we decide to shout ourselves several more before trying out Beppu's indoor sand baths.

On arrival at the baths we are given summery cotton kimonos called yukatas to change into and instructed to lie down in adjacent sandpits. Beautiful Japanese women then begin to shovel loads of black sand over us.

'Rosie,' I say, shifting under three inches of soil, 'I sort of feel like I'm being buried alive in a shallow grave.'

She chuckles. 'Me too. Wouldn't it be a terrible way to go?'

'Mmm,' I reply as sand rains down upon my legs.

'I've been thinking I have to learn that whatsit manoeuvre so I don't choke to death,' she says matter-of-factly.

'What are you talking about?'

'The other night I was eating a celery stick while watching an old *Seinfeld* episode and I laughed so hard I almost choked on my celery! So, I thought it could be handy to know that manoeuvre.'

It could be the sake I've been drinking most of the afternoon, but I suddenly feel an ocean of sadness for my friend and my eyes fill with tears.

'You're not always going to be alone, you know,' I say, my voice quavering. 'You'll find someone who loves you very much, Miss Rose.'

'Cut your fucking soppiness out right now!' she yells. 'If I could kick you in the shins, I would.'

I laugh. 'Oh, mate, I can't even lift my hands up anymore to wipe the tears away. This is the pits!'

'Literally!' she quips.

We listen to the scrape of the shovel on the cement and the dull thudding sound of the sand as it is deposited on top of our bodies.

'You know how you were telling me last night about the Jeremy watershed moment you had in the monastery?'

'Yeah.'

'Was it all worth it?'

'What?'

'The sadness of the past year to get to that point?'

'No,' I reply immediately.

We both laugh and laugh.

'I wish I'd let go of it all eight months ago. I just hold on to things for too long.'

'You know when I think you were at your happiest?' asks Rosie.

Another shovel load hits my neck. It's now impossible to look across at her.

'Any time I wasn't buried under three feet of volcanic sand!' I exclaim.

Ignoring me, she continues, 'When you were in the *Anne of Green Gables* merchandise store on Prince Edward Island.'

'Ha!'

'It's true!' she says. 'I remember you standing there in that *I Love Gilbert* t-shirt, holding up a tea towel printed with the recipe for raspberry cordial, and you were just glowing!'

'That was one of the best days of my life, being in that shop.'

'It's the things from childhood, isn't it, that take you back?'

'Mmm. I don't think I could move to Prince Edward Island, though. Too cold.'

'London was cold and you loved living there,' she says.

'Yeah, true. I did love London. It seems so long ago now, Rosie.'

'I know! So long ago. And yet . . .' She pauses. 'It's still there.'

111

'What do you mean?' I ask, sensing a gossamer thread of thought, which I dare not tread upon lest it break.

'I think I was happiest when I was in London,' she says.

'London was amazing,' I reply, feeling the sand's warmth seep into my bones. 'And you'll always get work there,' I say casually, knowing this conversation is now a delicate dance.

'Yeah, I'll always get work there,' she echoes softly.

We are now both up to our necks in sand, and the women with shovels are walking away.

'Fuck me! I hope they're coming back soon!' Rosie exclaims, snapping out of her daydream.

ᴑᴇᴑ

Later that evening, we lounge around in our ryokan. Rosie sits by the large, open windows and lights a cigarette, something she only does when she's either super relaxed or super stressed. She exhales smoke into the night air.

'You're not fooling anyone, Luce,' she says, looking at me.

I glance up from the magazine I'm reading on the futon.

'Least of all me,' she adds. 'Come on, what have you got behind that magazine?' Suddenly she leaps up and walks across the tatami towards me.

'It's a local magazine, *OL Style*!' I say, clutching it tightly. 'OL is short for "Office Lady",' I explain as she rips the magazine from my hands.

The book I'd been hiding falls into my lap, and she picks it up and reads the cover. '*The Five Love Languages* . . . Heaven help us all,' she says, shaking her head at me and tossing the book back on my lap. 'Once you're finished with that, give it to me and I'll burn it.'

'Just so you know, I'm hovering between "Quality Time" and "Acts of Service",' I tell her.

'Speaking of which, give us the list.'

'Oh, that's right,' I say retrieving a piece of paper from the back pocket of my jeans and handing it to her.

Earlier in the evening, she'd tasked me with finally writing the list of top five attributes I'm after in a partner.

The smoke curls from her cigarette as she reads my list aloud. '*Kind, intelligent, attractive, funny, adventurous, compassionate, a good communicator, generous, reliable, considerate* . . . You know who you're looking to meet?'

'Who?'

'Jesus.'

I gaze up at her.

'Jesus could be in London,' I say.

11

When my taxi from the airport pulls up outside the house four days later, I see Mum sitting on a plastic chair in front of the shed, bawling.

'Mum, what's wrong?' I ask, dropping my suitcase and running up to give her a hug.

'Your father's having an affair,' she sobs.

'No he's not,' I say with complete certainty.

'How do you know?' she asks.

'No-one would want to have an affair with him,' I say adamantly.

'No-one except an ex-girlfriend!'

I look at her, puzzled. 'No! Not Ruth!'

'Not Ruth? More like definitely Ruth! She's been trying to get her mitts on your father since the day we got engaged!'

'Mum, you sound like a crazy lady. Where's all this coming from?'

'Lucy, there is no bloody Jockey Club!'

'What?' I say, surprised.

'There was an article in the paper today about how they're converting the old Jockey Club building into a facility for the PCYC. It said that the Jockey Club folded five years ago!'

'That's weird, but there must be another explanation,' I say, scratching my head. 'Dad wouldn't even know where to start with having an affair.'

Mum wails.

'Where is he, anyway?' I ask, glancing around the driveway. 'And why are you sitting out here, Mum?'

'I don't know where he is. I went looking for him after I read the article but he was nowhere to be found. He's probably down at the car wash checking out Ruth in her bikini. Then I got your text saying you'd landed and I wanted to catch you as soon as you came up the drive, so I came out here.'

The sound of Glenda barking inside the shed startles us both and as we swivel around the roller door slides up and Dad steps out. Glenda races between his legs towards me.

'Well, isn't this lovely, Brian? I know there's no Jockey Club and now I've caught you red-handed!' She yells in the direction of the shed, 'Show's over, Ruth—you can come out now!'

'Calm down, Denise,' says Dad. 'Ruth's not in there.'

'Well, who is?' asks Mum, craning her neck. 'Not Helen from next door?'

'No-one's in there, Denise.' Dad sighs and rolls the door down. 'It was just me and Glenda.'

'Are you doing home brewing on the side or something, Dad?' I ask.

'No, I just hang out in the shed when I need some space to think.'

'What?' asks Mum, as if she'd prefer he'd confessed he and Ruth had a love child.

'I've been going to the Men's Shed down at Archer Park. I've had the blues, and the boys have been good to me. We do woodturning and make traps for the myna birds and restore old bikes for the Endeavour Inn—heaps of practical stuff. And we all chat over our sausage sizzles.'

'So why aren't you there now?' I ask.

'Well, the Men's Shed only operates on certain days. So when I need some time alone, I use *our* shed. I've bought a few woodturning tools to use here as well.'

'This is the dizzy limit, Brian!' exclaims Mum. 'Why didn't you tell me you were feeling lousy? We could have talked it through or gone on a holiday to New Zealand or something.'

'You're always so busy with your Qi-Gong or your tai chi or your African drumming and chanting, I figured it was best just to deal with it in my own way,' Dad says. 'You'd be surprised how many blokes start going to the Men's Shed because they're a bit down. But after a few weeks on the power saw building cubby houses to raffle, they're right as rain.'

'Oh, their poor wives,' says Mum, shaking her head. 'And you—poor you, Brian,' she adds quickly. 'Depression's a shocking thing. What do they call it, the stray dog or the black cat or something?'

'The black dog, Mum,' I reply.

'That's right, the black dog,' says Mum, patting Dad on the back. 'Well, let's go put the kettle on, shall we?'

I put my hand on Dad's shoulder. 'Isn't it hot in there, Dad?'

'It's bloody hot, Lucy,' he says, picking up my suitcase. 'I hid in there when I heard your mum start ranting about that newspaper article. I'm glad you came home when you did. I was dying of thirst and didn't dare face her without you. Anyway, how was Japan?'

'Oh yeah, it was great, you should see . . .' I begin, but notice Dad's attention has been drawn elsewhere.

'Oscar!' he yells, letting go of my suitcase and running down the driveway towards Oscar like a five-year-old who's just spotted Santa.

I look over at Mum to share the absurdity of Dad's reaction, only to see she too is running towards Oscar with outstretched arms.

Even Glenda joins the fray, jumping up at Oscar, her tail wagging furiously.

'We've missed seeing you, mate,' says Dad, shaking Oscar's hand, then gripping his elbows and taking a step back to admire him, like people do in the movies. 'What is it now, about three weeks since we last caught up?'

'Yes, it'd be about three weeks, Brian,' says Mum, her hand on Oscar's bicep. 'He only left a couple of days before Lucy went off to Japan,' she continues, giving me a wonky wink that looks more like she's struggling with an eye full of sunscreen.

Oscar smiles at me and I grin back, chuffed he's here. 'Man, anyone'd think *you* were their kid returning home,' I say, laughing.

Oscar places his hand over Mum's momentarily, sweetly signalling that she should release her grip. This kind gesture endears him to me even more and I glance briefly at the cement and smile as he walks toward me and wraps his arms around my shoulders.

As I step back from him, I notice Mum and Dad standing off to the side, watching us. They're grinning from ear to ear, looking from Oscar to me like we're Torvill and Dean and have just taken out the gold medal for figure-skating. To my great annoyance, I'm blushing.

'Do you want to come—?' I say at the same time as he says, 'Do you want to take—?'

God, I wish those two would move!

'Do you want to take Glenda for a walk up Mount Archer?' he asks, giving her an enthusiastic back rub as she looks up at him adoringly.

'That'd be lovely, Oscar,' says Dad. 'Just let me put my joggers on.'

'He's asking me, Dad!' I exclaim.

'I know!' says Dad, chuckling as he walks up the stairs with my suitcase. 'I couldn't help myself.'

Mum remains glued to the spot, still beaming at Oscar.

'How was Japan?' Oscar asks me.

'Yeah, awesome,' I reply. 'It was a great trip. Just what the doctor ordered.'

'Come on, Denise!' says Dad, ushering her up the steps. 'Let me show you this bowl I turned.'

I shake my head at them as Mum strains to look back at us. 'They're out of control,' I say to Oscar.

'They're the best.' He smiles. 'You're lucky to have them both,' he adds wistfully. 'I miss Dad.'

⁊℮꙲

We arrive at the base of Mount Archer in the late afternoon. The sky is a swirl of burnt orange and pale pink through the gum trees. The air is crisp, with a faint smell of wood smoke.

'So, when did you discover Mount Archer?' I ask as we begin our ascent with Glenda.

'Kate and I came here a few weeks ago.'

'How did you know I was coming back today?' I ask.

'I didn't. I just happened to see your taxi pull up.'

We continue to scale the mountain, the sound of our footsteps crunching on roadside gravel intermingling with the afternoon chorus of birdsong and the occasional passing car.

'Lucy,' he says suddenly, looking across at me, 'I wish there was a better way to say this, but I really, really like you.'

His words set my heart spinning like the Gravitron and I consider him with a quizzical smile.

'Meeting you has changed how I feel about Kate,' he says quickly. 'I still care about her, but, man, I'm falling in love with you.'

I inhale sharply and stare at the road. My heart is now back flipping like a cage on the Mean Mother Zipper.

'But I don't know what to do,' he continues, with some measure of distress, 'because you live in Rocky, and I live in Sydney, and Kate lives in Sydney, and we still hang out.'

Holy shit! I think. He's falling in love with me? Wow! This is brill—oh no, he mentioned Kate too, didn't he. Bugger.

'What do you think about it all?' he asks.

'I think you need to figure out what you want,' I reply. 'And you need to do it independently of anything I say.'

'What do you want for yourself, though?' he asks.

'I want to finish writing my novel by the end of the year,' I reply. 'And then I want to settle down somewhere and have someone in my life and feel like I'm doing worthwhile work.'

'But where do you want to settle down?' he asks.

'I don't know yet,' I reply.

'And what worthwhile work do you want to be doing?'

'I'm not entirely sure, but when I was in Japan I had some time to think without the pressure of family and friends and it clarified for me that all I want to concentrate on for the moment is finishing *Diamonds in the Dust* while making enough cash not to starve.'

'Are you still in love with that guy? That was him, wasn't it, in the café that day?'

'No, I'm not in love with Jeremy. I'm cured of that, thank God! I'll always hope he's doing well, but I'm not in love with him, if you know what I mean.'

'I do,' says Oscar. 'I think I started falling for you that very first night we met. And every time I see you it's like I struggle to breathe or something.'

'Oh, Oscar,' I say, grinning at him. 'I really like you too! I think you're the most gorgeous man. It's just all taken me by surprise and, you know, you've still got something happening with Kate and I don't know how to read this. You still have feelings for her, don't you?'

'Perhaps,' he says miserably. 'Yes. But . . .' He pauses.

I stay quiet. Though I instinctively feel sympathetic towards his situation and the agony he's going through, and long to tell him that he sets my world on fire, I also know he needs to make a decision without me affecting it one way or the other.

'The crazy thing is,' he continues, 'I've only hung out with you a few times, but I've never enjoyed someone's company as much as I enjoy yours. I feel so content when I'm with you. I can't explain it. And the worst part is that I think I'm sounding keener than you.'

'No, Oscar, the worst part is that you're saying these things to me and you've got a girlfriend in Sydney who you also care about and who cares about you,' I say and carry on walking up the mountain.

'I wish I'd met you ten years ago,' he says quietly, catching up to me. 'I think you're the most beautiful, warm, funny woman I've ever met.' He puts his arms around my waist and pulls me towards him.

Despite all my best intentions, I collapse into his embrace, my mouth melting into his like I'm some swooning contestant on *The Bachelor*. And even though I know what I'm doing is wrong, it feels so infinitely right.

I'm vaguely aware of a car rounding the bend towards us, but the awareness takes a back seat to the wave of desire gripping every cell of my body. We cling hungrily to each other and if I hadn't had a nightmare experience with gravel rash at a B&S in my early twenties, I'd be pinning him down on the road. So much for my moral high ground.

Out of the corner of my eye, I notice the car decelerate and I feel a surge of dread. There's only one person in Rocky who drives a fluorescent green ute. It's Ruth. She's spotted us fair and square and grins broadly and waves out the window at us as she drives past.

My heart sinks as I pull away from Oscar. Ruth will have a field day with this. And it'll serve me right for succumbing to a man with a girlfriend, something I never thought I would do.

'That's not going to be great,' I remark grimly as we watch her tail-lights disappear down the mountain.

Oscar leans in to me again, but I push him away.

'Oscar, you've got a lovely girlfriend who'd be devastated if she knew what just happened. And Ruth just saw us. The woman invented blackmail. She'll tell anyone who'll listen. She'll hold us to ransom.'

Oscar suddenly turns pale. 'Would she tell Mum?'

'She's probably heading straight there now.'

'Shit! I have to talk to her!' he says.

We run down the mountain, Glenda leading the way, jump in my Corolla and zoom across the old bridge like it's about to crumble into the Fitzroy River.

It's dusk as we pull up at Ruth's carwash and find her sitting on a collapsible chair, blowing smoke rings.

'Ruth,' I say.

'Lucy,' she replies with a big grin.

'Ruth,' Oscar says.

'Oscar.'

'Ruth, please don't tell anyone,' blurts Oscar.

'Why not?' asks Ruth, smoke snaking from one nostril. 'Not over with Kate?'

'No,' he replies. 'And I don't want to hurt her.'

A colourful cacophony of screeching parrots flies above us in the fading daylight. Ruth shifts triumphantly in her seat.

A heavy exhaustion engulfs me, and I suddenly yearn to be a million miles away from this man.

'I'm going, Oscar,' I say. 'See ya, Ruth.'

'Lucy, wait,' says Oscar, following me as I walk away. 'I don't want you to go. I fly back to Sydney tomorrow. Can't we hang out?'

'What? And sleep together so you can then go home and sleep with Kate? I don't want this, Oscar. I don't want to be the girl in between. And I don't want to be the reason for someone else's heartache.'

I get into my car and drive off without a backward glance.

12

I look across at the lane to my right. Mum's swimming free-style so slowly she may as well be floating. To my left, Rosie's been down in the shallow end, ostensibly stretching out cramps, but really perving on the lifeguard. She's been at it so long that her hair is now dry.

I swim up and splash her with water. 'You're not fooling anyone, Rosie, least of all me,' I say, smirking and flipping her kickboard off the ledge and into the pool. 'Come on.'

Rosie and I kick side by side down the lanes.

'So why did I get twenty missed calls from you last night?' she asks.

'Because I was extremely distressed and severely jet-lagged, and so emotionally overwrought that I cried through *Antiques Roadshow*.'

'Shit,' she says. 'What happened?'

'Oh, there was this woman with a little blue porcelain

dog and it was part of a set of dogs and her twin sister had the other one, but then her sister died of leukaemia and she couldn't . . .' My voice begins to shake.

'Oh, mate,' says Rosie, 'do you want to stop?'

'No,' I reply, resting my head on my board and continuing to kick. 'Anyway,' I say, taking a deep breath and staring ahead, 'she'd desperately wanted to track down her twin sister's dog because then they'd be forever united, if not physically as twins then in china, you know?'

Rosie nods.

'But she couldn't . . .' I stifle a sob. 'She couldn't find the dog.'

We reach the end of the pool and push off again.

'Luce,' says Rosie, 'what really happened?'

'Oscar and I kissed halfway up Mount Archer, but he's still going out with Kate, and I hate it that I did that while he's seeing someone. And I'd been feeling really good after Japan, not overthinking things and being positive, and now I feel gutted and am waging a massive internal war with myself.'

'Why?'

'If Ruth hadn't happened to pass by I would have slept with him in an instant, even knowing he's got a girlfriend. I wanted to. I still want to. But I knew I couldn't. I knew I couldn't do that to myself—or to Kate. But now he's under my skin, despite all my good intentions. So he's got the both of us falling at his feet.'

'But you didn't fall at his feet.'

'No, I didn't. But I wanted to. I would have washed those feet. Holy shit!' I say, standing up as we reach the shallow end. 'Maybe he's Jesus.'

'Luce, if he was I'd have had him in the pool turning this whole thing into wine,' says Rosie with a chuckle. 'Oscar is fucking far from being Jesus. You know that!'

'Yeah, I know,' I reply.

'Anyway, Jesus is in London, remember?' she says, raising her eyebrows at me.

'Oh, Rosie, I can't go to London,' I say. 'I've got no money.'

'Who's going to London?' asks Mum, bobbing up in the adjacent lane.

'Rosie, perhaps,' I reply.

'Are you, Rosie?' says Mum.

'Thinking about it,' she replies. 'It feels like it could be time for a change.'

'Lucy . . .' says Mum sternly, the effect of her frown partially offset by the old-fashioned swimming cap she's wearing and the goggle marks around her eyes.

'I know, Ma, I know—I'm not going to London,' I say, exchanging a glance with Rosie before we launch off the wall again.

'Can't believe Ruth caught you kissing Oscar. Of all people!'

'I know, it's the worst! She'll be blabbing to everyone who comes through the carwash.' I take a deep breath. 'Far out.'

'What you need is a circuit-breaker,' says Rosie, 'and I've got just the answer.'

'A thirty-cent cone from Maccas?' I ask.

'No, but let's get one after this.' She pauses. 'I think they're fifty cents now,' she says. 'Nah, let's go to Romancing the Rock. I read about it in the paper today. It's adventure dating and it's come to Rocky for the first time and I think we should be part of it.'

'Where's it at?' I ask quietly, looking around to see if Mum's within earshot.

'The Whipcrack Hotel, seven o'clock.'

'Okay, I'll come,' I reply.

'Shit, that was a lot easier than I thought it would be!' she says, laughing.

'I want to get out of the house, Rosie. The last thing I need is another night in with Mum and Dad watching Joanna Lumley on the Trans-Siberian bloody Railway or some old bloke nearly losing his shit over the value of a coin collection.'

Rosie smiles at me, then asks, 'Good kisser?'

'Perfect,' I reply.

⌒e⌒

'What time are we meeting Dad at the vet?' I call out to Mum, who's in the change room showers.

'In ten minutes,' she calls back, and I hear her turning off her taps. 'Better get a move on!'

'Is something wrong with Glenda?' asks Rosie, looking concerned.

'I don't think it's serious. She had a bad limp in her front left paw last night and winced when I tried to look at it. Dad booked her in to see Henry this morning, and Mum and I are going too.'

Reassured, Rosie says goodbye and I change into a short cotton dress—an outfit I favour because it can be worn sans bra. After rummaging through my swimming bag for my undies with an increasing sense of panic I search the cubicle. They're not there. I sigh and walk out of the change room to see Mum standing on the grass. She's washed and combed her hair and it appears flat and damp. I don't know why, but seeing my mum with washed and combed hair awakens a certain poignancy in me. Right now, though, I'm less touched and more concerned.

'Ma,' I say urgently, 'I'm not wearing any undies.'

She considers me for a second.

'I must have forgotten them,' I add.

'Well, what are you going to do about it?' she asks.

'I don't know,' I reply. 'And we're due at the vet any minute.'

'Oh, Lucy, you can't go to the vet with no undies on!' she says with conviction, as if I'm the one who'll be on the examination table with a sore paw. 'Here.' She hands me her mobile. 'Ring your father straight away and if he hasn't left already, ask him to bring your underpants to the vet.'

'Okay,' I say, dialling his number.

Luckily Dad's still home and instantly agrees, asking no questions, for which I'm grateful.

cec

I'm still giggling as I drive Mum's car to Pets and Vets, amused by the prospect of getting around town without any underwear.

'You would be wearing the shortest dress you own too, wouldn't you?' says Mum, indulging me with a chuckle.

'And no bra!' I add, successfully nailing a parallel park.

I open the door of Mum's low-rider Audi, and as I'm flinging my legs to the bitumen I look across and see a council worker on a little dirt devil doing roadworks. His eyeline is literally at crotch level and I gasp as he loses control of his pedals and bunny-hops through the potholes.

'Mum!' I exclaim. 'I need to get inside!'

I push open the glass door and rejoice to see Dad in the waiting room.

'Here you go,' he says, taking my undies out of his pocket and throwing them at me.

I catch them in one hand and slip into the bathroom to put them on, still laughing to myself. You're thirty-two, Lucy! I think.

'What do you reckon she's got in that box?' Dad asks Mum, looking at a woman who's just walked in. 'A cat,' he says. 'I bet it's a cat.'

Mum glances at the cardboard box the woman's struggling with.

'No, I think she's got a whole litter in there, Brian.'

They both turn as the door opens again and a man enters carrying a foxy chihuahua.

'What do you think's wrong with that dog, Denise?' asks Dad. 'Sore paw, like Glenda?'

'No, I think it's got something wrong with its ear, Brian,' replies Mum. 'See how it keeps flicking its head?'

'Ha!' exclaims Dad as a young woman who'd been sitting with her back to us stands up and walks towards the reception desk, nursing a sedate bundle wrapped in a chequered tea towel. 'No prizes for guessing what that is!'

'Yes, she's definitely got a rooster there, hasn't she?'

I look at them in wonder. Who knew you could be so easily occupied sitting in the waiting room of the vet clinic? I know where to take them in future for a morning out!

Henry walks into the reception area from his surgery talking to an elderly man with a parrot on his shoulder. I'm relieved Glenda's name is called out before Mum and Dad can diagnose the parrot.

Dad and Henry embrace heartily over the examination table.

'So, are you still keen for Kakadu?' asks Dad enthusiastically.

Henry glances at Mum.

'Oh, Denise knows everything now,' says Dad.

'Does she?' asks Henry, wide-eyed.

'Well, I don't know anything about Kakadu,' says Mum sharply, glaring at Dad.

'I thought I'd mentioned it,' he replies casually. 'The Darwin Men's Shed have invited us Rocky blokes up for ten days or so of fishing around Kakadu.'

Henry looks at Mum again and says, 'Don't breathe a word of it to Maureen. I've still got a month to break news of the Men's Shed to her.'

'I won't, Henry,' says Mum quietly, moving across to Glenda. 'So, what's going on with this kelpie of ours, do you think?'

∽

Mum and I drive home in silence. I sense it's best I keep quiet. She's upset, and it's not over Glenda's mild paw strain, for which Henry prescribed a juicy bone and a few days' rest.

I give Mum a hug and put the kettle on, then head to my room and sit at the computer to check my email. There's only LinkedIn notifications and Jetstar fare frenzy alerts, and I hear the kettle whistle, breaking the unbearable silence in the house. If I didn't think it was highly inappropriate, I'd set off Roomba.

I make Mum a cup of Complete Calm tea, which Rosie claims is just chamomile mixed with lemongrass, and she accepts it wordlessly, staring into space from her chair at the kitchen table.

I return to the computer, and type *Cher's top 30 quotes* into Google.

I re-enter the kitchen. 'Ma,' I tell her, desperate to dispel the heavy cloud of sadness, 'in a situation like this, Cher would say, "Men should be like Kleenex—soft, strong and disposable!"'

Mum begins to cry gently, breaking my heart. There is nothing worse than seeing your mum or dad cry, particularly when you don't know how to help them.

'No she wouldn't,' she says as I walk towards her. Her face is streaked with tears. 'Cher would say, "Husbands are like fires—they go out when they're left unattended."'

13

'You know this is going to be a sea of high-vis and Broncos jerseys,' I say to Rosie as we step into the Whipcrack Hotel just on seven o'clock.

'Don't be so judgemental, Lucy,' she replies. '*You* go for the Broncos *and* you're a bogan at heart.' She steers us towards a group of people huddled in a corner of the beer garden.

'Mmm,' I reply, then suddenly stop in my tracks and grab her arm. 'Ben's over there!'

'Oh yeah,' she says casually. 'I invited him.'

'Why?' I ask, incredulous.

'Because he's a fun guy and I ran into him at the IGA this afternoon.'

I feel like turning around and leaving but he's already waving at us.

'Good evening, ladies and gents,' says Colleen from the bottle-o, Video Ezy and Bits 'n' Pizzas. 'I'm Colleen, your host for tonight's—' she holds up a piece of paper and with great solemnity reads '—Romancing the Rock adventure dating event.

'So, if you all take out your mobiles, you'll see that a message and a photo of your first date for tonight has just come through. You have to find each other in the pub—that's the adventure part. Then you'll have ten minutes to—' she raises her fingers to signify air quotes '—"get to know each other", after which you'll receive another message telling you to move on to your next date and a picture of who it is. Clear as mud?'

We all nod at her nervously.

'Alright,' she says, picking up her handbag, 'if you need me, I'll be at the pokies.'

I look at the picture on my phone. It's my cousin Dave and he's standing right beside me. We decide to catch up over a steak. Just after I order, take a seat and happily accept a Guinness from Dave, my phone pings with date number two.

It's sixty-three-year-old Brad McMaster, who used to be Dad's paper boy and did odd jobs for Mum at All About Town. He's delighted to see me and accepts my invitation to join Dave and me at our table for tea.

Brad, perhaps believing I still drink UDLs, buys me three and tells jolly stories of picking me up from school when I was a teenager and dropping me home. His tales are hardly scintillating yet we all roar with laughter, attracting the attention of Rosie, who appears to be on a date with the newly separated Todd Doherty. Given his intricate knowledge of my financial position, Todd will definitely not be wanting to pursue me.

'Hello, Todd,' I say, standing up as he wanders over. 'How are you going?'

'Good, Luce. Gee, I didn't think I'd see you here,' he says with a sheepish grin.

'Me either,' I reply. 'I didn't think I'd see myself *or* you here.'

'Yeah,' he says, scuffing at the cement floor. 'Cherie and I split up, so . . .'

'Oh, I'm sorry,' I reply, feigning surprise, even though half of Rocky knows his wife's been cheating on him with Doug Albright from Carpets Galore. 'Well, look, do you and Rosie want to join us for a bite?'

'Oh, I'd love that,' he says quickly. 'If it's okay with you, Rosie?'

We look over to see she's already sitting down, eating garlic bread.

'What can I get you girls to drink?' asks Todd, gesturing towards the bar.

'Two rum and Cokes!' calls Rosie. 'Holy Moses, Luce!' she adds, eyeing the collection of cans I've accumulated. 'You've got about fifteen bevvies on the go there.'

'Yeah,' I say, finishing off a UDL and pushing two across to her. 'It can be darn thirsty work, this adventure dating.'

I'm feeling in quite good spirits when I look over my left shoulder and spot Ben on a date with a latecomer . . . Ruth.

Rosie follows my gaze. 'You're not the centre of the fucking universe, Luce,' she whispers. 'They're going to be talking about other things besides you. Just enjoy yourself.'

She's right, and when my phone buzzes with a picture

of my third date for the evening I'm thrilled to see that it's someone I don't know.

I find Shaun standing by an enormous vase of flowers in the hotel foyer. He is drop-dead gorgeous, with sandy-coloured hair, a strong, dependable jawline and misty green eyes.

I think he finds me attractive too, because he stares and stares as I approach.

'Lucy?' he exclaims.

'Yes,' I say, holding up a picture of myself on my phone. 'Yes, it's me.'

'Lucy Crighton?'

I nod modestly. Clearly, he recognises me from *The Headline Act*.

'Shit!' he exclaims, lifting me from the floor in a bear hug. 'Gee, it's good to see ya!'

Bewildered, I return his embrace.

'Oh fuck, pardon me. Sorry, Luce, sometimes I forget! You might remember me as Shauna Jasperson?'

'Shauna?' I say in disbelief. 'Shauna Jasperson! We used to sit next to each other in grade—'

'Three,' he says tenderly. 'Oh, look at you, you stunning woman! Why isn't there a ring on that finger? And what are you doing in this hellhole?'

'It's a long story, Shauna—sorry, Shaun. Do you want to come back into the beer garden? There's a bit of a crew there, we're having dinner.'

'Thank you, sweetheart, but I'm bailing,' he says, patting me on the shoulder. 'I didn't expect much of the whole show, but for crying out loud . . .' He gestures behind me and

I turn to see Ruth shaking a vending machine, successfully dislodging a packet of barbecue-flavoured Samboys.

I shrug my shoulders. 'The steaks aren't bad.'

ↄⅇↄ

By nine o'clock the cover band is playing the best of the eighties and nineties, and Romancing the Rock is winding down.

After Brad McMaster gropes my arse in a fond farewell, I return to my chair and clink glasses with Rosie, Ben and my by-now-fairly-inebriated cousin, Dave.

'Here's to the remaining adventure daters!' cries Ben jovially as we take a sip of our UDLs, a parting gift from Brad. 'What a night, hey?' he continues, looking around and slapping his thigh to 'You Shook Me All Night Long'.

'This cover band has been playing the same covers here since we were twenty-one, Luce!' says Dave, laughing.

'I know, Dave,' I reply, grinning across at him.

'Shame Oscar isn't in town!' shouts Ben to me. 'He'd love this pub!'

'Yeah!' I yell back, feeling rather tipsy. 'We'll have to bring him one night!'

The lead singer in the cover band announces they're going to take a short break and Dave wanders off in search of food.

Ben drains the last of his UDL and places the can on the table. 'There's a party in my mouth and everyone's invited!'

Rosie starts laughing and I look at him quizzically.

'As Christine Anu says, "Why don't you come join my party?"' he says, opening his palm to reveal two tiny white tablets.

'Ben!' I exclaim, staring at his hand. 'We can't be taking ecstasy on a Thursday night at the Whipcrack! Who are we going to party with? Those old guys over there playing Keno?'

'Suit yourself,' Ben smiles. 'All I can say is I dropped one twenty minutes ago and this night is now fan-fucking-tastic!'

'I'm in,' says Rosie, taking one of the pills and swallowing it before I've had time to blink. 'It's either hanging out with us or your cousin,' she adds, nodding over my right shoulder at Dave, who's walking towards us with a kebab and a can of Jack Daniel's.

As the cover band step back on stage, I swallow the pill.

'Yes!' shouts Ben, fist pumping as the guitarist strums the first chords of 'Run to Paradise'.

'Come on!' he says, taking Rosie and me by the hands and leading us onto the dance floor.

The band work through their catalogue of Paul Kelly, Cold Chisel and Crowded House, and by the time they reach Hunters and Collectors we're having the time of our lives. When, forty minutes later, they launch into 'The Horses' by Daryl Braithwaite, we're ecstatic.

'How fucking lucky are we?!' shouts Rosie, jumping up and down to the chorus. 'Look at us! We're dancing in this glorious pub, in the best town on earth, to a fucking brilliant cover band playing "The Horses"! Woohoo!' She lifts up her top and flashes the appreciative lead singer before running off to the bathroom.

At the song's conclusion, 'Copperhead Road' starts, but Ben and I are buggered. We leave the dance floor and slide into a booth opposite each other.

'Lucy,' he gushes, 'the bull statues around town here are just fantastic.'

'I know!' I say with feeling. 'So much love and care has gone into those statues.'

'And the people in Rockhampton are great,' he continues. 'I have not met a bad person since I've been here.'

'And you won't, Ben, I can guarantee you won't meet a bad person here.' I look across to the dance floor fondly. 'Only good people live here. Even Ruth's got a certain charm.'

'I just kissed the lovely Pat,' says Rosie, coming over to us and leaning on the table.

'Oh, which one's he?' I ask.

'*She's* the delightful redhead playing the pokies,' she replies.

'That's fabulous, Rosie,' I say, smiling up at her generously. 'Good for you, my good-looking friend.'

'Actually, I'm going to get the lovely woman's number—and a ciggie,' she says, blowing me a kiss and skipping off.

'I love Rosie,' I say to Ben, who's watching her duck and weave across the beer garden.

He turns around and we hold each other's gaze. 'You have such beautiful hair, Lucy,' he remarks, reaching across the table and twirling his fingers through my curls.

'Thank you,' I reply, smiling. 'Thank you, Ben.' I pause. 'Want to go get a Subway?'

⁊℮◦

The next morning, I wake with a pounding headache, an urgent thirst and a hand around my waist.

I frown as I realise I'm in one of Helen's bedrooms and then gasp as I look over my left shoulder and see Ben. He opens his eyes lazily as I sit up.

'You were spectacular!' he says.

I swallow hard and lie back down. The last thing I can remember is sharing a six-inch meat-and-cheese with Ben, then slow-dancing with him as he sang 'Wonderwall' in the cab queue. I groan as memories begin crowding into my throbbing head. There's a flash of me unbuckling Ben's seatbelt and him putting his hand up my top, and of me pinning him against the fridge after we devoured leftover lasagne. I remember texting Mum that I was staying with Rosie, then . . . nothing.

Ben reads the mortification in my eyes.

'Relax, Lucy, I'm just joking,' he says, withdrawing his hand from my waist. 'We got off to a good start and I'd hoped to try some of my charming moves but you passed out. Nothing happened.'

'Thank God!' I say, a little too emphatically, just as my foot brushes against my jeans, which are curled up at the base of the bed. I reach between the sheets and pull them on. 'Sorry, Ben,' I add, feeling nauseous with the sudden movement. 'I don't normally ever just black out like that. Bloody hell.'

'It's okay,' he says. 'We had fun.'

'Ben, I—'

'I know,' he says. 'I want Oscar to know about this just as much as you do.'

I now feel violently ill. Ruth must have told him.

'Oscar?' I ask quietly, attempting to look puzzled.

'He'd skin me alive,' he continues. 'It's been obvious since that first barbecue he's half love-sick over you. Whenever he's at Mum's he's always wandering over to the window to look down at your house.'

'But he's got a girlfriend,' I say.

'Yes, but he's definitely into you,' he replies, staring at the ceiling. 'Look, don't worry. There's nothing worth saying about this. Nothing happened.'

I remain silent, thinking.

'You're a great chick, Lucy,' says Ben eventually. 'Of course I love old Oscar, but don't take any crap from him.'

'What are you—?'

'I'm not really trying to say anything. Except that Oscar's a guy who can have any girl. Through no fault of his own he's used to getting what he wants, even if he doesn't know it.'

Maybe Ruth didn't tell Ben after all. This is the only thought I wish to consider right now, not the deeper and potentially more distressing observation about Oscar that Ben's just made.

I look over the side of the bed and see my top.

'Your mum?' I ask with alarm, pulling my top on and standing up.

'In Sydney with Oscar,' he replies. 'Good thing too. The kitchen's in a bad way after we tried to make banana bread.'

'Banana bread?' I shake my head in disbelief.

'Yeah, you insisted. Said your banana bread won ribbons at the local show or something. You wouldn't come out of the kitchen!'

'Oh God!' I say, rubbing my forehead.

'So we put on one of Mum's Phil Collins CDs, and when "A Groovy Kind of Love" came on you burst into tears and ran to the bedroom.'

I look at him, feeling equal parts aghast, embarrassed and thoroughly entertained.

'I found you asleep in your underwear,' he adds.

'That song always gets me,' I reply, as if it's the perfect justification for my behaviour. 'Sorry, Ben,' I add, walking to the door. 'Sorry I put you through all that.'

'You didn't put me through anything,' he replies. 'Don't be sorry.'

I turn the door handle. 'So we're not going to ever mention this again?' I confirm.

He nods. 'Lucy,' he says as I open the door, 'do you like him? Oscar?'

'Yes,' I reply. 'I like him.'

ॐ

I skulk in to Mum and Dad's and it sounds like World War III has broken out in the kitchen, with 'Kakadu . . . selfish . . .' ringing out in Mum's voice, followed by 'bloody chakras . . . stupid bongo drums . . .' in Dad's. I sneak into the lounge room, grab my car keys, then tiptoe back out the front door and drive to Rosie's.

'Ben?' she asks, opening her front door.

'Yes and no,' I reply. 'Pat?' I ask, noticing the red marks on her neck.

'No,' she says, letting me in.

'Todd Doherty?' I ask, puzzled. 'Did you link back up with him?'

'No,' she answers as we walk into her kitchen.

'Who then?' I demand, before my mouth falls open and Rosie starts to laugh quietly.

'Dave!' I exclaim.

'Shhh!' she says. 'He's still in there.'

'My cousin Dave?' I whisper. 'Hilarious!'

'I tell you what, Luce, under that flanno is a wild cowboy! The moves he was pulling on—'

'Stop it, Rosie, you'll make me sick,' I say, putting my hand over her mouth.

I sigh heavily and lean back against the sink as she pours a glass of water and hands it to me.

I gulp it down and then say, 'Rosie, do not be leaving me in this state today. If you do, I'll be calling Oscar. I'll be calling Jeremy. I'll be contemplating throwing myself off the top of Mount Archer. The works.'

'You're over Jeremy,' she says.

'I wouldn't put anything past me today,' I reply.

She rubs my back. 'I'm fucking famished, Luce.'

'Me too. What's open this early?' I ask.

'Red Rooster. We could dine in.'

'Oh, mate,' I reply. 'We are sinking to new lows in this town.'

'I know,' she says. 'What am I going to do about . . .?' She nods in the direction of her bedroom.

'Leave,' I say.

'Oh, I can't just leave! That's rude and awful.'

'Well, write a note then.'

She rips a piece of paper titled *Shopping List* from behind a magnet on the fridge, and hovers above it with a pen.

'Can you write it?' she asks, looking over at me.

'Me?'

'Well, he's your family! Just pretend you're me.'

'Oh, righto,' I say and scribble across the page.

'Luce! I can't just write "Good on ya, Dave!"'

'Do you want to pursue something with my cuz?' I ask, eyeballing her.

She shakes her head quickly and we leave the note under an orange on the kitchen table.

⁊ⴰ

Sitting in a booth at Red Rooster, Rosie and I murder a family pack of chicken rolls, nuggets and chips.

'Right, so you're eating now, which means you can talk. I cannot believe you woke up with Ben!' she laughs.

'Neither can I!' I exclaim. 'Those bloody pills! What the hell did we take?!'

'You've also got to remember that we each had about eight UDLs.'

'I definitely kissed him,' I say. 'I think he had his hand up my top at one stage. And I remember body slamming him against the fridge door and nibbling on his ear.'

She lowers the chips from her mouth and starts shaking with laughter. 'Lucy Crighton, you are out of control! You do know that Ben's related to Oscar?'

'I didn't mean it! It was those pills!' I put my head in my hands. 'What have I done?'

'He says you didn't shag him, so that's okay,' Rosie says quickly to counteract my distress.

'No, thank goodness,' I reply.

'Ben's not going to say anything,' she continues. 'And he's leaving in a few days to walk the Camino.'

'What?' I ask, startled.

'Yeah, he told me last night. He's pretty lost. Poor bugger. I think he's hoping some sort of answer to all his questions will be whispered to him as he's trekking through the Pyrenees.'

'Maybe it will be,' I say, feeling sad for Ben, but also relieved I won't risk running into him.

'There never is,' says Rosie. 'Only what you make up in your mind.'

I mentally sift through the events of the last twenty-four hours, assessing whether the news of Ben's imminent departure paints what happened between us in a new light.

'Lucy, get over yourself and stop worrying,' says Rosie sternly. 'You were trying to bake banana bread at three in the morning, I was in the bath with your cousin Dave, and Ben was trying to get you in the sack. It was the pills talking, nothing else.'

I nod and push the chicken roll away, feeling suddenly ill at the image of Rosie and Dave in a bath.

In better spirits after our Calippos, I drive us to the cinemas over on the north side and watch the only film screening that afternoon: *Hotel Transylvania 2*. Such is my fragile state that I cry when Dennis leaves the hotel and flees to the forest, while Rosie sleeps through most of it.

'Luce,' she says as we emerge from the darkness of the cinema into the dusk of the car park, 'I'm gonna move to London.'

14

The next morning, I awake at an ungodly hour to the sound of Roomba outside my bedroom and Mum bustling about on the back deck, singing Foreigner's 'I Want to Know What Love Is'. My feelings of outrage over Roomba are somewhat offset by my relief that she's sounding brighter.

Last night, after I got home from the cinema, I'd found her in tears again. And for some strange reason she'd emptied the cutlery drawer onto the kitchen table and was sifting through the spoons. I did what I always do when I don't know how to cope with Mum. I called Max and put her on the phone to him. Within minutes she was chuckling down the line.

'While you're off gallivanting around Kakadu, I'm going to China with Max to tour the Fancy Pants factory outlet, and I'm going to tack on a Qi-Gong trip through Mongolia with Master Ray and his students,' she'd said to Dad without drawing a breath, then firmly shut the TV room door, wiped away her tears and replaced the cutlery drawer without a second glance as to whether the knives matched the forks.

'Mum!' I yell out now as she continues singing. 'What are you doing?'

'I'm recharging my crystals, Lucy,' she replies, as if it's perfectly obvious what she's up to at 5.30 am on a Wednesday. 'I need to take advantage of this morning light.'

'It's too early, Ma!'

'Rubbish!' she calls back through the flyscreen. 'Glenda and I have already been out for a walk, had a cup of tea and hung out the washing.'

'Jeez, that dog's multi-talented,' I say. 'We'll have to post a video of her hanging out the washing on YouTube.'

I close my eyes, hoping to rejoin those happy souls in the Land of Nod, then jump in shock at the sound of Mum whispering, 'Come and sit outside with your poor old ma.'

'Hooly-dooley, Ma!' I exclaim as she starts laughing, her forehead and nose pressed against the flyscreen of my window like Freddy Krueger. 'You frightened the wits out of me!'

I join her outside on the swinging chair, the day still breaking before us on the back verandah. Despite the winter winds, the hardy bougainvillea continue to bloom, adding flashes of brilliant maroon and pink to the burnt orange hues of sunrise.

'There's something nice about watching the clothes dance in the wind, don't you think?' asks Mum.

'Yeah, there is,' I reply. 'I think it's because you're achieving something, there's an outcome at the end of it.' I snuggle up to her. 'It's getting cold.'

'It is,' she agrees. 'There's flannelette sheets in the cupboard, you know.'

'Mmm,' I reply.

'How was your night at the Whipcrack with Rosie?' she asks. 'I feel like I've hardly seen you since then.'

'Yeah, good,' I say. 'Rosie's pretty set on London.'

'Is she?'

'Yeah. She's a bit over Rocky.'

We swing in silence, both grim at the prospect of losing Rosie to England. Still thinking of her, I say, 'Dave Conroy was at the Whipcrack.'

'Ah, lovely Dave!' She smiles. 'Have they had much rain out that way?'

'A few inches,' I reply.

'Remember when he used to chase you around and try to pull your pants down?' she says. 'I think I've still got a photo of you two having a bath together as whippersnappers.'

I wrinkle my nose in disgust, then smirk as I think how it's not my pants he's trying to pull down these days, and that Rosie isn't the only one who's bathed with Dave.

'I went and saw Meredith yesterday,' says Mum. 'She's not good at all.'

'Isn't she?' I ask.

Meredith is a sweet, gentle soul who used to spend a few hours each week repositioning clothes on mannequins at All About Town. I think even she knew her work wasn't essential, but she loved being with Mum and always said I looked fabulous when I played dress-ups with the stock as a little girl. Earlier this year she had a stroke, and now she's living in the high-care ward of a nursing home with people almost double her age.

'No,' says Mum. 'It makes me sad to see her like that, just lifeless and empty when she used to be so sprightly and independent.'

'Does she still recognise you?'

'She always smiles and tells me how busy she is, but I don't think she really knows me. I hold her hand but I'm not sure if it makes any difference.'

Mum looks beyond the trees in the backyard to the mountain range, now aglow with the rising sun. Lately, I've noticed a subtle shift in her. She's starting to take naps in the afternoon and is getting weary again by the early evening, and as we swing back and forth I get a keen sense that this person, whose presence I love but have taken for granted for so long, won't always be around.

I can remember having the same sensation of impending loss with my grandma. One day when I was about fifteen years old I was studying at our dining room table and looked up from my books to see her in the kitchen, emptying plates and cups from the dishwasher into her wheelie walker basket and shuffling along with them to the cupboard. I took the whole scene in and freeze-framed the moment, hoping to preserve it in my mind. These moments, which range from the heartbreaking to the hilarious, help me to map my journey. The beauty and the sadness, I think, lies in the moment of recognition, when you realise what you're seeing is so stirring, yet so fleeting.

This morning, I freeze-frame Mum, hoping I'll always recall this image of her, sitting beside me, staring distantly at the breaking day and the dancing clothes.

ॐ

I spend the rest of the morning working on my novel, and am pleased with how it goes. My heart sinks, however, when I go to the ATM to get twenty bucks out for a coffee and am greeted with a screen telling me I have 'insufficient funds'. It's well and truly time for me to get a few more freelance jobs.

That afternoon, I walk along Quay Street with the one-and-only business card I have left. When I rang Rosie to tell her about my ATM fiasco she said one of her patients had mentioned a production company that has just started up in Rocky. Though I suspect all they'll be doing is producing low-budget TV commercials for places like Bits 'n' Pizzas and Gone Bush, I haven't made any money since my vet articles—and I figure producing ads is better than washing cars with Ruth. I've also realised that devising any sort of plan requires cash.

A sign with orange lettering against a gleaming white background announces my arrival at Matchstick Productions. I square my shoulders, take a deep breath and tell myself to be confident. I have years of experience working as both a radio and TV producer. They would be lucky to have me. I slide the business card from my wallet and walk inside.

'Hello,' says a friendly woman behind the reception desk. 'Can I help you?'

I take heart in her conviviality and hand over my card, saying, 'Hello . . . Ah, my name's Lucy Crighton. I've worked for TROPPO FM, Sky News in Perth, WIN TV in Port Douglas, *The Headline Act* . . .'

The woman nods encouragingly as I list my former employers.

'And I'd love to work for Matchstick Productions,' I conclude enthusiastically.

'Ah, look, that all sounds great,' she says, thumbing my business card, 'but we actually produce . . . matchsticks.'

'Oh,' I reply, overcome with humiliation and hilarity simultaneously. 'Sorry.'

As I leave Matchstick Productions I burst into laughter. The only downside, I think, as I lean against my car cracking myself up, is that I just gave my last business card to a timber mill!

⁓

Arriving home I walk along the side of the house, following the sounds of Mum and Rosie on the swinging chair, flipping through the latest HomeHints catalogue.

'The thing is, Denise,' Rosie is saying, 'as you get older your knees go, so this Weed Remover with Ejector would actually be quite handy because it allows you to remove weeds while standing, see? Look at this picture. No more bending.'

'Hmmm,' replies Mum. 'Could be a very useful tool. Your mum might also like one, Rosie. I wonder if they'd give us a discount if we bought three.'

I roll my eyes and stay there a bit longer, listening to them discuss Mum's upcoming trip to China and Mongolia and Rosie enthusing about going to London.

When they start talking in lowered voices, it can only mean one thing and as I lean against the brick wall I hear Mum say, 'Rosie, you know Lucy can't go to London.' The creak of the swinging chair fills the silence between them. 'She needs to finish this damn novel and figure out what she wants to do next. And I just don't think London's the answer.'

'Well . . .' Rosie begins then stops. 'She's on track with her writing. She's been working really hard.'

'I know,' says Mum with a sigh. 'It's taken a lot out of me, this book.'

'And hello to you both!' I declare jauntily, stepping onto the back verandah.

'And hello to you!' cries Mum brightly, making me think she should definitely audition for the next intake at NIDA.

'I can't see that you both have much to discuss about me anymore!' I say with exaggerated cheeriness.

They remain deathly silent. 'Do you?' I ask, hesitant.

'So,' says Mum ignoring me, 'when do you start with Matchstick Productions?'

'Oh, Rosie!' I say. 'You stitched me up!'

'What?' Rosie asks.

'Matchstick Productions produces matchsticks!' I exclaim.

'Oh, it doesn't!' says Mum, starting to laugh.

'I must have looked like the biggest joke in town rattling off my CV to the poor woman there.'

They're both giggling now. And I can't help but be pleased to see Mum looking happy.

'You're the pits, Rosie!' I say, and though she claims she genuinely thought it was a media production company, she's laughing so much she's incoherent.

I sit down opposite them and am laughing too when I hear the familiar sound of Helen's VW backing out of the driveway. Suddenly, my jovial air dissipates.

It's been three days since I last saw Oscar, although it feels more like three weeks. I'm determined not to contact him, although every second moment I have to fight the urge to send a text before stopping myself, because there's no point getting in touch when he and Kate are probably out shopping for sheets. And besides, what would I write? *G'day! Lots of love from your girl up north!*

'Have you heard from Oscar, love?' asks Mum in a forced casual voice, her timing, as always, uncanny.

'No, Mum.'

'I had a chat with Helen when I was getting the mail this morning,' says Mum. 'She was telling me how busy Oscar's been negotiating new Bev's Buffet franchises in Sydney. She doesn't think he'll be up here for a few months now. And did you know Ben's just left on some big walk through France and Spain?'

'Oh yeah, he did mention he was going soon,' I reply, looking at the pavers to avoid catching Rosie's eye. 'Where's Glenda?' I ask, changing the subject.

'She was here earlier. She's probably snuck onto your bed.'

$\sim\!\!\infty$

As Mum predicted, Glenda is sprawled on my mattress, her little white head on my pillow. The sight of her fills me with joy and I lie down on the bed and shamelessly spoon her.

'If you were the Bachelor, you'd choose to end up with me,' I say, kissing the fur between her ears. 'I'm sure of it.'

I must have fallen asleep, because I startle awake at the sound of a brisk knock on my bedroom door to find the room completely dark and Glenda suddenly alert.

I look up to see Dad standing in my doorway.

'I know you don't care, but I thought you should hear it from me first,' he says. 'Tiffany Bloxsom just won a Logie.'

As I tighten my grip on Glenda's chest Dad sighs heavily, then leaves.

'Don't worry,' I say to Glenda. 'You can be assured I would choose you if I was the Bachelorette.'

'Mate,' says Rosie, walking into my room, 'are you talking to your kelpie?'

'Yes,' I reply.

'Move over,' she says, shutting my door and lying beside me and Glenda. 'I know what's going through your head, Luce, but you don't need a Logie to be bloody awesome. And you weren't enjoying Melbourne regardless of Jeremy.'

I'm surprised by how totally unfazed I am at the mention of Jeremy, then my heart sinks as I think of Oscar.

'Fuck him,' says Rosie, reading my mind.

'Well, I'd—'

'No, you've got to scratch him off the list. Ben mentioned Oscar's still seeing Kate, so he's made his choice and you've got to forget him. He's gone. Never existed. We can't even say his name anymore.'

I look at her glumly. 'I didn't have much of a list, Rosie. I'll scratch him off it but he was the only one there.'

'Ah well,' she says. 'My list is looking pretty blank too.'

'So you think that's that then?' I ask, knowing deep down that it is.

'Yep,' says Rosie, adamant.

'Mmm. It's probably for the best,' I say. 'He can't just click his fingers and have me.'

'But he's not clicking his fingers, Luce.'

'Sometimes I wish you weren't so good at pointing out the obvious,' I say, and we both laugh. 'I just don't see how things are going to work out for me anymore, Rosie. I'm not a hot twenty-three-year-old, I don't have my semi-glamorous TV job in Melbourne, there's only so many times I can pass Brian and Denise off as my flatmates. It's over. I think I'm out.'

'What happened to your Japanese Zen from the Buddhist monastery?'

'I left it on Mount Archer,' I say.

'Well,' she says, 'I still believe in you. Look at all you've achieved so far in your thirty-two years. You've tried. You've put yourself out there, and that's more than a lot of people can say. You've lived with your heart on your sleeve, and that can get you in strife sometimes, but for you it's the only way to live.'

'If you were a guy,' I say, smiling at her, 'we would have been married at eighteen.'

She laughs. 'Yeah, and divorced at twenty-five.'

'Rosie, are you *really* going to London?'

'Yes, and I think you should come too, no matter what Denise and Brian say. You can keep writing your novel there and get a part-time job. I'll get work as a dentist no problems, and I looked up the UK immigration website last night and even though we're over thirty now you can still stay for up to six months on a tourist visa. Why don't you come and see if you can find a job and then get sponsored?'

I close my eyes and cross my arms.

'If you run into trouble, I'll put you on as my dental assistant and get them to pay you cash in hand,' says Rosie, poking me in the ribs. 'We had a ball together when we lived there, Luce.'

'Do you think you can ever go back, though?' I ask. 'Can you ever relive that first-time experience? Those Bruce Springsteen "Glory Days"?'

'I don't see why not,' she replies. 'I mean, of course we're older, but does that mean we have to live in Rocky and be content with nine-to-five jobs and *Friday Night Football* just because that's what most of our friends are doing?'

'No, I guess not,' I say.

'What frustrates me about you, Luce, is that you've got everything going for you, but you won't allow yourself to see it,' says Rosie, shifting on the bed. 'Regardless of whether leaving Melbourne was the right or wrong move, don't you think you've punished yourself enough for that?'

'Mmm,' I reply.

'You have to trust that you can make a plan.' She pauses before shaking her head at me. 'Sometimes I just don't think I get through to you.'

'You are getting through to me,' I reply.

'It doesn't have to be London, you know—you can write a novel anywhere. You could move to New York. You could go any place you made up your mind to. You could even go back to Melbourne or try some time in Sydney . . . But if you go to Sydney, don't make it about Oscar. You've already made that mistake with Jeremy.'

'I know,' I say.

'Just don't stay here,' she says, walking to the door. 'Don't become institutionalised like that poor bugger in *The Shawshank Redemption*.'

We hear Dad talking to himself in the hallway as he passes my bedroom. 'The two of them are curled up in there with Glenda,' he mutters. 'It's all terribly unhygienic.'

Rosie raises her eyebrows at me. 'Know what I'm saying?'

15

Rosie's comments about me not becoming institutionalised rattle me so much that straight after she leaves I ring Tom Baker, the manager of local commercial station TROPPO FM and my first-ever employer, to see if there's any work going. I'm surprised when he asks if I can come in straight away and greets me with a big hug, telling me my timing is absolutely perfect, and can I help him cover a one-month holiday contract because the producer he's organised has dropped out at the last minute. Next thing I know I've got a job starting on Monday producing *Afternoons with Desley Delaney*.

Mum and Dad are over the moon when I tell them and Rosie is so thrilled she says she's shouting me dinner at Ribs 'n' Rumps on Saturday night. Ironically, I'm the most focused and productive I've ever been as I work on my novel for the rest of the week. On Sunday arvo, I lie on the couch, my feet on Rosie's lap, coping with yet another hangover, and Mum is sitting on her favourite armchair looking the happiest I've seen her in months.

'Why Cher, Mum?' I ask, contemplating the framed picture of Cher above her in the lounge room.

'She's had a hard life, love,' says Mum, glancing up at the wall. 'I first read about it in *New Idea*. All that business with Sonny and his addictions, but look at her now: strong and confident and empowering women everywhere.'

'What was that concert of hers like—the one you went to back in '84?' asks Rosie.

'Oh, it was the most marvellous night!' says Mum, her eyes shining with memories. 'You know she came out on an elephant wearing suspenders?'

'Who was wearing the suspenders?' I ask. 'Cher or the elephant?'

'Cher, of course!' she exclaims. 'The elephant had enough bling on it to open a Cash Converters, though,' she adds.

'Are you looking forward to starting work tomorrow, Luce?' says Dad as he walks into the room and settles into his recliner.

'Not really, Dad,' I reply, eliciting a snigger from Rosie.

'Well, that's not the attitude to have, is it?' says Dad, snapping me back to reality.

'Producing is not really what I want to be doing with my life, Dad.'

'You're not really in a position to be choosy, though, are you? Tell me, honestly, how much have you got in the bank?'

'When the money comes through from the Japan articles I wrote I'll have fifteen hundred. And I'm going to save all of my TROPPO money.'

Rosie's attempt to stifle her laughter is dismal. I give her a shove.

'Right, that won't last long,' says Dad, reaching down and pulling up the lever to send his legs horizontal. 'Lucy, you might think money's a dirty word, but you have to have it to survive, to exist. Then you can do your writing, or drawing, or whatever you want to do.'

'I don't think money's a dirty word, Dad, I'm just trying to be true to myself.'

'I know, Lucy,' says Mum, leaning forward in her chair. 'I know you're very talented and you'll do well in whatever you put your mind to. It's just the practicalities of living in the meantime.' She bites her fingernails. 'It's hard, isn't it?'

'It's not hard at all,' says Dad. 'Denise, right now, Lucy needs this job. And who's to say something permanent won't come up? She can write that novel in her spare time.'

Mum nods. 'Oh, I agree, Brian.'

I catch Rosie nodding too.

'The thing is, Luce, you've got to have a purpose in life,' says Dad. 'For a good while there I was down and out, as you know.'

'Well, we didn't really, Dad,' I point out.

'No, we had no idea, Brian!' cries Mum. '*And* no idea about Kakadu,' she adds under her breath.

'Were you down and out, Brian?' asks Rosie, interested.

'Yes I was, Rosie. But since I joined the Men's Shed, I feel like I've got something to do. I'm being useful to the community.'

'Yep, yep,' I say, 'but producing radio at TROPPO isn't my purpose in life, Dad.'

'Well, it might not be right now, but sometimes you just have to do things you're not that passionate about. And if you want to study medicine or vet science or whatever, you can start looking into it while you're earning a bit of dosh.'

'Are you still thinking of medicine, darl?' asks Mum nervously.

'No. I don't think I'm cut out to treat people's piles and ingrown toenails. I think after this month at TROPPO I'll do an ESL certificate and teach English in Vietnam.'

'Brilliant!' Rosie slaps the couch. 'I think that's a great plan, Luce!'

'And how much would that pay?' Dad asks me wearily. 'You want to be able to put a deposit down on a house, don't you? And have a family?'

I feel the cold hands of hopelessness and despair claw my shoulders, and I look at the floor.

'Brian!' says Mum, desperate to keep me on an even keel. 'Lucy will have lots of joy in her life, just let her take one step at a time.'

'Yeah, Brian, give her a bloody break,' says Rosie.

Mum considers me in earnest for a bit and then asks, 'If someone could wave a magic wand and you could be anywhere, doing anything, what would that be?'

Bless Mum for continuing to ask me these questions, when I know my answers bring her and Dad so much anguish. 'I wouldn't mind presenting a travel show about tea, and finishing my book.'

'I could see how a show like that would have huge appeal,' says Mum loyally, not betraying for one second that she'd dearly hoped I'd respond, 'I'd love to do a DipEd and marry Matt Kennedy, the local solicitor who's always fancied me, and have babies and put a deposit on that charming Queenslander in Agnes Street.'

'Tea's the second-biggest drink in the world apparently,' continues Mum. 'I read in the *Women's Weekly* only last night about this mum and her daughter who set up fair trade tea fields in the Gold Coast hinterland. It was quite interesting actually.'

'I wouldn't mind reading that article, Denise,' says Rosie.

'Look, Lucy's flat out buying a *cup* of tea at the moment,' says Dad. 'Anyway, all this talk is too silly. What I'd like to know is whether anyone's putting on the kettle?'

'I will, Dad,' I say, and clamber off the couch. I feel annoyed with myself for engaging in the same old frustrating discussions. My parents didn't try to influence my decision to follow the creative path. When I finished high school they were supportive of me studying journalism, despite their lack of knowledge about it.

They were thrilled when I started working at TROPPO FM—having listened to it all their lives—but as I continued to pursue gigs around the country, they became ever more perplexed about the workings of the media, baffled at the industry I'd chosen.

Bewildered, they'd shake their heads when I regaled them with stories of jobs being advertised then withdrawn; of emails going unanswered; of losing sleep about daily deadlines. Over the past decade, I'd watched their view of my profession change from one of innocence to cynicism.

'Oh well, you won't hear back from them,' Mum would reply after learning I'd messaged a former colleague on

LinkedIn, and Dad would say, less tactfully, 'Love, that boss of yours doesn't even know you're alive.'

Mum's bugbear was when movers and shakers would tell me I was talented and that I'd 'crack it one day' and then walk away. 'But what good is it?' Mum would cry. 'We all know you're talented. But what does it mean?'

By that stage I didn't know either.

Understandably, when I persist with ambitions of presenting TV shows or writing books, Mum and Dad harbour grave concerns. Perhaps they're just being more realistic than me, their drifting dreamer.

As I hover above the boiling kettle, the steam condensing in what I hope to be anti-ageing droplets on my face, Mum and Rosie appear on either side of me.

'By the way, have you checked your email, darl?' asks Mum lightly.

'Today?' adds Rosie.

'What are you two up to?' I ask, looking from one to the other. 'If you've tried to sign me up to eHarmony again I'll delete the account.' I whip my mobile from my pocket and tap the email icon.

We all peer at the screen as my inbox refreshes. There are a few emails from friends and LinkedIn notifications. I continue to scroll down, wondering what they've been plotting.

'Lo and behold it appears I have an email from . . . the HomeHints catalogue?' I look at the two of them suspiciously.

Rosie grins back at me as the email loads.

'*Dear Lucy,*' I read aloud. '*We are delighted to confirm that your application to become a casual copywriter for the*

HomeHints Direct catalogue has been successful. Please find attached a list of our upcoming products for the Spring issue. As outlined in the attached information document, 200-word descriptions are ideal. Please invoice us $100 per description. We look forward to working with you. Kind Regards, Marjorie Beaumont, HomeHints Direct.'

I laugh as I glance up from my phone to see Rosie and Mum high-five.

'We saw it advertised in the catalogue when you burst in on us,' says Mum. 'It was after you tried to draw out that non-existent money, and we weren't to know you'd get fill-in work at TROPPO FM.'

'Yeah, and we knew you'd think it was beneath you to apply, so I hacked into your Gmail account,' says Rosie. 'You really should change your password by the way, Glenda1234 is ridiculous. Anyway, I found your CV on the desktop, submitted it, and here we are.'

Rosie and Mum grin at each other and then at me. I can't help grinning too. Tiffany Bloxsom may have her Logie, but who cares? I'm the new casual copywriter for HomeHints and my two biggest fans in the world couldn't be prouder.

I throw my arms around them and we group hug in the kitchen.

'God almighty!' says Dad, walking in on us. 'What does it take to get a cup of tea in this place?'

'See if you can nab us a staff discount, hey?' says Mum, her eyes glistening as we return to the lounge room.

16

Over the next three weeks I discover that my dread about going back to TROPPO FM was largely unfounded. Being among the bustle and banter of work colleagues has been really positive. I'd forgotten the comfort to be found in the ritual of turning up at a happy workplace every morning and saying hello; of making small talk while making tea; of the little nod-and-smile exchange when passing people in the corridors. The regular pay cheque is also nice, and I've managed to write a few blurbs for the HomeHints catalogue in the evenings and on weekends, so my bank account balance is looking much healthier.

I'm even quite enjoying producing—skimming through the papers and online news sites every morning, diving into my trusty contacts book to track down talent, devising quirky talkback topics and writing introductions and questions for Desley.

Originally from Melbourne, Desley is a gun presenter and is quickly learning the ways of Queenslanders, although I still rib her about the time she ordered a dirty chai from Bits 'n' Pizzas and the waitress responded, 'So, you want a dirty big chai?' I also need to provide copious notes on the screen for her during our Friday sports segment, and constantly remind her that when she refers to rugby, she is not referring to rugby league.

⌒ℯᕲ

'Hearing your favourite recipes using leeks on 1300 599 444. Ah, Joyce is on the line from Blackwater . . . Hello, Joyce!'

'Is that you, Desley?'

'Yes, got you loud and clear, Joyce.'

'Oh, Desley, I just wanted to say that I haven't grown beets in years.'

'What's that, Joyce?'

'I haven't grown beetroot in years,' Joyce says.

'Ah, right, Joyce,' says Desley. 'That's interesting. But we're actually talking about leek—101 ways with leeks.'

'Who?'

'Thanks, Joyce. Joyce from Blackwater getting a little confused there, but wonderful to hear from her just the same, and we might talk about beetroots tomorrow. I used to have lovely beetroot lattes on the weekend at the Vic markets. Thanks for the suggestion, Joyce! But what about you, Terry, calling in from Yeppoon today—any secret leek recipes you can share?'

'Is that you, Desley? Oh, I beg your pardon, I've rung in for Wally Ryan's gardening talkback.'

'Well, you're half an hour early there, Terry, but stay on the line, Lucy'll grab your number and you'll be first off the post when we open the lines for Wally.'

'Lucy,' says Desley, buzzing me through the intercom during the next ad break, 'have you got the weather bureau up? We've got ten seconds.'

Fuck! I focus again.

Despite the welcome distractions of work, my head is still full of Oscar, my thoughts oscillating exhaustingly between fondness and reminding myself he already has a girlfriend. So why, almost a month after I left him standing at Ruth's car wash, do I care in the slightest whether he misses me? Why does my pulse quicken when I hear a car pull in to Helen's driveway? Why hasn't my heart caught up to my head in recognising the situation as hopeless?

'Lucy,' says Desley again, causing me to frantically check the rundown for what I've missed. Puzzled, I look up to see her winking at me from the other side of the glass. 'I think someone's got a visitor!' she sings playfully.

Desley is convinced that Lachy Campbell, the online producer, is smitten with me. I'm not so sure, though Lachy does consistently hang about the studio as we're putting the show to air, and agreeably plies me with homemade food at every turn. He's an affable guy, no doubt, and the fact that he is walking towards me with a chocolate muffin is delightful, but I have absolutely zero interest in him. Whatever the case, I'm willing to play along in the interests of Desley and me having something to chat about in the kitchenette.

'Hey, Lachy, how are you going?' I ask between screening talkback calls on the humane disposal of cane toads.

'Fantastic!' he says. 'Chocolate muffin for you and Desley to share at half-time?'

'Awesome, thank you—I'm starving!'

'I thought you might be,' he says, turning to leave. 'See ya during the news.'

Forty minutes later, after Desley hosts a heated discussion on bringing back daylight saving, he slides a tray of spring rolls and dipping sauce onto my desk. To be honest, if it meant kissing him to keep this food train coming, I could probably stomach it.

'Spring roll for a roll in the hay, hey?' quips Desley as she walks out of the studio during our five-minute news bulletin.

'These are very good,' I say, smiling while keeping an eye on the clock.

'So what do you think?' she says, perching on the edge of my desk in that way people from big cities are wont to do.

'Oh, I'm not sure how long I'll be around Rocky, Desley, so I'm not looking to start anything with anyone.'

'Hmmm. About that—next week is your last with me. What are your plans?' she asks.

'Don't know yet,' I say, hearing the newsreader move onto the sports headlines. 'I've got a few options, but I'm just waiting to see what happens.'

'You know, Lucy,' she continues, unperturbed by the fact that she's on air in less than half a minute, 'I suspect you need to learn that commitment isn't always evil.'

I dodge answering and tell her I've got fifteen seconds to track down our expert on how to look six-foot-five when you're only five-foot-six.

☙

On Thursday night, in celebration of getting paid, Rosie and I head out to do some late-night shopping on account of her telling me my current pairs of jeans are only fit for the farm and I need to buy me some new Lee's. Despite her steady stream of talk and jokes, I can tell Rosie is distracted and she seems a bit tetchy.

'What do you think of these?' I ask, pulling back the curtain in the Red Dirt Denim change room.

'Hot!' She nods approvingly. 'Turn around. Yep, they're the winners. Get 'em and then let's go to the food court.'

As we walk towards Paradise Plaza's familiar medley of carveries and juice bars, much frequented in our youth, I decide to air the niggling annoyance I've carried all afternoon.

'Rosie, is there something about me which screams commitment-phobe?'

She pauses, clearly unsure how to answer, so I continue, 'I only ask because Desley made a point of telling me today that commitment isn't always evil. And I don't really know why she said it.'

We hover around a spare table that's being wiped down. 'I don't believe I'm a flaky person,' I say, taking a seat. 'I always aim to do my best.'

Rosie slides in opposite me. 'I do think you sometimes give off a bit of an untouchable air.'

'What, like I'm too good for everyone?' I ask, astonished.

'No, like you're just unattainable for anything—work, love, life . . .'

'No I don't!' I reply, stung.

'Do you want me to keep going or not?' she asks.

'Can I get a doughnut first to soften the blow?'

'I understand what's behind it,' she continues as I return from Donut King. 'You feel like you don't want to regret making the wrong choice with work so you make none. You don't want to get burnt again in a relationship so you search for perfection because you know, subconsciously, you won't ever obtain it, and therefore you'll never have to risk being hurt.' She pauses. 'I know you're putting up a force field to protect yourself, but to everyone else it just looks like you're hanging back—and, yes, that you're a commitment-phobe.'

'I don't hang back,' I say defensively.

'Studying for medicine—did you ever look at one uni website?' she asks.

'No,' I reply.

'Teaching English as a second language. Did you download any course forms?'

'No,' I say, unsure whether Rosie's interrogation is productive or patronising.

'Living in London. Have you seriously considered coming with me?'

I look at the half-eaten doughnut on the table, unable to answer, tears welling in my eyes.

'I've got to grab a couple of things from Woolies,' says Rosie, getting up.

I don't know where to start contemplating Rosie's analysis, so I lean back in my seat, cross my legs and numbly watch the comings and goings of the food court without registering anything.

'Earth to Lucy!' calls someone loudly, causing me to jump in my chair.

'Oh, sorry, Lachy,' I say, looking up to see him standing grinning at me with a trolley full of groceries. 'You startled me!'

'I know,' he says with a chuckle. 'You were a million miles away.'

'Something like that,' I respond, sitting up straighter. 'How's things? Got the groceries, I see.'

'Yep, got the groceries,' he replies. 'Oh, hey, did Tom talk to you this afternoon?'

'No,' I reply, feeling anxious at the prospect that Tom might want to extend my contract beyond next week.

'Connor Silver's coming to town!' says Lachy, his face lighting up with excitement.

'Connor Silver?! 'Velvet Kisses' Connor Silver from the eighties with the big blonde mullet? Why?'

'Well, not Rocky exactly, but Capella. His band's playing there.'

'Capella? That's bizarre. When?' I ask.

'This Saturday!' he replies. 'The concert's only just been announced, and I think it's sold out already, but we can get media passes for it.'

'Does Tom want me to go?'

'Well, I'm going to interview Connor, but Tom wants to make a big deal of it for online, so he wants both of us to head there.'

'What about Desley?' I ask. 'Isn't she a big Connor fan?'

'Yeah.' He nods. 'Tom asked Desley, but she's going to a wedding in Melbourne this weekend.'

'Ah, right. Oh well, it could be fun,' I say cautiously.

'Yeah, I think it'd be unreal! Anyway, I'm sure Tom'll talk to you about it tomorrow.'

'Cool,' I say, relieved to see Rosie walking towards us.

'Alright, better get these cold things in the fridge,' he says. 'See ya, Luce.'

'See ya, Lachy,' I reply, noting the enormous amount of produce it takes to keep Desley and me fed.

'There's absolutely no fucking ham hocks in this town!' yells Rosie as she approaches me. 'Every bastard in Rockhampton is making pea and ham soup! So much for living in the bloody beef capital of Australia!'

I should let it slide, but I don't. 'It's pig, though,' I say, getting up. 'Ham is from a pig, not a cow. Beef is cows.'

'Fuck off, Lucy,' she says.

I wish I was tougher, but I'm not. I start snivelling out the front of Best & Less.

'Oh, mate,' she says, stopping and putting her arm around me. 'You know I love you to the moon and back.'

I rest my head on her shoulder. 'Maybe you could buy a chicken,' I say, trying to smile. 'And make chicken soup.'

'I'm sorry,' she says, rubbing my back. 'I'm sorry. I'm sorry.'

We retreat to a bench and silently watch the passing parade of shins and calves.

Rosie sighs heavily. 'I ran into Trent the Tradie this morning. It's only been two months and he's already bloody engaged to that new girl. I didn't think it'd piss me off so much. I'm sorry if I've taken it out on you.

'I'd sort of been holding off from booking my London ticket to see if I could convince you to come. But I know now you won't.' She looks at me with tears in her eyes.

'I'm leaving in five weeks,' she says. 'I can't wait to get out of this fucking town, Luce.'

'I know,' I reply. 'I know.'

↝

I wake the next morning feeling emotionally and physically exhausted. At Mum's urging I'd made my bed with flannelette sheets before hitting the sack and it was the wrong move. I tossed and turned into the early hours, overheating like a car on Christmas Day. I even had nightmares, sitting up in a horrible rush to the image of someone gripping my neck and pushing me underwater. I decide I need to go easy on the late-night *House of Cards* episodes and switch my linen back to breathable cotton.

I also need to cut back on the caffeine. Since I've been working at TROPPO FM and writing copy for the HomeHints catalogue at night, I've been completely under the spell of that cunning java vixen and having three coffees a day. When in her clutches, I'm on top of the world, my nervous system shaping up to move mountains, bursting with ideas for talkback topics and segments. Then, a couple of hours later, I look around the office with beige-tinted glasses and wonder if everything isn't pretty dull, really. The upshot is, I can't go on the way I am, so today I replace my afternoon coffee with a Panadol and make an appointment to see a psychologist after work.

Now, with the show having gone to air, and Desley having gone for sushi, I sit at my desk, stretch my arms above my head and yawn. When I open my eyes I'm startled to see Tom hovering in front of me. Tom is the quintessential hoverer. He hovers around until you say hello, hovers until you say goodbye and does a lot of hovering between.

'Hello, Tom,' I say with a weary smile.

'Afternoon, Lucy. How are you?'

'Well, thanks. The show was good today. Lots of talkback on becoming a republic and fluoride in tap water. I think tomorrow we're going to do "your favourite useless kitchen utensil" and 101 ways with lemons.'

'Yes, wonderful, terrific! Spoken to Lachy?'

'Oh yeah, I ran into him last night. He told me about Connor Silver.'

'Yes, yes, mmm, yes, ha!' he says, hovering. 'So, ah, would you be interested in going?'

I've been anticipating this question and given it a great deal of thought. Other than him being a mega rockstar from the eighties, and once owning Hamilton Island, I know nothing about Connor Silver, so seeing him in the flesh could be a buzz. On the other hand, it involves being trapped in a car with Lachy for a three-and-a-half-hour return trip, so I've resolved not to go.

'Well, not really, to be honest,' I answer. 'I had a few things planned for the weekend, so . . .'

'Oh right, yes, yes, right. It's just that we have no-one else to accompany Lachy and the orders are coming in from Sydney that we really have to get behind this.'

'Oh, okay. Is TV going out?' I ask.

'No crews allowed. Connor doesn't want any filming inside apparently. Photos yes, and the chat with Lachy fine, but no filming.'

'So you'll want me to take stills?'

'You've taken some beautiful shots for our website so I thought you'd be the best person—after Desley, of course, who's a massive Connor fan, but she's got a wedding in Melbourne. But if you absolutely can't . . .'

I think of Rosie and Desley's commitment taunts. 'Okay, I'll do it,' I say. What the hell.

'Terrific! That's terrific! Wonderful! You can take the station car and we've arranged accommodation for you both above the Capella pub so I'm sure you'll have a fantastic trip!'

'Sure, it should be good. Alright, thanks, Tom. Goodbye.'

'Goodbye,' he says, though he remains hovering for a good thirty seconds.

ᴄeᴐ

The psychologist, Beth Carmody, is kind, a good listener and a bearer of insights, which is everything I could have hoped for in my forty-minute consultation. There is a box of tissues on the table between us, and a clock on the wall behind me, which I glance at surreptitiously as I blow my nose.

I tell her about Oscar, and how living at home and working back in the office of my first-ever employer makes me feel a little like a failure. I confess to constantly sabotaging myself with thoughts that I've missed the boat on having a career, and that I'm afraid of how I'll feel if my novel is rejected. I also tell her I'm worried I won't have enough money to make changes and that my parents think I'm unrealistic about what to expect out of a job and that, though they don't say it, they believe I'm wasting my time writing a book.

At this point, I burst into tears and she hands me the box of tissues and waits for me to pull myself together. Then she points out that if I think I have a genuine, burning desire to do things differently, I'll walk over hot coals to make changes. She asks me to consider whether or not I enjoy this feeling of being stuck—whether it has become like a second skin, a habit I can't shake, a faulty mode of thinking I've fallen into because negativity and apathy are easier tracks to tread.

She also asks gently whether I'm taking a lazy approach to my life.

And though I don't reply, I suspect the answer is yes.

17

After my appointment with Beth, I have the best night's sleep I've had in ages, so I'm feeling refreshed and re-invigorated as Lachy and I drive along the western roads to Capella, the sunburnt landscapes opening up before us.

I gaze out the window as we pass ghostly gums, their gnarled branches like witches' fingers against the blazing blue sky. There's a peacefulness in this harsh and rugged terrain, and as we continue further inland, the shifting sun bathing the barks in dappled light, I feel my mind relax as I soak up the scenery.

'Mind if I put on a playlist?' asks Lachy, turning down the radio.

'Oh sure,' I reply, smiling at him and bracing myself for something like Nickelback. I'm pleasantly surprised when he plays Old Crow Medicine Show, and a fine selection of Gillian Welch and Dave Rawlings Machine. My mood lifts and I make a mental note to add some alternative country to my repertoire of what Dad describes as my 'awful bloody mournful music.'

'Well, I've thoroughly enjoyed your DJ session, Lachy,' I say as we whiz past the *Welcome to Capella* sign. 'I'll have to get those albums off you.'

'Yeah.' He grins. 'From time to time you do actually hear a good song on commercial radio. I've been thinking a lot about this interview tonight. I mean, Connor Silver's an Aussie icon. At some stage everyone's owned a copy of "Velvet Kisses". There's so much to talk about.'

'Yeah, you just have to narrow it down, I suppose.'

'Are you excited?' he asks.

'What?'

'Are you excited to see him?'

'Ah, yeah, I am,' I say. 'But it's more getting out here that excites me. I love hitting the road.'

'I know what you mean,' he replies. 'I miss my skate-boarding days.'

This is why I'm not attracted to Lachy. He says things like that.

'Oh!' I exclaim as we get out of the car. 'It's bloody freezing!' We scoot inside the old weatherboard hotel and stand at the bar. A woman eventually appears and gives me a key, then tells me Mr Campbell and I are in a room straight upstairs. I frown, but assume she's made a mistake and Lachy and I have a room each. However, when I ask, the woman shakes her head and tells me the lady at TROPPO FM said a room with two single beds was fine.

'Man, you'd think they'd have organised separate rooms

for us,' I say to Lachy as I gaze at the two single beds, which just fit in the tiny room with about a metre to spare.

'Me too, but it's TROPPO, isn't it?' he says, looking much too delighted for my liking.

'True,' I concede. 'Oh well, doesn't matter. I suppose we'd better get to this concert.' I throw my bag on one of the beds.

'Hang on,' he says, unzipping his backpack. 'I just have to change.'

I look down at the floorboards while he whips off his t-shirt, then glance back up after he sings, 'Ta-da!' to see he's wearing a skin-tight black skivvy bearing a faded and cracked iron-on of Connor from his Bad Attitude band days.

'Where did you get that?' I ask.

'It's Desley's. She insisted I wear it.'

'It's shocking, Lachy,' I say, shaking my head as we close the door behind us.

⁓

Connor Silver and his band, Sterling Silver, raise the roof at the Capella Cultural Centre. Spirits are high, literally, with one man dousing himself in Bundy and Coke. The crowd love it. And why wouldn't they? It's not often a chart-topping artist with a spectacular blonde mullet puts on a show in the Central Highlands.

At the end of the concert, Connor sits onstage to sign autographs for a queue of several hundred people. Weaving among them with my camera, I take happy snaps of little girls in braids and boots, middle-aged men in Harley-Davidson leather, straight-talking, Wrangler-wearing teenagers and, to my great delight, a couple of sapphire hawkers from the nearby gemfields who thought they'd try their luck with Connor.

Half an hour later, I find Lachy leaning against the wall at the back of the venue.

'Can you tell Connor I'll do the interview when he's finished signing?' he asks, looking a bit pale.

'Yeah, no worries.'

I walk up to the stage and sit down beside Connor Silver. 'How's it going, Connor?' I say, smiling at him.

'Good, mate, how are you?' he asks, between signatures.

'Yeah, good. I just wanted to let you know that Lachlan from TROPPO FM will be doing an interview with you after all this. He's at the back of the room.'

'No worries. Who's this for?' he asks, handing me a white bra.

'Whose is this?' I ask the crowd.

'It's for Kathy with a K, love!' a woman wearing a purple-and-black flannelette shirt calls back.

'Right, Kathy with a K,' he says, signing one of the cups and flinging it back into the outstretched arms of its owner.

'What about this one?'

I look to the burly bikie who handed over the tea towel.

'Roger,' he replies.

And so we go on like this for the next forty minutes— people handing things to me for Connor to sign, and me handing them back. Connor and I share the odd joke, and I'm surprised by how easygoing he is.

At one point I stand to stretch my legs and he signs my jeans.

'Oh, Connor!' I say, looking down at him, annoyed. 'These are my brand-new Lee's!'

He laughs and continues signing.

When the last of the autograph hunters and sapphire hawkers have left, I tell Connor I'm going to get Lachy for the interview. I find him at the back of the hall, but just as I reach him his phone rings and he looks like he's going to take the call.

'Time to do this interview, Lachy,' I say with some urgency, conscious that Connor might not want to hang around for too long.

'I'm sorry, Lucy,' he says quickly. 'I can't do it.'

'What do you mean?' I ask.

'I have to answer this,' he says, thrusting the recorder into my hands. 'You'll have to do it.'

'I can't do it!' I exclaim. 'I know nothing about Connor Silver! I was only two when "Velvet Kisses" went to number one!'

He shoots me an apologetic glance before raising the phone to his ear and walking out of the venue.

On my way back to Connor I feel like I'm shuffling towards the gallows. I honestly know nothing about this man—nothing.

He smiles and taps me on the head with his marker pen. 'Let's do the interview, hey?' he says, jumping down from the stage and heading towards the back of the building. 'Where's your man?'

Oh God. Fuck! I think as we turn the corner into a small room. A fridge stocked with VB sits against one wall, and off to one side of the fridge are two chairs. 'Ah, well, it turns out he's had a family emergency,' I say, inwardly cursing Lachy, 'so I'm going to do the interview instead.'

'Cool. Want a beer?' asks Connor, opening the fridge and offering me a can of VB.

What the hell am I going to ask him? What is going to come out of my mouth here? I wonder as we sit down. I turn on the recorder and check my levels, trying to dredge up something—anything—about this man.

'Sitting down to do an interview with Connor Silver here. Welcome, Connor, thanks for doing the interview.'

'Thank you, it's my pleasure,' he replies, taking a swig of his beer.

'So, you look like you get a lot of enjoyment up there. Have you always performed musically?'

'Yeah, mate, I've been doing gigs from a very young age, since I was fifteen. The stage is like my theatre . . .'

I'm panicking so much I hardly take in a word he says.

'You really do look like you get a buzz from performing musically. You've always performed, from a young age?' I ask.

Connor gives me an odd look, then starts laughing. 'Ah, if you listen back to my previous answer, you'll hear me say that I've been performing since I was a kid.'

'Oh,' I reply, gutted. 'I'm sorry. Hamilton Island's lovely, isn't it.'

We chat for forty minutes, with me making mistake after mistake, incorrectly referring to his band as Stainless Steel, and him looking at me in good-humoured horror when I ask him to explain the meaning of the word 'zeitgeist'.

Given the circumstances, he's very kind and generous,

and I actually think my complete unpreparedness may have been refreshing.

At the end of the interview, we hug and Connor says with a chuckle, 'Now, if you're brave, you'll just broadcast all of this.'

I apologise again and tell him that now I've met him I'm going to buy 'Velvet Kisses' on LP.

'You know, you've got a lot to offer,' he says as we return to the hall.

I grin. Connor Silver thinks I've got a lot to offer. Maybe things are going to work out after all!

I'm busting to see Lachy, and after searching around I find him back in the pub, perched at the bar. He apologises for dropping me in it but I tell him it ended up going okay and Connor said I had a lot to offer. Lachy's excited for me, but I sense he's also a little disappointed that he missed the opportunity.

'I got this for you,' I say and slide him a signed VB coaster.

'Oh, Luce—thanks!' he says, and reads what Connor wrote on the coaster: *Lachy, mate, the next one's on you! Cheers, Connor*. 'Awesome, Lucy, this is going straight to the pool room!' he says.

'I thought you'd like it.' I smile.

He takes a sip of his beer. 'Did you get something signed for Desley?'

'Yeah,' I reply. 'I feel a bit bad, but all I could find at the last minute was this Woolies receipt in the back of my jeans, so he signed that too!'

We laugh, and I feel on top of the world. I'm proud of my courage. I still can't believe I was brave enough to do that. It definitely wasn't the world's best interview, but it was certainly my own, and not one I think Connor will forget too quickly either.

I buy us both another drink.

'Hey, Luce?' he says earnestly, swivelling towards me.

Oh, man! That's right. I forgot about Lachy's crush. Stuff it, I think—maybe I should just kiss him. It might help banish Oscar from my mind forever.

'Yeah?' I say.

'Do you think Desley likes me?' he asks.

'Desley?' I say, gobsmacked.

'Yeah,' he replies shyly. 'That's who called me when I was going to do the interview.'

'Ah . . .' I say slowly.

'Why do you say it like that?' he says, blushing slightly.

I laugh. 'Lachy, Desley is convinced that you're keen on me!'

'Ha! Well, I was for about three days, but I could tell you were all over the shop; you don't know whether you're coming or going. Trouble!'

'So all that food,' I say, as if I'm DCI Barnaby piecing together evidence at the end of *Midsomer Murders*, 'that was actually meant for Desley?'

'Well, you *and* Desley. By the way, you can eat a lot!'

'Yeah, I've always been a good eater,' I say and am surprised to find my ego slightly bruised. 'So, Desley, hey? But she's from Melbourne.'

'I know, that's the only thing. But she can angle park properly and she goes for Queensland in the State of Origin.' He smiles into his drink. 'I think she's pretty cute.'

'I thought she was with that Craig guy from the Beef Australia committee?'

'No, that finished months ago. I saw him about three in the morning at Subway the other night, kissing some chick. I think she runs the car wash on the corner of —'

'Fitzroy and Albert streets. That'd be Ruth.'

I take another swig of my beer, thinking.

'So, does Desley often call you?' I ask, still attempting to make sense of it all.

'No,' he replies. 'That's why I thought it was important to answer. She'd had a few drinks at the wedding. She wanted to know all about the concert.'

'Ah,' I say, smiling. 'The old had-a-few-drinks phone call. That's a good sign. So what's the plan, man? I don't think you're going to win over Desley with muffins and spring rolls alone.'

'No?'

'No. She's from Melbourne, Lachy! Think more macarons and macchiatos. You need to ask her out for coffee.'

'Right,' he says. 'What, like to Bits 'n' Pizzas?'

'No, take her somewhere classy, like Cup of Jo on Bolsover Street. Jo Fleming just opened it. Desley will love it.'

'Thanks, Luce,' he says, and we clink glasses.

∽

Later that evening, I struggle to fall asleep and shift about, restless.

'What about you, Lucy?' asks Lachy suddenly, cutting through the silence. 'A good-looking girl like you'd have a few fellas hanging around.'

'Oh, not really,' I reply.

'Not really's not really an answer,' he says.

I laugh. 'Well, it's sort of a long story.'

'Tell me about it,' he says. 'I'm not going anywhere for at least six hours.'

I figure I have nothing to lose, and reconstruct the Oscar timeline for Lachy, from the initial knock on my front door to the incident on Mount Archer and, finally, leaving him all those weeks ago at Ruth's car wash.

I tell him about my confusion, Oscar's confusion, and how a quiet acceptance of it all is now sinking into my bones. When I finish pouring my heart out, there's silence.

'Lachy, are you asleep?'

'No, no, I've been listening,' he says. 'Have you heard of the weather map test?'

'No.'

'Okay,' he says, 'you know when Jenny Woodward presents the weather on ABC News?'

'Yeah?'

'Well, at the start of the weather, a big map of Australia flashes up and you can see all the capitals and the big cities.'

'Mmm.'

'After you've looked at Rocky, where do you look next?'

'Sydney,' I reply immediately.

'See, there you go,' he says, triumphant. 'If you were completely over Oscar, you wouldn't be glancing down at the Sydney temps.'

I sigh. 'Well, you're a guy. What do you make of it all?'

'If you want the truth, it sounds to me like the ball's in his court. He's obviously into you, but you live in Rocky and he lives in Sydney and so does the woman he's seeing. Things are just too easy for him to make any massive changes, especially when they involve hurting someone he likes.'

'Yeah, I know you're right.'

'But what would you do if he made a grand gesture and said, "How about moving to Sydney and being with me?" What would you say?' asks Lachy.

'I don't know,' I admit. 'It's too hypothetical. There's too many variables. And besides, he's not going to say that. We haven't spoken in a month, and I've been trying to just carry on like he's died.'

He yawns. 'Sounds dramatic, but all I'm saying is that sometimes it takes guys a long time to realise what they actually value and what they actually want in a partner.'

'I guess,' I reply, not finding any hope in his words. 'Thanks, Lachy. You're a good listener.'

'Still can't believe Connor Silver signed your jeans,' he says.

'I know! My brand-new Lee's, bloody ruined,' I say, though at the same time I'm marvelling at life's unpredictability. Just when you think you're making a mess of everything, out comes a superstar from the eighties to tell you over a VB that you've got a lot to offer.

ॐ

Halfway between Capella and Rocky, I play Lachy audio from my conversation with Connor and he almost drives off the road with laughter at my embarrassing faux pas.

'You can't play that!' he gasps.

'I know!' I agree. 'There's no way I could play that!'

But as we pass the fields of cattle and crops, I gaze out the window and wonder whether there's any way I *can* salvage my Connor Silver interview. By the time we arrive back at the TROPPO studios, an idea is taking shape . . . I could turn my disaster into a piece on how *not* to interview Connor Silver.

I write a script for Lachy to voice as if he's just heard my interview with Connor, and is taking me through step by step, telling me what I could have done differently. Lachy's a champ and absolutely nails his lines. We also record my reactions to his suggestions, and I then cut the whole piece together, including audio of the exchanges between Connor and me to which Lachy refers. At the end of our efforts, we play the piece back through the studio speakers and laugh and laugh. I sound like an absolute dill, but I couldn't be happier. I have always felt most alive making people laugh, and if it's at my expense, then all the better.

My train-wreck interview is played the next day, to much hilarity, on TROPPO FM-affiliated stations dotted around the country. Soon I'm fielding congratulatory phone calls and emails from one-time colleagues at WIN TV and *The Headline Act*. I even receive a flattering Facebook comment from Tiffany Bloxsom. I sense this is what it's like to be flavour of the month, and I admit to feeling ten feet tall.

Then Lachy receives a call from Connor's publicity manager, who asks, 'Who on earth is this Lucy Crighton? And why did she stick the boots into Connor when he'd been so generous to her?'

Lachy looks across to me as he replies that I had no idea the announcers would interpret the piece as Connor picking on me and then proceed to take my side. He said I'd naturally assumed listeners would be laughing at my incompetence and not pointing the finger at Connor.

After Lachy debriefs me on the call, I'm devastated to think that what I've put together could be misconstrued, especially given how friendly Connor was to me. Apparently his publicity manager had caught the interview on TROPPO FM in Brisbane, and immediately called Connor, who told her he'd had a lovely chat with me in Capella and that I was sweet. 'Well you should listen to what she's done with your interview!' she'd replied.

The consensus in the office is that Lachy handled the phone call extremely well and I am grateful for his clear, confident, pragmatic advocacy on my behalf. I am, however, gutted that Connor might think I've set him up.

Back at home that afternoon, I find the business card for the guy who was travelling around with Connor's band, operating the merchandise stall. I sit down at my laptop and begin writing an email. Twenty minutes later, I am still typing, pouring my heart out telling Connor I never meant him any harm, and sobbing into the keyboard.

'Who are you writing to?' Mum asks after walking into my room and seeing my tear-streaked face.

'Connor Silver,' I reply between sobs, still tapping away.

Mum looks at me as if I'd said I was writing to George Jetson from *The Jetsons*.

I press 'send', knowing deep down there's a slim chance Connor will ever read my heartfelt apology, or that our paths will ever cross again.

18

With my TROPPO FM contract over, I heed Beth's advice and vow to be completely disciplined about writing *Diamonds in the Dust* in the mornings and to do any work for the HomeHints catalogue in the evenings.

A week goes by and I'm really happy with my progress. I've been waking up early to take Glenda for a walk, writing till one, followed by making lunch and then laps at the pool and writing again. I've been allowing myself one episode of *Marcella* after dinner and then get stuck into any Home-Hints copy.

Right now, though, I'm whizzing around the aisles of Woolies, one hand on the trolley, the other holding Mum's grocery list. I'm always slightly ashamed at how content I feel in Woolies. As soon as I enter the store my mood lifts. I don't know if it's the music or the lighting or whether it's that it reminds me of being very little and carefree, scooting off to retrieve boxes of cereal and laundry detergent, listening out for the familiar jangle of Mum's keys against her handbag to track her down. Whatever the origin of my sense of wellbeing, it's embarrassing, and I wish I could shake it.

I'm in the dairy section, attempting to decipher Mum's handwriting, when I hear a voice that, ridiculously, sets my heart racing. I spin around to see Helen walking towards me, a huge smile on her face.

'Hello! I haven't seen you in ages!' I say as we hug. To be fair, because I've been trying to block out thoughts of Oscar I've been avoiding Helen like the plague, timing my runs to the mailbox and reversing out of the driveway when I know she's safely inside.

'Yes, it has been a long time, Lucy,' she says. 'Jolly well done to you on the Connor Silver interview! Oscar and I heard it in Sydney.'

'Oh, really?' I say. So he did hear it! I think.

'Yes, Oscar must have played it half a dozen times, chortling away like a mad thing. We both thought you were just delightful and so funny.'

'Ha, thank you,' I say, grinning as a piece of me crumbles at her kindness. Little does she know how much credence I place on her words, and how I wish, for some unknown reason, that I could tell her.

✑

Until I'd run into Helen, I'd been so distracted by my Connor Silver rollercoaster that I hadn't been thinking of Oscar as much, but as of this afternoon he's back, leading a marching band through my mind. Would he like me more, now that

I've interviewed old Con dog? I foolishly wonder as I walk Glenda to Rosie's unit. If I studied medicine, would I be more attractive to him? I continue to undermine my own confidence until I stop in my tracks and say aloud to the towering eucalypts, 'Lucy! You've got a lot to offer as you are! Remember that!'

After tying Glenda's leash to a fencepost in the shade, I let myself into Rosie's unit. The sound of The Wombats leads me to her bedroom, where she greets me wearing a puffer jacket and flinging clothes backwards from the wardrobe in the direction of an open suitcase on her bed.

'Rosie,' I yell above the music, 'what's going on with the aircon?'

'I'm trying to acclimatise for London,' she yells back.

'You're mad! I've got goosebumps!'

'Well, I've got a goose-down jacket on! You're the one who's mad!'

Knowing this conversation will go nowhere, I spot her remote and switch off the air-conditioner.

She turns down the music.

'How's things, stranger?' she asks, unzipping her jacket and tossing it onto the pile of clothes. 'All going well with your new bestie Connor?'

'Hardly,' I say and sit on her mattress. 'I doubt I'm making his Christmas card list. Anyway, it's *you* who's been hard to track down this week!'

'That's because I've been spending every minute trying to track down fucking tracksuit pants. Big W, Best & Less and Kmart have all sold out. The first sign of cold weather in this joint and everyone goes friggin' nuts!'

'What about—?'

'Target? Yeah, Target came through with the trackies. Although they're maroon and three sizes too big.'

'Ah well, they'll be good for watching the State of Origin at the Walkabout!' I joke.

'Yeah. And by the time I've had a few years of pints and pies over there I'll probably need the size sixteen.'

We both grin and I realise how much I'll miss our silly conversations. Then Rosie's expression turns serious and she tells me she's flying to London in a week.

As I look at her in horror she explains that she wasn't planning to leave so soon but then a friend in London emailed to say a great room in a Putney share house was just about to come up. She tells me she's already joined a recruitment agency as well, and the woman at the agency assured her Aussie dentists are still highly sought after.

'Oh, Rosie, I can't believe you're leaving me,' I say, burying my head in her suitcase and attempting to zip up the lid around me. 'There's nothing for me in this town. You're, like, the best and only thing I've got going.'

'Don't be ridiculous, Luce,' she replies, laughing. 'You've got a hell of a lot more than me going for you. You just have to let yourself see it.' She pauses. 'And if I *am* the only thing you've got going for you, then jeez, heaven help you! Besides, you've got your mum and dad and Glenda.'

'They'll always be here.'

'Well, you know you can join me. Anyway, what have you been up to these past few days?'

'Oh,' I say, taking my head out of her suitcase. 'I've had the focus of a Jedi master with this novel, Rosie. I've written three chapters since I left TROPPO. And I'm that bloody busy writing for HomeHints I've hardly had time to wash my hair!'

'Well, I'm pleased to hear that,' she says.

'Though who in their right mind would want to buy flippers with a torch in the end of them I don't know,' I say.

'Ha!' she says. 'What'd you call that one?'

'Flippin' Good Idea!' I reply. 'Hey, do you want to go to the Gardens Kiosk with me and Glenda and get one of those cordials in the plastic kangaroos? I'm cashed up.'

'You had me at kiosk,' she replies.

⊙⌒⊖

As we sit beneath a canopy of fig trees in the gardens taking selfies with our plastic kangaroos, my phone chimes with a Facebook notification, which says Jeremy is engaged. I'm surprised that I feel almost relieved. Relieved to know I've heard the news I'd secretly feared hearing for so long and how it completely pales into significance compared to my sadness about Rosie's imminent departure.

Congratulations, Jeremy! I post on Jeremy's Facebook page, genuinely meaning it.

I swivel my phone around to show Rosie and she grins and high-fives me.

19

Marjorie Beaumont's appetite for my copywriting appears to be insatiable, and as a result I've been up most evenings this week, penning what I hope are witty captions for absurd appliances. A reflective iron board cover? *Eye-on You!* A sonic denture cleaner? *Sink Your Teeth Into This!* Fish deboning tweezers? *Make No Bones About It!*

Tonight, though, I'm staying as still as I can because my gorgeous little niece Isla is lying beside me.

Max and Brooke and the kids have driven up for a couple of days before Max and Mum fly out to China and I've been totally focusing on Jack and Isla after I finish writing at midday. I adore their company, and I know they love mine too, although I do take a back seat to Dad with Jack, and I'm definitely second fiddle to Peppa Pig and, bizarrely, a UK reality TV medical show called *Embarrassing Bodies* with Isla. I've caught her a couple of times this week with

Max's iPad on my bed, watching British doctors perform the most outrageous surgery. 'What is this one?' she'd asked with the cursor hovering above an episode titled 'Erectile Dysfunction'.

'Oh no, Isla,' I'd said quickly, 'that's all about doodles.'

She'd then stared me down and, with a cheeky glint in her eye, replied, 'I want that one!'

As if that wasn't bad enough, this morning I returned to my room after a shower to hear a Pommy medico say, 'And if you're still constipated, then we'll have to flip you over and put coffee up your bum.'

'Isla!' I'd exclaimed, grinning down at her in mock horror as she giggled up at me. 'What on earth are you watching?'

Later today, as I'd lain beside her reading, she'd pressed pause on *Little Princess* and said to me, 'Alright, Lucy, flip over, it's time to put coffee up your bum.' We were in stitches.

∞

I wake the next morning to find Isla and Jack have gone to see *Trolls* with Mum and Dad, and Brooke and Max have left for a drive to the beach. After the carnival-like atmosphere of the past few days, the house is now beautifully calm. I'm staring into the fridge when I hear my phone buzz on the bench with a message. My heart thuds when I see it's from Oscar.

Hey, Lucy, just wanted to say congratulations on the Connor Silver interview. I've heard it like three times in Sydney! Well done! By the way, I'm up this Friday. It would be great to see you if you're up for it?

I read his message again. And again. If I'm up for it? What the hell does that mean? I wonder before texting him back. *Sure, Oscar! We're all heading out for dinner at the Wild West Saloon on Friday night if you'd like to come. Rosie is leaving for London on Monday!*

I stare out the kitchen window above the sink. Did that mean anything? I ask the mountain range. Probably not, I answer in my heart and delete his message to prevent further analysis. Just then my mobile lights up again.

Sounds great, Lucy. Is it okay if Kate and Mum come too?

Of course :) I reply, and then erase his number from my phone.

ᴄᴇᴏ

Later in the morning, as I lie reading in bed, a third text message comes through. It's from Rosie. She's written one word. *London?*

I look around my familiar old bedroom, scanning the walls I've allowed to comfort yet confine me for so long. I know in my bones it's time to move on. As Rosie pointed out, I can write my novel anywhere. And I've managed to save almost all my TROPPO FM and HomeHints money so I have a decent cash buffer now. I tell myself I will probably never feel one hundred percent certain that the path I choose is the right one, but that's not a dilemma unique to me. I just have to make a choice.

I decide to clean my room thoroughly while I mull over what I'm going to do. I start off by attacking the cardboard boxes that have been underneath my bed for years. I cough through the dust storm I create as I drag them out. Sitting on the floor going through them, I shake my head at the sight of photos, journals, notebooks, maps and trophies dating back decades. And though I'm tempted to slide the boxes back, I also feel compelled to cull the past.

Sifting through the first box I flick through photos of my travels with Rosie in Italy, Spain, Thailand and Croatia, as well as snaps of us living in London.

I chuckle at one particular shot of Rosie and me in Spain. We're sitting beside a stream, each nursing a bottle of wine and eating bread and cheese—a couple of carefree twenty-five-year olds enjoying their youth and funding their adventures with ridiculous jobs. We look so happy—and so ludicrously young.

I skim through a journal I'd kept during my time in the UK, and pause on one of the entries. My observations about working as an au pair for a posh British family in Hampstead make me grin, but as I continue to read my heart sinks as I realise with dismay that the thoughts and concerns I had as a twenty-five-year-old are eerily similar to the ones I have now. My mind has the same self-defeating and second-guessing patterns that it did more than seven years ago.

I flip through another journal, and see a consistent theme of confusion and lack of confidence. I can now see how my limiting beliefs have played out in many aspects of my life—with my finances, with regrets about *The Headline Act* and with Oscar. And I see how my thought patterns continue to undermine my future, causing me to feel incapable of choosing one path over the other and making a plan.

I take a deep breath and glance at the pile of self-help books stacked on the floor beside my bed. They tower so high an Olympic pole-vaulter would struggle to clear them.

There's Wayne Dyer's *Excuses Begone!*, Gordon Livingston's *Too Soon Old, Too Late Smart*, Louise Hay's *You Can Heal Your Life*—and many many more. And I haven't really benefited from reading them. I stack them all into a box for Vinnies and take it out to my car.

After that I go through my wardrobe and ruthlessly cull clothes and shoes. What thirty-two-year-old wears lace-up Rockports? Out they go!

I turn the room upside down and by the time I'm finally finished the shelves are sparse, there's hardly anything in the bedside dresser, and the wardrobe is bereft of daggy clothes and old hangers.

After heaving two more boxes into the car boot I dust and scrub the room from top to bottom. Two hours later I lean back against the wall and think, Fuck it! I'm going to move to London!

⁓

On the drive home from Vinnies, my mind is alive with images of Buckingham Palace guards and parks beside the Thames. There are red buses and scurrying squirrels jumping from one synapse to the next as I consider the prospect of returning to London. Then, in the next instant, as I spot a car with Victorian plates attempt to reverse angle park outside a bakery, I think of Desley and how content she is to live in Rocky. I wonder then whether it's me who's been looking at Rocky through a faulty prism. Now that I'm on the verge of deciding to leave, I question whether I'm shooting myself in the foot, thinking I'm too good for the small-town life and that the grass will be greener in the UK.

I pull over near the water tower that overlooks the city and recognise that Rocky is a new adventure for Desley, a town that holds no history, a place full of undiscovered delights. But to me Rocky is a pair of ugg boots—super comfortable, sturdy and secure.

Would the new Lucy be wearing ugg boots in this next chapter of her life? I ask myself. No, I decide as I pull out of the parking bay. She will be wearing stilettos.

⁓

When I arrive home I find Max staring blankly into the fridge and persuade him to come for a walk with Glenda.

'Have fun breaking that news to Mum,' Max says with a smile after I tell him of my decision to move to London.

'Can you help me, please?' I ask as we walk briskly beside the Yeppen Lagoon. 'You're the golden child. It'll be easier if you back me up.'

'Hmm,' he says, 'remember that time you told me the spa at Rydges had no steps and I jumped in and almost broke my legs?'

'Max!' I begin, before he talks over me.

'And that time you dobbed me in to Sister Carmel for putting mangoes up the bishop's exhaust pipe?'

'I thought his car would explode!' I protest. 'Anyway, what about that time we were on the beach and that Rottweiler was pelting towards us and you put me in front of you like a human shield?'

Max chuckles.

'And the time Mum caught us looking at Christmas presents in the boot of the Commodore and you blamed it on me!'

He's suddenly serious. 'That was bad! We were naughty.'

'I know; Mum was *so* upset.'

We walk along, both sombre at the prospect of Mum being that upset again.

'Alright,' he says eventually. 'I'll back you up.'

⁓

Mum and Dad do not take kindly to the idea of me moving to London, despite the backing of their golden child and my admitting that I've already bought a ticket. They tell me I'm being unrealistic and that to move to London without a job is madness. They point to the uncertainty of the UK economy post Brexit and the volatility of world affairs. Mum reminds me how much I hated the cold weather in Melbourne and says, 'How on earth will you cope with London's constant drizzle and darkness?'

'I don't know why you're still searching,' she says to me, close to tears. 'You were always such a happy little girl. I never dreamt you'd be the one I worried about.'

Deep down, I know she's concerned the move will just place me one step further from her dream of seeing me settled with someone and having bubs. I think she's also upset that, try as she might, she can no longer understand me.

I tell her that I need to get my life back, that I can work on my novel anywhere and that, while I might fail spectacularly, at least I'll be trying again. I promise her I'll continue to write for the HomeHints catalogue in London and start looking for a job on arrival; that I'll come home at the first sign of political unrest or influenza; that I'll give myself a timeframe and if things aren't working out, I'll return.

Max, for his part, tries to make light of the fact that Mum, Dad and I are all bustling about packing identical red Samsonite bags for different trips, and joking about what would happen if Mum got to China and opened her suitcase to find fishing lures and Bushman mozzie repellent. His humour falls completely flat for once.

That's when I decide to put on Cher's *Believe* album in the lounge room and ask Mum if she'd like to dance.

She bursts into tears and says she will miss me terribly and that she's got so used to me being around that it will be an awful shock not to have me here.

I tell her I love her very much, and I'm not planning on starving or living in squalor or letting myself get murdered.

Mum says she isn't worried about that so much as my falling in love with a Pom and moving with him to the Outer Hebrides. She says she can't bear the thought of not being able to see me and my children easily, and I tell her to take a deep breath and understand that I have no intention of living in the Outer Hebrides. She hugs me just as 'Strong Enough' finishes playing.

'Lucy,' she says, 'you will be the death of me.'

∽

'You've told Rosie, I assume?' asks Dad the next morning, peering at me over the pages of *Queensland Country Life*.

'No, I thought I'd surprise her tomorrow night when we're out for dinner,' I reply, grinning. I can't wait to see the look on Rosie's face when I tell her I'll be touching down in Heathrow three days after her.

'So, you're happy as Larry now, Dad, aren't you?' I ask. Now that I've got an escape route I wonder whether I gave enough time to Dad while I was living with him and Mum.

'Oh well,' he says, lowering his paper, 'I must admit that London came as a shock, but Denise insists you're doing what you think's best and if it means—Shit! What's happening with Glenda while we're all away?'

Upon hearing her name, Glenda sidles out from under the table and lies at my feet.

'Oh, my little mate, I'm going to miss you,' I say, feeling a bit teary. 'But I promise I'll be back. And Mum and Dad will look after you almost as well as I do.'

Mum walks into the kitchen, wearing togs, and says to Dad, 'Kennels for a couple of weeks until we get back,' before searching through the laundry basket for a towel.

Dad rubs his chin. 'I'll take her to the Men's Shed sometimes, if you like. A few of the fellas bring their dogs along and they spend the first ten minutes sniffing each other.'

'That'd be good, Dad, thanks. She might help you out at the sausage sizzles at Dan Murphy's on a Saturday morning.'

'Ha!' laughs Mum. 'I can just see her behind the barbecue with tongs!'

'Christ almighty, I don't think we'd be selling many sausages with Glenda at the helm,' scoffs Dad. 'Men's Shed'd go bankrupt!'

⁊ℰᴐ

The Wild West Saloon is its usual hair-raising, Bundy-rum-swilling, hay-and-manure-scented self on Friday night for Rosie's and my joint farewell party.

On the drive there, I'd blurted out my London news to her, unable to contain myself, and she'd reached over and hugged me so hard I almost veered into the BP.

Mum and Dad, at peace with my decision, enjoy the spectacle of bulls bucking cowboys five feet in the air and the unbridled, party-like atmosphere found ringside at the rodeo arena.

I suppose I've always taken the Wild West Saloon for granted, assuming it was normal to have bulls stampeding around a sand-filled stadium out the back of a pub. But the expression on Oscar's face when he and Kate approach Rosie and me by the steel barricades—just as a man is flung sideways before narrowly escaping the hoof of a one-tonne Brahman—reminds me that it's not your average watering hole.

'You wouldn't get this in Sydney,' I say after we've hugged, feeling a bit overcome at seeing him again. I lean in to Kate's light embrace, the scent of her delicate perfume heightening the sense of guilt I suddenly feel as I inquire how she's been.

'There's a platform over there with a bird's eye view of the ring if you'd like to check it out,' says Rosie to Kate after we've exhausted our small talk.

'Sure,' she replies and I glance at Oscar as they walk away.

He looks fit and handsome, with his hair cut shorter and his skin tanned, and as we chat and laugh it almost seems like we're picking up a conversation from yesterday. I feel an undercurrent of sadness at the thought of not seeing him for what could be years, but remind myself that new horizons and new adventures await.

He asks about my writing, and I tell him how much progress I've made and how I've also been conjuring up copy for the HomeHints catalogue. He's thrilled to hear that *Diamonds in the Dust* is coming along and urges me to keep going and not to give up. We lean against the side of the rodeo ring and watch a knee-high cowgirl in spurs and a safety helmet race around on the back of a poddy calf, and when he turns to talk with Kate as she and Rosie return, I take a step closer to Rosie and curse my thumping heart.

Later in the evening, Oscar and I are seated opposite each other in the steakhouse when Dad raises his glass, wishing Rosie and me all the best in London and urging us to 'make every post a winner'.

Oscar looks at me with a devastated expression. *You're leaving?* his eyes say. *But . . .*

But what? I respond with my gaze. *Yes, there is a connection between us, and maybe you do love me. But you love Kate too. And I'm moving to London, so there's no future for us.*

I clink glasses with Kate and then him and he looks away, knowing there's nothing more to be said.

Not long after, the night takes a very unfortunate turn when, upon hearing our chorus of cheering, Ruth, who'd been sitting a couple of tables behind us with Colleen from the bottle-o, Video Ezy, Bits 'n' Pizzas and Romancing the Rock wanders over drunkenly to see what the fuss is about. On hearing that Rosie and I are London bound, she roars with laughter and slaps the table, saying, 'Ha! You played that one well, Oscar!'

When everyone looks at her quizzically, Ruth blurts out. 'I thought for sure when I sprung you and Lucy snogging on

Mount Archer road that she'd be shacking up with you in Sydney by now. Was he a lousy kisser, Luce?' Then, as she realises Kate is at the table, she slaps a hand over her mouth. 'Jesus Christ! Catch ya's later.'

Kate gets up abruptly and runs towards the bathroom, Oscar nearly knocking his chair over as he races to follow her.

I desperately wish that one-tonne Brahman would storm through the barricades and sit on me. By the look on everyone's faces, I can't leave the country quick enough.

20

I board the Qantas flight to London buzzing with the sense of anticipation I always experience upon heading overseas.

'Congratulations, Luce,' I say aloud, to the alarm of the passenger beside me, and pat myself on the back. 'You've done it.'

As our plane descends into Heathrow twenty hours later, I gawk out the window at the huge expanse of inky blackness below, and my veins surge with adrenaline as I spot the red circle of the London Eye, the unmistakable outline of Tower Bridge, the dazzling city lights.

By the time I'm walking across Putney Bridge a couple of hours later, I'm grinning from ear to ear. I am back! Back among the red double-decker buses and the high street fashions and the screech of the tube. I can revel once more in the magic of Soho, the edginess of Angel, the magnificent sweeping buildings and electrifying atmosphere of Piccadilly

Circus. I am walking around with other people who've chosen to spend time in one of the most exciting cities in the world. Yes, it's freezing, but even the breathtaking cold is exhilarating. And there isn't a bull statue in sight.

I double-check the address on my phone, then stop and gaze up towards the top-floor flat of a three-storey apartment block just off Putney High Street. My spirit soars at the thought of seeing Rosie, and I race up the building's internal staircase two steps at a time.

The buzzer by the green door is answered by a scruffily good-looking, athletic Scotsman wearing an Arsenal jersey and ill-fitting long johns, which bunch at the crotch, blouse at the thighs and hug the calves.

He grins cheekily as my glance shifts upward from his legs. 'You must be Lulu.'

'Lucy,' I reply.

'Joe,' he says. 'Welcome to the Putney Palace!'

'Thanks,' I reply and follow him inside. 'Terrific location.'

'Yes, it's not bad, is it?' he says as we pass a hallway bookshelf lined with well-thumbed Lonely Planet guides before turning into a boxy lounge room.

'I've been here two years,' he says loudly over the blaring TV football commentary. 'Shit!' he yells, cracking his knuckles. 'You're missing a good game, ref!'

After watching the match for a few minutes he turns back to me and says, 'Rosie's not here, unfortunately. She's gone to a bar up The Shard with the others.'

'Oh, right,' I say, as if I know exactly what he's referring to and thinking how, when she's not looking into someone's mouth, Rosie's attention to detail can be poor.

Still, I feel disappointed that she must have mixed up my arrival date.

'Amazing views,' he responds, momentarily switching his attention from the game again.

I swing my backpack to the floor and glance around the room, which bears the telltale markings of an antipodean London share house. Two faded couches face each other from opposite walls. A smallish TV balances on a stack of magazines near a fireplace, above which is strung a collection of holiday snaps. I feel like I'm back in 2009.

Joe turns to me after a whistle sounds.

'Sorry, not much of a host, am I? This is a must-win for Arsenal. They've been rubbish so far.' He picks up my backpack and flings it over his shoulder. 'Quick tour of the rest, then I'll show you Rosie's room, yeah? I'm sure you're exhausted.'

He leads me into the kitchen, where cereal boxes are lined up on top of a microwave and an assortment of crockery balances precariously in a dish rack. An electrical cord drapes from speakers on a bench hanging low above a toaster. It's a scene that would send my dad into a health and safety fit.

'Help yourself to anything marked *Joe*,' he says, opening the fridge door.

I shake my head as I take in the various milks, beers, jam jars, salad containers and tins bearing the names *Nick*, *Bec*, *Carl*, *Tina*, *Sam*, *Baillie* and *Fiona*.

'Jeez, how many people live here?' I ask.

'About eight, give or take. Hard to know, really. Follow me.'

We turn right out of the kitchen and come to a halt in front of a door at the end of the hall. He knocks gently before entering the darkness and flicking on the lights, revealing a decent-sized room with two single beds.

I get a shock and stagger back as a woman abruptly sits up and rubs her eyes, blinking into the brightness.

'Sorry, Hyuna,' says Joe. 'Time to go, babes. Your flight leaves in four hours.'

'Shit!' Throwing off the blankets, she leaps out of bed fully dressed—including sneakers—and makes a beeline for a backpack propped against the wall.

'Sweet girl,' says Joe, smiling whimsically. 'But that's the problem with you travellers, isn't it? You all have a plane to catch sometime, don't you? Anyway, this is Rosie's room, so this is you, Lucy. The new Hyuna.'

My semi-stunned silence is replaced by the dim roar of the television.

'The shower's opposite you!' says Joe, before running back into the lounge room.

Sitting down on the floor at the foot of the bed, I glance around the room. I take comfort in the familiar sight of Rosie's pink suitcase atop the wardrobe and her extensive collection of makeup strewn across a chest of drawers. A wave of fatigue suddenly overcomes me and I yearn for bed, but the effort required to get there makes it seem unattainable. Instead, I lean back against the frame and close my eyes.

'We won!' yells Joe, jolting me awake as he appears in the doorway. 'Goodnight!' he shouts, vanishing again before I have time to reply.

Dizzy with tiredness, I stumble into the shower, then stagger back to the bedroom, where I collapse on the bed Hyuna had so recently vacated.

Five hours later, I awake to a familiar voice. 'Fucking hell!' exclaims Rosie. 'You're here!'

⁓

A week later, having settled into a routine with my writing, I'm walking to Waitrose in the Putney Exchange when I pass a bookstore called Scribe, which has a sign in the front window advertising for full- and part-time staff. For several moments I stare at the notice before deciding it could be great fun to work in a bookshop, and upon going inside I'm heartened to discover that the store has a lovely vibe.

Perhaps on account of our 'across the ditch' camaraderie, Penny, a Kiwi woman with a smile twitching at the corners of her mouth, takes an instant shine to me when I approach the front counter and enquire about work. She asks if I like kids' books and I nod, thinking she may as well have asked if I like sausage rolls. Conscious of wanting to keep on track with my novel, I counter Penny's offer of a full-time job with a request for three or four days per week. We settle on three and a half days and I agree to start in the children's section the following morning.

From my very first shift I adore working at Scribe, due in no small part to the fact that I adore Penny, who has a wicked sense of humour and is incredibly encouraging. After I tell her about all the books I loved reading to Jack and Isla, Penny suggests I do a Storytime session every Friday morning, reading picture books to kids. Storytime is soon the hottest ticket in Putney and sometimes I wonder, as I watch all the Aussie nannies and their posh British charges crowding around well before the eleven o'clock start time each week, whether it isn't my broad accent that's the drawcard. I often look down as I'm reading to see the kids staring up at me wide-eyed from the carpet, their mouths gaping, half stunned and clearly not understanding a word. The Aussie nannies are always laughing, though.

With a weekly wage coming in from Scribe, I'm able to write on my days off without anxiety over affording rent or the odd pint, and with Rosie away travelling with some old dentistry friends in France for a couple of weeks, I've been devoting every spare moment to my book.

I'm feeling so happy with my novel's progress and so positive about life generally that I suddenly yearn to speak with Mum and Dad and tell them how well I'm doing. I often think of them, particularly on Friday afternoons when the floors are being vacuumed and I'm reminded of Roomba. Mum would be back from Mongolia by now and Dad from Kakadu.

Later that night, I text Mum to say that I'll be calling, hoping Max had taught her how to use Skype, as he'd promised.

'Hello? Hello?' she shouts on answering my call, appearing upside down on my screen. 'Is that you in London, Lucy?'

'Yes, it's me, Mum!' I say, wondering who else she'd think it might be.

'Oh, Lucy,' she says, 'look at you. All the way over there with the Queen.'

'Mum, if you can swivel that camera around on top of your computer, you'll be the right way up on my screen.'

'Lucy, I'm not going near that camera! It's taken your father and I half the morning to try and mount it properly. As it is we've got it hanging on by a lick of Blu-Tack.'

'Hello, Lucy!' Dad yells into the camera, his face so close to the computer that I can make out the blackheads on his upside down nose.

'Hello, Dad! How was Kakadu?'

'Just marvellous, Luce. Caught some bloody big barra too.' He takes a step back from the camera. 'Anyway, glad you're looking well, love. Glenda and I are off to the cattle sales now. Come on, Glenda!' he shouts.

'Oh, Dad, let me see Glenda!' I exclaim as she starts barking.

'Here you go,' he says, holding her so close to the camera that all I can see is her panting tongue and then, 'Righto, we're off!' he shouts, lowering Glenda to the floor and walking out of shot.

'Bye! So tell me about Mongolia, Mum.'

'Oh!' she says. 'If I did one arm sweep, I did a million. I was up at five-thirty every morning and meditating until eight. I kept getting told to return my thoughts to nothingness, but it's hard to return to nothing when you've slept all night on a slab of wood with six others in a sleeper train! Oh, Lucy, you've no idea . . . And there's no changing of the sheets between passengers, mind you. They just shake the sheets out and put them back on. And the hotel in Beijing! Well, didn't I cause a ruckus there! First of all, the windows didn't shut properly, so I had sheets of rain coming into the room, and then I turned on the taps in the bathroom and left to try to pull the windows closed in the bedroom, and when

I came back the bathroom was flooded because the pipes weren't connected underneath the basin.'

'Oh, Ma!' I exclaim. 'It sounds like you had the trip from hell.'

'Well, believe me, I felt like telling Master Ray to go to hell by the end of it. It's well and truly cured me of Qi-Gong, Lucy. No more navel gazing in a yurt for me, thank you very much.

'Anyway, tell me your news now and cheer me up.'

I tell her about Penny and the bookstore, and how I love working in the children's section with Margie, a lovely South African woman around my age, who swears in Afrikaans when orders are delayed and dreams of opening her own bookstore in Cape Town, and conducting Storytime on a Friday. I speak effusively of Putney and the parks, and how the other day I spotted squirrels.

She laughs when I say Rosie's been larking around Europe like she's on a Contiki tour and is delighted with my latest caption for the HomeHints catalogue, *Sure to Appeal*, for a banana storage container.

After we stop laughing she brings me up to speed with Rocky's social pages—she saw a snap of Todd Doherty and Cherie having lunch at Bits 'n' Pizzas the other day, she tells me, which might be a sign of reconciliation—and complains that you can't drive two metres without seeing a flyer of Ruth in her bikini plastered to a light pole advertising her annual Suds 'n' Thuds disco at the car wash.

As I hear kookaburras cackling in the background, I feel a sudden pang of homesickness, but am careful to remain cheery, and remind myself that the buzz of living in London outweighs the sound of laughing birds.

On the days we overlap, I enjoy standing behind the counter chatting with Margie. Between customers, she tells me that she misses braai, which turns out to be Afrikaans for barbecue, and we vow to have braai in Kensington Gardens before the summer's end.

As the weeks go by, and Margie and I grow closer, she tells me one day that she's desperately in love with a gorgeous black man called Dennis, who doesn't even know she's alive, and I tell her that I'm happily in love with my life in London and that Dennis must be a few stubbies short of a sixpack not to notice her. She looks at me with a baffled expression but laughs anyway.

Being a prominent bookstore in well-heeled Putney, Scribe often attracts big-name authors for readings, and I sometimes turn from stacking shelves to see the likes of Julian Barnes and Michael Morpurgo walk into the store as if it's no big deal. My exposure to these inspiring writers and their wonderful books and passionate readers spurs me on with my writing, and three months after arriving in London I finish the first draft of *Diamonds in the Dust*.

'Fucking yeah!' says Rosie when I share my exciting news with her as we tube surf to Hammersmith to see Radiohead. 'I'm so proud of you, Luce. You did it!'

'Yeah,' I reply, grinning. 'I did it.'

'Best decision we've ever made, doing this, wasn't it?'

'I know!' I say. 'As if you'd ever see Radiohead in Rocky!'

213

'No, I mean the decision to live in London again. Look at us, we're fucking thriving over here! You've finished your first draft and I'm having a ball jumping on trains to Paris. We're killing it, Luce!' She makes a face. 'I'll probably need to pick up the drill again soon to afford it all, though.'

'Did you hear back from the recruiters?' I ask.

'Yeah, they got back to me,' she says. 'But they all want me to work full-time! It's like your dad's been talking to them or something! How are your parents going, anyway?'

'They're so funny.' I smile and shake my head. 'I skyped them this arvo to tell them about finishing my book but the reception was a bit dodgy. I heard Mum yell out to Dad to turn off the toaster in case it improved things!'

Rosie laughs. 'They're classic, Luce. I actually miss my cups of tea with Denise and stirring up Brian. How's Glenda?'

'Oh, she and Dad are inseparable! It wouldn't surprise me if they go down to the jeweller and get those BFF heart necklaces.'

'Do you ever hear from Oscar?' Rosie asks, giving me a jolt; she hasn't mentioned his name for the longest time.

'No.'

'Ben messaged me on Facebook this morning. He's been travelling around Spain after finishing the Camino and he's coming to London in a month or so for a few weeks.'

'Oh, how did he go on the Camino?' I ask.

'Good, I think. Said it was both soul-soothing and sole-destroying. But he spelt sole s-o-l-e.'

'Ha! He's hilarious, Ben.'

'Yeah.' She smiles. 'Anyway, it'll be fun to see him.'

The following week I muster up the courage to ask Penny if she'd mind reading the first draft of my novel. Penny replies that it would be an absolute pleasure and that evening she sends me a text saying she is totally hooked on the Foster family, and she thinks I have a lot of talent. I take a screen-shot of her message, and make it my wallpaper.

Over the next month, Rosie continues to head off on various European jaunts, and even though I feel a pang of envy when she comes back raving about snorkelling around Mykonos, I'm enjoying the process of rereading and revising my manuscript. Penny gave me some really good feedback and her suggestions have helped steer my fossickers in the right direction.

I'm also kicking goals with Storytime, which has become so popular that I now take two separate sessions. After an exceptionally busy Friday, made extra manic by the arrival in store of Rick Riordan's latest release, Rosie and I decide to hit the pub and then the shops along Oxford Street.

'Tell ya, when I do pick up the drill again there'll be no shortage of work for me in London,' Rosie says, glancing at the gaping mouths of some passers-by.

'You should come to Storytime while you're not working. You're probably the only one who'll understand me!'

'You're really enjoying the bookshop, aren't you?'

'It's the best!' I say happily. 'It's so cute seeing kids hooked by a story. And you know Penny?'

Rosie nods.

'She loves me! And I love her!'

Rosie giggles.

'Sometimes I have to restrain myself from telling her how much I love her,' I add. 'I worry I'd come across as unprofessional!'

'Is she available?' Rosie asks.

'She's a grandma, Rosie!' I exclaim. 'Happily married for forty years. But it's made me think that maybe this is what it'll be like when I meet the right guy. He'll like me, and I'll like him, and it'll all be very straightforward.'

'You are such a dag!' says Rosie, laughing.

Up ahead I see a crowd gathered on the pavement outside Topshop. 'What's happening up here? Must be a big sale on.'

'Let's have a look,' says Rosie, and we insert ourselves into a throng of teenagers wearing chokers and midriffs and ride the escalator down to the basement, where we find a Little Mix concert in full swing.

'Hilarious!' yells Rosie as we stare at a stage surrounded by racks of vintage tops, handbags and screaming fans.

'How random! Can you imagine Little Mix doing this in Paradise Plaza?'

'I don't even know who Little Mix are!' Rosie responds. 'Are those chicks wearing scrunchies?!'

We make our way through displays of shoes and accessories and join a crowd of girls dancing metres from the stage, taking photos of the group with their flower crown Snapchat filters.

'Perrie!' Rosie screams, mimicking their calls. 'We love you, Perrie!'

I look across at her and grin. And as we sing along to lyrics we don't know and jump up and down with the twenty-somethings on the tiles in Topshop, it occurs to me to get in touch with Cher and let her know that you can, in fact, turn back time.

21

I appear to be in a casual relationship with Joe.

It started innocently enough. About a month ago, while Rosie was off on what she swore would be her last European mini-break before getting serious about work, I went to the Jolly Gardeners with Margie and Sally, an Aussie nanny from Bundaberg. Sally ended up getting so drunk I offered her Rosie's bed for the night. Unfortunately, she snored like a freight train so I went and curled up on the couch with a blanket. Not long after, Joe happened to walk into the lounge room and offered me his bed, saying he'd sleep on the floor. He stayed there half an hour before accepting my invitation of an upgrade to the mattress. Since then, we've been frequently sharing that mattress, and the power shower, and even the kitchen table on one rare occasion when no-one else was home.

At first, when Rosie got back from Prague, it was hard for me to gauge her reaction to me and Joe. I assumed she wouldn't care less, but one morning over a cup of tea she told me she was worried Joe would hurt me and she couldn't deal with me having a broken heart again on her own. I told her I was fine and that it was fun to have a casual fling with no pressure or expectation, but she wasn't convinced. She said she knew me too well to believe I wouldn't get emotionally involved, and that I was not built for casual affairs. She didn't think I was capable of shutting off certain sections of my heart.

Margie, on the other hand, felt that I should absolutely partake in a glorious, liberating romance abroad, if for no other reason than that sex was good for the joints.

Joe makes me laugh. He shows me exactly where to stand on the platform to board the least crowded carriage in the train and has introduced me to hidden Putney gems, including the Cat's Back, a charming Edwardian pub that still has lock-ins. Sometimes I worry that he's more into me than I'm into him, but I enjoy his company immensely, and Margie said perhaps that's enough.

⌒⊘

Rosie has finally accepted a job and, to my endless amusement, it's full-time. When I'm not waking up with Joe, I'm emerging from slumber to the sounds of Rosie spraying deodorant and drying her hair. She hates that I'm able to skip off to the bookstore eight minutes before it opens and routinely curses me of a morning—today being no different.

'Could you keep it down, Rosie? I don't have to get up for two hours.'

'Oh, mate, this is fucked,' she says, tugging on her boots. 'You can get screwed.'

I dive under the covers as she pegs a hairbrush at me.

'Don't forget tonight,' she says, halfway out the door.

'What's—? Oh, that's right. Where are we meeting again?'

'Spotted Horse. Six-thirty.'

⁓

When I walk into the Spotted Horse at six, Ben is perched at the bar drinking a snakebite. Sporting a tan, a beard and his ever-engaging grin, he jumps from his stool and envelops me in a bear hug. On this cold London night, he radiates warmth and I'm so pleased to see him.

'You look great, Ben!'

'So do you! London suits you, hey?'

'Yeah, I think so,' I reply, taking off my jacket. 'It's been four months now. Your hair goes flat over here. Anyway, how have you been? How was the Camino?'

'Incredible. It's hard to explain, but I highly recommend it. Sometimes it was crap, and I couldn't wait for it to end. But then other times it made all the sense in the world and I didn't want to ever stop walking.' He begins to laugh. 'Not sad to say goodbye to those boots, though. Bloody hell, I was nursing blisters for months.' He glances over my shoulder and I grin as his face lights up like a billboard on Times Square. 'Hello! Here's trouble!'

I turn to see Rosie approaching and Ben greets her effusively, with the same barrelling embrace he'd given me. She returns his broad smile and her eyes flicker with a cheeky glint.

'You look like a lumberjack!' she teases.

'Part-time lumberjack!' he jokes.

She rolls her eyes. 'Oh, don't mention part-time, Ben. Those were the glory days.'

'What do you mean? Don't tell me you're . . .?'

'Full-time. Yes, I'm fucking full-time. Never thought I'd see the day and it's everything I thought it would be. It's the absolute pits!' She grins at him and elbows me. 'Meanwhile, this one here's having the time of her life reading kids' books and can get to work in about two seconds.'

'Cider?' I ask.

'Love one,' Rosie replies. 'Oh, and she finished her novel too! Has Penny got back to you about the publisher, Luce?' Penny, proving yet again that she was an angel come to earth, had sent my revised manuscript to a publisher friend of hers.

'Not yet, but she will. Penny won't let me down. She loves me and—'

'I know, I know,' says Rosie, giving me a little shove, 'and you love her.'

'Congratulations, Luce!' says Ben, when I return from the bar with our drinks. 'You're so bookish.'

'Ha! Can you be hot bookish?' I ask.

'I don't know about hot bookish, but look at this, there's a "chocolate brookie" on the menu! Ha! What do you think that is?'

'Don't care—it sounds delicious and I'm ordering one,' says Rosie and we all move with our drinks to a table by the window.

Tucking into plates of battered haddock and chips, steak and ale pie and honey mustard sausages, we swap both dishes and tales, and as we each take up a spoon and share a chocolate brookie, which turns out to be a fabulous combination of brownie and cookie, I feel thoroughly happy to be with my best friend and a man who seems to make every moment he's in more brilliant.

Eventually we get talking about what Ben wants to do next and it's clear he isn't quite sure.

'I want to be wild,' says Rosie suddenly, putting down her spoon. 'I want to live in wild places and break the rules and tell people who deserve it to get fucked and run my own race and just cut loose and sleep with whoever I want, and work whenever I want.' She flips a coaster on the side of the table and catches it again. 'That's what I want.'

Ben looks at her as though he's slightly star-struck and says, 'Yeah, maybe that's what I want too.'

⁑

'I always thought you and Oscar were made for each other,' says Ben as we zigzag home, thoroughly pissed. 'I never saw him so happy as when he was around you, or so preoccupied when he wasn't. He was always looking out that bloody window to your house.'

'He also has a girlfriend,' I remind him.

'No he doesn't—he and Kate broke up ages ago.'

I feel a twinge of guilt as I remember the scene at the Wild West Saloon. My lasting image is of Kate sitting on the footpath around the side of the pub, crouched over, head in her hands, and Oscar sitting beside her, neither of them saying a word.

'Oh, Ben,' I say quietly, 'those days are long gone now.'

'Yeah and she's shagging Joe, a Scottish dude we live with,' adds Rosie. 'He's a mechanical engineer. Handsome too.'

'Mmm,' I confirm. Ben's remarks have sent me reeling sideways, as if a wave I'd had my back to, and never saw coming, had unexpectedly crashed over me.

'What's news from Brian and Denise?' Rosie asks me, obviously sensing my need for rescue.

I seize the lifeline gratefully. 'They're crazy. Dad's been getting arthritis in his fingers and Mum read the best cure is to take medicinal marijuana, so they're importing packets of hemp seeds from America to sprinkle on their muesli every morning.' I laugh. 'I think they're high as bloody kites half the time.'

Rosie laughs too. 'Could you imagine Denise after a bit of hooch? Hilarious.'

'Oh, man, I do not want to know what that would be like,' I reply.

'Where's your fella tonight then, Luce?' asks Ben after a while.

'Ah, he's gone to an Arsenal match,' I say. 'Mad keen on the football.'

I feel ashamed for not telling Joe about our gathering. Subconsciously, I think I didn't want him and Ben to meet, although as we reach the Putney Palace and all stagger up the stairs it looks like it's inevitable. Inside, I head straight to Joe's bedroom and am so enormously relieved at not finding him there I wonder whether we shouldn't just break up as soon as he gets home.

Having no desire to contemplate this thought in my drunken state, I join some Germans on the couch, and watch a Graham Norton rerun.

Faintly, above the applause and the ad breaks, sounds of Rosie and Ben clanging about in the kitchen drift through to the lounge, and when the Germans turn off the telly, I hear Rosie say, 'But, Ben, we're like chalk and fucking cheese!'

'I know! But we could go together like cheese and fucking biscuits!' Ben replies.

22

Joe's arm feels heavy around my waist and he shifts slightly as I place my hand on his wrist and slink from beneath his grip out of bed and to the bathroom. I walk quickly across the cold tiles and steady myself against the cool porcelain basin and when I look in the mirror I see crescents of grey beneath my eyes. Then, having no desire to hold my own gaze, I drop my head and stand for several moments staring at the cracked enamel of the basin.

'Luce,' says Joe quietly, knocking on the door and opening it gently when I don't respond. 'Are you okay?' He comes over and wraps his arms around my shoulders. 'What's the matter?' he says, kissing my neck.

I turn around to face him. 'Nothing's the matter, Joe,' I say abruptly. 'I just had too much to drink.'

'Ah.' He smiles sympathetically. 'Do you want me to carry you back to bed? I've always wanted to carry you into bed. Here, let me try . . .'

'No thanks, Joe,' I say, laughing lightly as I move away towards the door. 'I think I might head to Notting Hill this morning. Fresh air is the answer for me.'

᦯꙰ꙮ

I've always enjoyed walking around the Notting Hill markets and with slivers of blue sky now cutting through the grey, the day holds promise and I too feel brighter.

A couple of streets from the Portobello Road crowds, I stumble across a quaint café with flowers falling from window boxes onto whitewashed walls, and I order a coffee and croissant to have at a table by the door. Patches of dappled sunlight filter down in pockets throughout the room and as I shrug off my jacket, I grin at the thought of Rosie and Ben. Knowing her, there won't be any shades of grey this morning; she'll either draw him closer or send him packing, and I can't predict which she'll choose.

In terms of suitability, they actually make a hell of a lot of sense. They're both adorably mad and could each, with a flash of teeth and a wink, get away with murder. Yes, I think, they could be great together.

Half an hour later, as I'm wandering down a sloping street of antique stores, my phone pings with an email notification. My heart rate speeds up as I realise the message is from Jacqui Dundas, the publisher to whom Penny had sent my manuscript. But my hopes are quickly dashed. Jacqui writes that while she thinks my novel has great potential, the market is exceedingly tough and she's just taken on two other historical fiction authors. Unfortunately, she concludes, she will have to pass, but wishes me all the best in finding a suitable agent or publisher. 'All the best'—the three-word salutation that sounds so congenial but has such a spirit-sinking finality about it. I've heard of authors who could papier-mâché a pergola with the number of rejection letters they've received, but still, Jacqui's response stings.

Because I'm hungover, and feel flat as a tack from Jacqui's knockback, and horribly confused about my reaction to seeing Ben and hearing him talk of Oscar, I decide that instead of heading home and facing everyone, I'll go watch *Ghostbusters* at the cinema at Notting Hill Gate.

When I emerge a couple of hours later into London's version of a sunny afternoon I see several missed calls from Rosie. I call her back, and we decide to meet up for a walk in Hyde Park.

She finds me on a bench by the lake, gazing absent-mindedly at people larking about in paddle boats.

'Well, I didn't see that coming,' says Rosie, plonking down beside me, and because I know exactly what she's referring to, I double over in laughter.

'Feeling good or bad?' I ask when I catch my breath.

'Well,' she says, crossing her arms, 'for once, I don't fucking know.'

'Really?'

'Yeah, it's very odd. Normally I can get a reading on these things. But I can't read Ben. Well, I can't read how I feel about Ben.'

'Do you want to see him again?' I ask.

'I think so. I mean, he's really fun.'

'Yeah, he's a great guy. I was thinking about you two this morning. You could actually be perfect together!'

'I'm perfect already.'

We walk along a wide path lined with plane trees and smile as three little girls wearing stockings and pastel coats skip past us arm in arm, urging their trailing grandad to keep up. In the distance, between patches of oaks, we catch flashes of London's ubiquitous red buses and black cabs motoring by.

With a measure of disgust, Rosie tells me about the team-building day she's being forced to attend at Wandsworth Dental Practice the next morning, and how she'd much prefer to be drilling and filling to being assembled into a human pyramid by overweight former boy scouts who now call themselves 'change management consultants'.

When I don't respond with laughter, as I normally would, she glances across at me. 'What's wrong?' she asks.

'Nothing.'

'Why are you so serious then?'

'Oh, it's just that I'm meant to be wearing stilettos not ugg boots.'

'What the hell are you talking about? Are you stoned? Has Denise got you on the hemp too?'

'No.' I laugh and blink back tears. 'The publisher friend of Penny's emailed this morning saying she doesn't want my novel.'

'But that's okay, Luce,' Rosie says and pats my back. 'You always hear about those authors who had a million rejections. What about J.K. Rowling!'

'Yeah, I know. But I feel like I can't face Penny now. I think I'll give up on the Foster family.'

'Would the Foster family give up on you?'

'No,' I admit. 'They're fossickers. They never give up.'

We continue to walk in silence.

'Okay,' says Rosie eventually, looping her arm through mine. 'Let's break this down. Why can't you face Penny?'

'Because I failed her. She stuck her neck out for me and her publisher friend didn't like my book.'

'I bet Penny doesn't see it that way. I reckon she'd think it was perfectly normal to get knocked back on your first try. She thinks you have talent, doesn't she?'

'Yes.'

'Then don't worry about Penny,' Rosie says, hugging me. 'I'm sure she'll still love you.' She gives me a shrewd look. 'You're probably a bit rattled by Ben talking about Oscar last night, aren't you? Well, don't worry about always having to see Ben,' she continues. 'I've just decided that I don't want anything more to do with him.'

I remain silent, knowing for certain she's decided nothing of the sort, and is in fact just stating the proposition out loud to see how it might feel.

'You know what we need?' she says abruptly. 'Retail therapy.'

'Oh, I couldn't agree more!' I reply, instantly happier.

We catch the tube from Hyde Park to Piccadilly Circus and walk to Anthropologie on Regent Street, where I promptly forget my worries among the racks of whimsical cotton tops and boho chic homewares.

⁖⁖⁖

'When I get married, do you think Penny will come to the wedding?' I ask Rosie over a steaming bowl of chicken and coconut noodle soup at Itsu later that evening.

'Luce,' she says, and puts down her chopsticks, 'if you make her your bridesmaid, I will never fucking forgive you.'

'She's sixty-three!' I guffaw.

'Who are you marrying, anyway?' she continues.

That's when my phone beeps with a message from Joe with the ominous words: *We need to talk.*

ꞔഌ

When I arrive home, Joe leads me into his room and we sit on the bed, side by side. I glance at him, feeling the awkwardness between us, unsure what to do about it—unsure what I *want* to do about it. Abruptly he tells me that he hasn't been able to stop thinking about this morning and how distant I was, and he wonders why I'd be avoiding him.

He looks so distressed that I loop my arms around his waist and apologise, assuring him that the weird vibe he'd sensed earlier was only due to my being incredibly tired and horribly hungover.

He places his hands on my shoulders, gently pushes me away and considers me from arm's length.

'Luce, it hit me after you left this morning how much I care about you. It's sort of snuck up on me. I know we said we just wanted something casual, but I've realised that I want more.'

I gaze back at him, not sure how to respond.

'I want this to be long-term, Luce. But I don't know if you feel the same?' His eyes are searching mine.

I've never seen him look so anxious and I feel my stomach tighten at the thought of hurting this lovely man—and for what? Because of some silly notion of caring for someone who lives thousands of miles away and who I'm not even in touch with?

I hear myself telling Joe that I have no intention of breaking up with him or slowing things down. He grins at me with such enormous relief that I can't help grinning back.

We spend the rest of the evening in bed together, and as I snuggle against his chest and we laugh away at an episode of *Catastrophe* on his laptop, I tell myself I must have had rocks in my head to ever consider giving this simple, uncomplicated love away.

༈

Penny smiles at me kindly the next morning when I tell her about the publisher's email.

'Don't give up on *Diamonds in the Dust*, Lucy,' she says, as if she'd eavesdropped on my conversation with Rosie. 'Remember, if it was easy to get published everyone would be doing it. And different publishers are always looking for different types of books.' She picks up an armful of *Room on the Broom* and walks a few steps before turning to look back at me. 'Prove her wrong. Make your writing sparkle and shine so much that it demands publication.'

My heart swells with her words, and I vow to keep faith in my childhood dream.

Later that day, when Margie and I are both rostered behind the counter, I tell her of Joe's sudden keenness for commitment, and how despite my assuring him otherwise, deep down I'm not convinced I feel the same.

She says that when she'd faced a similar situation back in Cape Town, her mum had responded by quoting the first line of Elton John's 'I Guess That's Why They Call It the Blues'.

I smile and tell her our mums would get along like a house on fire.

∽ℯ∾

As if my conversation with Margie had summoned her, I hear from Mum that very evening.

'Hello?!' she yells after I answer her Skype call. 'Hello? I'm trying to turn this up, love. Hang on, I can't get it, we'll just have to yell.'

'Hello, Mum!' I say, grinning as Glenda jumps onto Mum's lap, totally obscuring her face. 'Oh, look at Glenda!' I say, then pause. 'She's a bit of a fatty boomba, Ma!'

'Don't talk to me about that!' she retorts. 'It's your father who's stopping by Bernie's pie van and sharing one with her every second day. I've told him to cut it out. You should feel the weight of her on me now! And I'm flat out watching *Grand Designs* of an evening; she jumps on top of me and I can barely move. Come on, off you get, Glenda. Well, at least move your head then. Ah, there you are, my darling. You look a bit pale, Lucy.'

'That's 'cause I live in London, Ma. It isn't exactly Townsville!'

'Are you eating enough red meat?'

'Yeah, I think so.'

'Don't ever be shy of putting a chop in your pocket, Luce,' says Dad, appearing on the screen suddenly.

'Dad, what have you been feeding Glenda?' I demand. 'She looks like she needs a stint with Jenny Craig.'

'Sorry, love,' says Dad, looking slightly shamefaced. 'We keep passing Bernie just as he's about to close and he insists on giving us leftover pies. Even waved me over last time I tried to drive past without stopping.'

'Can't you just avoid going near his pie van?' I say. 'Or freeze them for the Men's Shed?'

'Yeah, okay,' he says, calling Glenda as he heads out of the room.

After I hear the front door slam, I ask Mum how Dad's going. She says he's been good and has been spending more time at the farm lately, which is why he's passing Bernie's so frequently. She sympathises when I tell her it's getting dark at three-thirty in the afternoon now in London, and perks up when I say I stumbled across a half-price cashmere sale at The Library in Chelsea the other day and bought her a scarf.

'I also walked past The Ivy on King's Road—that was one of the places in the article you sent me on "Top 10 High Teas".'

'Oh, how lovely. Why don't you take some nice young man there for tea and scones, Luce?' She laughs. 'Or even Rosie would do!'

I feel a pang of guilt for not having told her about Joe and resolve to mention him as soon as she finishes talking, but when I go to speak the words catch in my throat and instead I ask her about Suds 'n' Thuds and whether Ruth tried to resurrect her wet t-shirt competition.

I'm not intending to keep Mum in the dark, but for some reason I fear that if I mention Joe to her there'll be no going back; he will creep into every future conversation and I don't feel ready for that just yet.

'You know that Oscar's been up here, asking after you,' says Mum unexpectedly.

'Oh, was he?' I say, super casual despite my quickening pulse.

'He asked for your London number. Do you want me to give it to him?'

'No,' I say and then steer the final minutes of our conversation back to the mutually happy ground of expressing how much we both love Glenda.

⚮

Rosie arrives home from work thoroughly disgusted with her team-building day. She has me in fits of laughter as she recounts a session on 'giving feedback'. Apparently, the new protocol at Wandsworth Dental is that you should seek permission from your colleagues before offering them feedback, as in: 'Excuse me, Kelly, can I give you some feedback?' Kelly can then accept or decline the invitation, depending on her frame of mind.

Apparently, following the session, a dental assistant had asked Rosie if she could give her some feedback, and Rosie said no, that she was fed up with feedback and to try her again in a fortnight.

After washing up our dinner plates, I return to our bedroom to find Rosie sitting on the edge of her bed, holding a small card and smiling. She glances at me and I follow her gaze to a vase of violet orchids on her dresser.

'Wow, they're beautiful,' I say.

She hands me the card.

Even if I saw you part-time I would be happy! B x

I smile, then leave her alone with her thoughts.

23

Over the next two months, I successfully banish Oscar to the back of my mind by recalling Einstein's famous quote that the definition of insanity is doing something over and over again and expecting a different result, and so Joe and I settle into a happy groove. I find his turns of phrase, such as referring to strollers as 'pushchairs', quite adorable. And he, in turn, is highly entertained by my banter with Rosie and my Australian expressions. 'Wouldn't shout if a shark bit him?' he echoes in bewilderment when I describe one of the managers at Scribe who's particularly tight.

I also point out all the amusing British idiosyncrasies he takes for granted.

'Listen to this,' I say when we're cooking together one night, and proceed to read from the top of a jar of pasta sauce: '*Do not use if lid depressed*. What if the lid's just having a down day? Surely you've got to give it another chance?'

To my great delight he responds with, 'You silly duffer!'

Joe gets into the habit of swinging by Scribe when I finish work, to stroll home with me. And I find myself looking forward to stepping out into the afternoon darkness, knowing he'll be there.

⚬⚬

On the bank holiday weekend, Joe takes me on a surprise visit to his parents in Fraserburgh, a quaint coastal fishing village in Scotland's far north-east. I still haven't told Mum about Joe, and as I stand with him among rolling green fields dotted with sheep and gaze at rugged cliffs that drop hundreds of metres into the ocean, I realise I'm perilously close to the Outer Hebrides.

'What are you chuckling at?' asks Joe, pulling me close.

'Oh, nothing,' I reply, kissing him to prevent further interrogation.

⚬⚬

We drive back to his parents' place and Joe points out the landmarks that are woven into the fabric of his past. I smile as we pass the football field where he scored the winning goal in the 1992 Scottish Junior North Premier League final, and laugh when we look down upon the stretch of coastline where he tried and failed to impress the local ladies with his kitesurfing. When I say that I'll have to show him around Rocky sometime, he responds lightly he'd love to see where I'm from and that if I ever want to go back to Australia he would follow me home like a lapdog.

⚬⚬

'Fraserburgh used to be the largest supplier of white fish to Britain, but now it relies more on tourism to keep it ticking over,' explains Joe's dad in such a thick Scottish brogue that I wonder whether I mightn't need to invest in a lip-reading course.

'Would you like a fancy piece?' he asks with a twinkle in his eye, then meets my dumbfounded look with a proffered plate of jam biscuits.

'We call cakes and treats "fancy pieces" in Scotland,' says Joe with a grin.

'Ha,' I reply and reach for the plate. 'I thought I might have to offer your dad a knuckle sandwich!'

Joe's parents guffaw with delight, although I later learn they had just as much trouble deciphering me.

Over endless cups of tea and fancy pieces, I recognise Joe in his mum's smile and his dad's eyes, and feel like I can place more of this man now I've met his family. I joke I'll no longer be a fancy piece if I continue to dine on fairy cakes and fresh butter, and so we spend a couple of days walking and exploring the Scottish countryside.

We visit the eerily atmospheric clifftop ruins of Slains castle, which apparently provided the inspiration for Bram Stoker's *Dracula*, and cruise on Loch Ness. I sample haggis, and take photos of seals that have fled the wintery North Sea and are sunbaking on the rocky Fraserburgh foreshore. I find such joy in these sights and sounds, so distinctly different from Central Queensland, that I don't even mind when a giant seagull, referred to as a scurry, flips our parcel of hot chips up and onto the pavement.

'How can you be laughing, Luce!' exclaims Joe, standing and shooing away the scurries with a curse.

'Don't worry,' I say, grabbing the back of his jeans and pulling him down beside me. 'When we get home we can have a jam fancy!'

'Mmm,' he murmurs, before kissing me. 'I fancy that.'

24

Back in London, Rosie ushers me into her room as soon as I walk through the door and tells me she and Ben barely spent a moment apart over the long weekend.

'That's great, Rosie!' I say, then, seeing her concerned expression, 'Isn't it?'

'Yeah.'

'What's the matter?'

'Well, he wears a singlet to bed which says, *I've got 99 problems but a bench ain't one*, and below that is a picture of a bench press.'

'Hilarious,' I say sincerely.

'He doesn't let the tea draw.'

'Maybe the tea's not creative.'

'He doesn't know what he's going to do next.'

'Neither do I half the time but you still love me, don't you?'

'Oh, Luce,' she says and buries her head in a pillow. 'I really like him. Fuck! He just sparks joy like that cleaning book by the Japanese woman.'

'Marie Kondo,' I reply, intimately acquainted with the bestseller.

'I really didn't want to like him so much, but then his bloody shoes got me.'

'What, does he wear great shoes? Oh, that was on your top five list, wasn't it? Something about wearing decent shoes?'

'Yeah, but that's not what I mean,' she says quickly. 'When you were gone, he stayed over, and I left early the next morning to get some milk, and as I was walking back, I was in two minds about whether I wanted him to be there when I got home. And then I got home and saw his shoes still outside my door and my heart did this little jump, and I realised that I wanted him to be there!'

She looks at me with such despair that I can't help laughing.

'He's even got a good Uber rating!'

'What's that got to do with it?'

'Haven't you heard the Uber-rating theory?'

'No.'

'When you meet a new guy or girl, you check their Uber rating, and if it's anything below a 3.5, then you start asking questions. Why are they getting marked down? Are they an arsehole when they're not with you? Is it only a matter of time before you find this out?'

'And what's Ben's Uber rating?'

'Fucking five!' she exclaims.

'Ha-ha!'

'Shit, Luce. I really, *really* like him.'

'But that's okay, isn't it?'

'No! It's not! I'm out of my depth. I've never liked someone this much.'

'Well, I'm absolutely certain that he likes you just as much, Rosie.'

'I know he does,' she says miserably. 'He tells me all the time—that's what frigging freaks me out too!'

⁓

Later that night, aided by wine, Rosie and I formulate a 'Ben game plan', which consists of her continuing to see him without freaking out.

We end up halfway sozzled and I eventually creep into Joe's room before remembering he's gone out to catch up with a friend. As I lie down I spot a note from him on my pillow with a drawing of a giant scurry. Beneath it he has written: *I love you, Luce*.

'I love you too,' I whisper as he snuggles beside me hours later.

⁓

Over the next month I observe Rosie and Ben fall madly, wildly, head over heels in love. They're so clearly besotted with each other it's hard to imagine any flames existed before they got together, and, like that line from *Captain Corelli's Mandolin*, it is inconceivable that they should ever part.

I too have a spring in my step, thanks to Rosie's great idea.

'It struck me when I was on the tube this morning,' she says one evening. 'You should send *Diamonds in the Dust* to some Australian publishers. They'd get the setting, and your sense of humour—they're Aussie!'

I look at her in wonder. 'Why didn't I think of that?'

I take a week off work to get my manuscript spick and span. Checking out agents and publishers in Australia, I see that several publishers actually encourage writers to email the synopsis and first three chapters of manuscripts. Crossing my fingers, I follow their submission procedure and press 'send' before I can have second thoughts, hoping against hope someone will respond without signing off 'all the best'.

After that, I decide to shelve my book and relax when I'm not at Scribe.

Over the next few weeks Joe is really busy with work, consulting on Heathrow's third runway proposal, and I end up spending a lot of time with Ben and Rosie. Ben's renting a room at mate's rates from a friend on safari in Africa. It's in a flat on Broadway Market, a shopping street that sits between Regent's Canal and London Fields in hipster Hackney and he's sharing with a guy in high finance who never seems to be home. They have a washing machine that works, a hot shower with great water pressure, and their light-filled lounge room overlooks Off Broadway, one of our favourite bars, on the corner opposite. When you step outside, you're in the heart of the East End's quaint cafés, gourmet food markets and indie music stores.

Neither Rosie nor Ben ever mentions Oscar around me, which I suspect is Rosie's doing. On one of my days off Ben and I go out for coffee and he asks me about Joe, and how things are going with us. I respond that we're fine, telling myself that love can sometimes be a slow burner, and that the dizzying infatuation between Rosie and Ben is always to be expected at the beginning.

I tell myself it doesn't matter that Joe and I never had the dizzying infatuation. Maybe it isn't even necessary. Maybe what we have is enough, and probably there are heaps of couples in the world who charged through the absence of the dizzying infatuation, and are still happily together.

∽⊘

Although we're under the same roof, it feels like forever since Rosie and I caught up alone, and so one evening we head to Somerset House for a festive fix of ice-skating beneath the glittering Christmas lights.

'Things all seem good with Joe, hey?' she asks as we glide along.

'Yeah, good,' I say, concentrating on the ice. 'I bet your mum can't wait to meet Ben.'

'I think she already likes him more than me. Whenever she calls he takes the phone and has big chats.' She grins like she always does when speaking of Ben. 'What does Denise think about Joe?'

'I haven't told her about him,' I reply as we skate towards a huge ornament-laden Christmas tree in the centre of the rink. 'If I do, she'll never stop asking me about him.'

'Luce, do you even like this guy?' Rosie demands abruptly as we skid to a stop in front of the tree. 'Because if you don't you've got to tell him. He's head over fucking heels in love with you.'

'I do love him. I *do*. But it's not like what you and Ben have. It's not like I think we're made for each other, or that the world would stop turning if we weren't together.'

'Can I give you some feedback?' she asks.

I nod.

'It's not like I think the world would stop turning if Ben and I broke up. I'd be sad as hell, for sure, but then someone else would come along. I don't buy into this whole soul mates thing. I just think if you're having fun with someone, then that's a good sign.' She smiles. 'And Ben and I have fun.'

'So I'm overthinking things?'

'Well, only you can know how you feel about Joe. There's no point staying in something if half the time you're plotting how to get out of it. But I've seen how he makes you laugh and, you know, he's a nice guy.'

'Rosie,' I say as we skate off, 'can I give you some feedback on your feedback?'

'Yes.'

'It was good,' I say.

'Ha, Vegemite breath!' says Joe, after kissing me at the kitchen table one morning. 'I'm starting to recognise it!'

I smile and angle the laptop towards him so he can see the screen. I'm in the midst of organising a trip to Spain for us as our joint Christmas present to each other. Joe's only ever been there on boozy bucks' weekends and said he'd love to see it with me. I've only overnighted in Barcelona, and can't wait to escape the drizzle and darkness of this bitterly cold London winter.

Half the fun of going on holiday for me is the planning beforehand, and Joe and I spend the rest of the day happily booking flights and ogling accommodation we can't afford. Both being fixated on food, sunshine and sand, we decide to visit San Sebastián, Spain's culinary capital, on the Basque coast.

We click on images of bars lined from one end to the other with pintxos and reserve a charming room in a pension located in the labyrinth-like alleyways of the cobblestoned old town.

With his friend returning to the Hackney flat the next day, Ben has pretty much moved into Rosie's room and I have pretty much moved into Joe's. We get around London as a puffer-jacketed foursome and I faintly perceive, with every Skype call home, that my yearnings for the chorusing cicadas and breaking waves are becoming less intense. One night, though, while Joe's at an Arsenal match and I'm watching an episode of *Outlander*, Rosie knocks on the bedroom door and sends my world spinning in a different direction.

'Luce,' she says, ashen-faced, 'Oscar's in the lounge room.'

I stare at her like a deer caught in headlights and she walks over and sits on the bed.

'This is what I'm thinking: I'll send Ben and Oscar off to the Nag's Head and tell them we'll meet them there later. That'll give us a chance to regroup and—'

'Shit, Rosie,' I say, shocked. 'What's he doing here?'

'I think he's having a break. He put someone else on to help manage Bev's Buffet. That's all I know.'

I look at her blankly, not really taking in one word she's saying. All I can register is that Oscar is only metres away.

'I had no idea he was coming, Luce,' she says and takes my hand. 'You don't have to go tonight, you know. There's no pressure on you to be there.'

'Mmm.'

'How about I tell them that we might join them later, hey?' she says, hopping up.

I nod and stare vacantly at the door after she closes it. Then I hear the sound of Oscar's voice drifting faintly from the lounge room, and sit up with a startle, knowing with every bone in my body that I will be there.

⁓

Half an hour later, after I've showered and dried my hair, I change into the new black dress I got from Zara and shrug on the overcoat Mum bought me before I left Rocky. Rosie and I then catch the tube in to Covent Garden, and I tell myself to downplay any excitement I feel at seeing Oscar by acting elegantly subdued.

The evening begins in a civilised fashion around a table at the Nag's Head. As soon as I step into the pub I think how achingly handsome Oscar looks, but then remind myself to stay cool. As I hug him hello I hope I'm conveying the message: *It's amazing to see you, but don't think you can fly in and turn my life upside down again.* But really, my heart is screaming: *I still love you, Oscar! Oh my god, I freaking love you like these British people love marmalade and bacon butties. I want to keep you in my pocket like a folded tube map. Please hang out with me until we're so old we have trouble hearing each other. Please don't ever leave!*

Oscar hugs me back, saying, 'You look amazing, Luce! It's so good to see you!'

I smile and take off my coat before accepting a sauv blanc from Ben. While everyone's talking I hold back and try to maintain a slightly aloof air, but only succeed in attracting puzzled looks from Rosie, who hustles me off to the bathroom at the first opportunity.

'I know Oscar's here and it's thrown you a bit, but holy shit you're acting weird!' she says to me as I stand next to her at the basins.

'What do you mean?' I say.

'Oh, just this whole ice-queen thing you seem to be doing. You're bloody boring! And you're going to turn into an ice-queen if you don't put your coat back on!'

'Is it that bad?'

'Oh, mate, if you weren't my best friend I would have moved with Ben to a booth!'

To the obvious relief of my companions, I return to being my normal self, and soon we're all laughing as Ben recounts his struggles to keep pace with a priest on the Camino. When I next hop off the bar stool, though, I overbalance and, instead of steadying myself on the table, I accidentally steady myself on Oscar's thigh. My hand lingers there a fraction longer than if I'd stumbled into my aunty, and when I look up at him, I imagine he sees the desire in my eyes.

An hour later, Rosie gives me another talking-to in the bathroom. 'Luce, pull yourself together! You're falling all over him!'

'Oh shit. I've really got to lay off the wine, Rosie. There's going to be hell to pay tomorrow,' I say.

'There's going to be hell to pay if you go home with Oscar too, you know? You're looking at him with such longing in your eyes!' Rosie replies.

'Oh God, I'm not, am I?' I cover my face in horror.

'Yep, you are. Let's get out of this pub, hey? Fresh air'll do you good. They've turned on the Christmas lights in Covent Garden—should we . . .?'

'Yes, we should,' I reply.

↶↷

As we walk into Covent Garden's famous piazza, I'm overcome with a love for life as incandescent as the red and gold bulbs twinkling on the tree soaring above us. I've always delighted in the traditions of Christmas, and when Oscar loops his arm through mine and we crane our necks to look up at the dazzling decorations, I think there can't possibly be a more perfect moment occurring anywhere in the world.

With Ben leading the charge, we stroll across to the Apple Market, which is festooned from one end to the other with mistletoe chandeliers.

'How about those two?' Oscar says as we stand at the back of the hall and watch Ben attempt to kiss Rosie beneath every one of the forty chandeliers. 'I've never seen him so into someone.'

'Well, it's Rosie, isn't it?' I say, grinning as Ben steals another kiss from my best friend.

I successfully negotiate the mistletoe gauntlet by engaging Oscar in intense conversation about Bev's Buffet's Brisbane expansion, wondering how he can take time off during the peak Christmas party season. It transpires that he's recently hired a guy with an MBA to share his workload because he was getting too stressed and needed a break. When I try to ask him more he changes the topic to *Diamonds in the Dust* and when I tell him I've finished and have sent it off to some Australian publishers he asks if I intend to write a sequel. I laugh and say there's no use thinking about a sequel if I can't find a publisher to take on the first one.

We're so caught up in conversation that we lose Ben and Rosie for a while and I'm beginning to panic slightly when Rosie texts to say they're outside the Apple Market. We link back up with them and then join the jolly crowds heading towards Covent Garden's Mulled Wine Festival.

'How awesome!' cries Ben as we near the ticketing area. 'My shout!'

'You don't have any money, Ben!' yells Rosie. 'You just told me.'

'Shit, that's right,' he replies. 'Ah well, I'll busk.' He takes off his beanie and puts it on the pavement, then launches into an error-ridden version of 'Six White Boomers'. His spirited mashup of Australian and English Christmas carols attracts smirks, sympathy and a small amount of shrapnel before one of the guys stamping people's arms to get into the festival offers him free entry if he shuts up.

When we finally get inside we end up in front of a friendly Irishman called Kevin, who dispenses generous serves of warm wine from cavernous steel pots and challenges us to try every one of his twelve variations.

After the seventh cup we're all sporting rosy cheeks and

dispositions, and Oscar asks if I'd like to check out the stall selling hog roasts. I say that I'd love to and we grab a wine for the road and weave our way towards the food vendors. Laughing at the frosty plumes of breath that feather our words, Oscar and I discuss books we've recently read, bands we've discovered and gripping podcasts we think the other would love, and rave about *Stranger Things*, which we've both been watching online.

In fact, we cover so much common ground that it reminds me of Dr Karl once telling a listener on Triple J that your brain is your main sexual organ. Consequently, I don't mind in the slightest that the queue for hog roasts is colossal.

'I love your laugh,' Oscar says to me. 'It's like you just don't know what might happen next with that laugh.'

I grin, elated; no-one else has ever said that to me.

From the back pocket of his jeans, Oscar pulls a crumpled piece of paper and says, 'Luce, I'd envisaged a more romantic setting than the queue for a hog roast, but I want to say that I'm hardworking, honest, fit, wear decent pants and shoes, and have good dental hygiene.'

'That's Rosie's top-five list, Oscar!' I say, doubling over with laughter. 'Didn't the dental hygiene thing give it away?'

'Oh, is it?' He grins. 'Actually, I didn't think *any* of it sounded much like you!' Then he lifts me off the ground with a hug. 'Well, what are your top-five requirements then, Luce?'

I'm ashamed to admit that it is only then, when I spot an army of people in Arsenal jerseys whooping their way through the crowds, that I think of Joe and how much I care for him, and how lovely he is to me, and his mum and dad, and the scurries and the sunbathing seals.

'I'm seeing someone, Oscar,' I say, and step back from him as he sets me down. 'We're going to Spain next week.'

'I know, Ben told me,' he says quietly. 'Do you love him?'

'I'm not sure,' I reply, suddenly feeling anxious. 'Sometimes I think so.'

'But sometimes not?' he asks.

Before I can respond he says quickly, 'Sorry, that came out wrong. Luce, I realise things haven't been straightforward between us. But when Ben said Rosie thought you might still have feelings for me, I knew I had to come and see you. I haven't been able to get you out of my mind since you left, and when you walked into the pub tonight, you took my breath away.'

I avoid his gaze, feeling wretched and lost for words.

'Do you want to be with me, Luce?' he presses.

'I don't know,' I reply. 'The timing's not right, Oscar.'

'The timing will never be right. But if you want something badly enough, you have to make it happen. Do you want something with me?'

'Oscar, you live in Sydney and I live in London and Joe lives in London too.'

'We could be together in Sydney,' he says with a pained expression.

I'm silent, surprised by what he's just said.

'What are you looking for?' he asks helplessly, searching my eyes. 'I don't know what it is you're looking for.'

I stall for time by sculling my drink, then say, 'My life is here now. I have Penny and the bookstore and . . .' As

I speak, I feel my head whir with words, and though I try to focus on Oscar, he and everyone around him have started to spin.

'I'm sorry, Loscar,' I slur into his neck as he steps forward to steady me. 'I thought move to London I'd wearing stilettos, but I can't shake ugg boot. Fucking ugg, Oscar.'

He laughs and strokes my hair. Mulled wine should be illegal.

'Take me home, Oscar,' I say. 'Need to go home.'

In the cab back to the Putney Palace, I lie with my head in his lap and cry drunken tears into his jeans. After he pays the fare, he helps me out of the taxi and steadies me as I stumble up the stairs. Inside, he and Joe have a brief conversation before Joe carries me into the bedroom and lowers me gently on the bed.

'Who was that guy?' he asks as he empties a sachet of orange electrolyte powder into water.

'That's Oscar's brother Ben,' I explain. 'No, Ben's brother Oscar.'

'Do you like him?' he asks, helping me to sit up and handing me the glass.

'His mum's our neighbour in Rocky,' I reply and hope that he doesn't notice I have dodged his question. I'm pretty sure he wouldn't be thrilled with the answer.

25

I wake the next morning knowing I need to resolve things with Joe. We're supposed to be flying to Spain together in two days and, after seeing Oscar, I know I can't get on that plane.

Joe deserves someone who adores him, not someone who isn't completely sure whether she's in love with him and is hedging her bets while she tries to work it out. If I went to San Sebastián, only half my heart would be present.

Later that morning, as we walk across Putney Bridge, I blurt out the sentences that have been circling in my mind like sharks.

'I'm sorry, Joe, but I can't go to Spain. I love you, but I'm not in love with you. I think we should break up. I'm so sorry.'

Joe looks at me with such utter shock that tears immediately spring to my eyes.

'What?' he says.

'I love you, Joe, I love hanging out with you, and I thought maybe what we had was enough, but I just don't think it is.'

'Luce,' he says, taking my hand, 'where is this coming from? You've never said anything at all about being unhappy.'

I can't bring myself to speak as tears trickle down my face.

'Are you unhappy with me?' he asks, gently brushing the tears away.

'No, I'm not unhappy with you,' I reply truthfully. 'I just have doubts sometimes, Joe, and I think you should be with someone who doesn't have doubts.'

'But having doubts is normal, isn't it? Don't you get through the doubts by just spending time with each other? We have fun together, don't we?'

'Yes,' I reply with a sob.

He looks at me in disbelief. 'What about our trips to the Borough Market and our runs around Battersea and bike rides over Albert Bridge? And the seals and jam fancies and the scurries?' His eyes are glistening with tears too now. 'Mum and Dad—' he begins, choking up. 'They love you.'

'I love your mum and dad, and the fun we have in London. I love you too, Joe—but not in the way you deserve.'

'Please don't do this, Luce,' he says, pulling me towards him. 'Please come to San Sebastián with me. We can talk about things there.' I feel his tears slide down my neck. 'Please,' he repeats.

I cry into his jumper and we stand there and hold each other for the longest time.

Eventually, I take a step back and say, 'I'll get my things out of your room. I'll start looking for somewhere else to live.'

'You don't have to go anywhere. You can stay with me forever. Don't leave, Luce—I love you.'

'You're a beautiful man, Joe,' I say. 'You deserve someone who loves you absolutely unreservedly.'

'I don't want someone different, Lucy. I don't want anyone else. I don't understand this at all.' He covers his face with his hands, then looks up, anguished. 'Is it that guy from last night? Is that why?'

'Yes,' I whisper agonisingly.

Joe looks at me, completely crestfallen, then turns around and walks away. I stand there watching him until his red jumper fades from sight. I feel so utterly miserable that if I weren't halfway across Putney Bridge and risked being swarmed by social workers, I would sink to my knees and sob. Instead, I put one foot in front of the other, stare down at the Thames and tell myself over and over that I did the right thing, and that Joe will be happier in the long run.

When I finally reach home, and fumble for my keys at the top of the steps, Rosie opens the front door and I collapse into her hug. She tells me she's been worried about me and suggests we head down the road to Gourmet Burger Kitchen for a debrief.

'I broke up with Joe,' I say as we walk.

'Oh shit, Luce.' She sighs. 'What happened last night? Oscar messaged Ben to say you were sick and that he was taking you home.'

'Nothing happened with Oscar. He brought me back in a cab, walked me up the stairs, then left.'

'Poor Joe,' says Rosie.

'I know—I hate that I've hurt him,' I say. 'But I couldn't

go on a holiday with Joe after seeing Oscar.' I burst into tears again, picturing Joe's devastated expression on the bridge.

Rosie puts her arm around me and I explain that as soon as I saw Oscar at the pub I knew my feelings for him were just so different from my feelings for Joe. I can tell Rosie's concerned I might be getting ahead of myself with Oscar, and she says how much she and Ben have come to like Joe over the last few months of hanging out together. I agree that he's an awesome guy and say how I'd hoped what we had would be enough and she admits that she and Ben worried Joe was more into me than I was into him.

I tell her what Oscar said at the hog roast stall and how he produced her top-five list from his back pocket.

'No way!' She laughs. 'That's classic, Luce.'

After walking in silence for a while, she looks at me and says, 'What are you going to do?'

'Well, first I need to move out and find somewhere to stay,' I say, the sadness of leaving Joe and our happy life in the Putney Palace now fully hitting me. 'Then . . . I don't know what will happen next.'

26

I book into an Airbnb bedsit around the corner from work, where I have a truly horrific night's sleep, worrying about Joe and feeling awful about hurting him so badly. The next day, just before I start Storytime, Rosie texts to say Joe has cancelled our flights to Spain and is on his way home to Scotland. She says to come around after work and she'll help me pack up my stuff.

Then, as I read *Slinky Malinki's Christmas Crackers* to children sporting jumpers adorned with Rudolph the Red-Nosed Reindeer and Santa Claus, my voice catches at the sight of strollers, which Joe always referred to as push-chairs. I don't regret ending our relationship, but I do regret the sadness I've caused him. After Storytime, I discover I'd missed a call from Oscar with a sweet message saying he hoped I was okay. Although I instinctively want to call him back, I also know that I can't just jump from one relationship to the next and follow Oscar back to Sydney. I need to put my own life in order, rather than relying on someone else to do it for me.

During our lunchbreak, Margie and I share pre-packaged sandwiches from Pret a Manger and I tell her I've broken up with Joe. She gives me a hug and invites me to join her and her brother at their Clapham unit for a Christmas Day braai. She then admits, blushing, that she's also invited Dennis but predicts there's more chance of hell freezing over than him turning up.

ༀ

That afternoon I start searching for more permanent accommodation and am nearing Westbourne Park to look at a room advertised on EasyRoommate by Paul, one half of a 'friendly Aussie couple with an adorable cat called Pepsi', when he texts me to say it's just been taken. I almost want to cry, but at least he's let me know.

I then change direction to inspect a 'room' in Acton, which turns out to be an electric cupboard, complete with swirly red windowless walls, a skylight and a massive hot-water system humming away in the corner. Perhaps more astonishing, though, is the trail of women who, after seeing the room, proceed to write their details on a clipboard proffered by two young guys, who are inspecting their potential roomies as closely as the women are inspecting the electric cupboard.

After that I set off to Earl's Court and dismally survey a single room with a dodgy cooking grill and dirty washbasin. It sinks my spirits so low I immediately turn and retrace my steps to the Underground, where I board the District line train to Putney. On the way, I conduct a Q & A session in my mind.

Should I head back to Rocky and hang out with Glenda and try to get work at Dymocks in Paradise Plaza?

No, you shouldn't, because Glenda has Dad now and you're about to turn thirty-three. You are not eight.

Well, if I can't go home, where can I go? New York? Yes, maybe New York is the answer—I'll go to New York!

What would you do in New York that's different from what you've done in London?

Okay, maybe I should stick it out in London. Maybe it's just hard at the moment because I'm unsettled, and I just need to hang in there a bit longer.

A bit longer for what? It's only going to get colder and you're not saving anything on your bookstore wage. Penny and Margie will always be your friends. What's the point of battling it out in London?

What about Rio de Janeiro? It looked spectacular in the Olympics. Or Cape Town? Margie said I'm always welcome there.

You're just plucking locations out of the sky now, Lucy. This train of thought is not productive—and speaking of trains, your stop's up next.

༄

In the evening, after I walk across Putney Bridge, I spot Ben stepping out of a pub on the high street. He crosses over and as we turn the corner towards the Putney Palace he says, 'If I could just go through life with that two-beers feeling, everything would be perfect!'

While Rosie and I are cramming my clothes into packing cells, Ben makes tea and sings Nick Cave's 'The Ship Song' in the kitchen.

'Here you go,' he says, appearing in the doorway with two cups. 'And yes, Rosie, I let the tea draw!'

☙

Rosie helps me lug my stuff back to the Airbnb room I'm renting and, after we've both lied through our teeth about how wonderful it is, we catch the Overground to Shoreditch. Between spoonfuls of Brick Lane butter chicken, I outline my plan to spend Christmas Day with Margie and the evening in Belsize Park with Penny.

Rosie nods approvingly, saying she's relieved I'll have company. She and Ben had booked flights to Dublin for Christmas around the same time Joe and I were organising our trip to Spain.

'Jeez, could you imagine sitting alone in that fucking awful Airbnb room on Christmas Day?'

'Oh, man, it'd be the pits!' I agree.

Rosie then leans back in her chair and tells me, with considerable casualness, that she won't be in London much longer.

'Ben's just killing time, figuring out what he wants to do next, but I know he's also waiting to see what I'll do next, and I want to be fair to him. He's been talking about making a fresh start somewhere and keeps raving on about Darwin and a postgrad environmental management course he'd like to do at CDU. So I've told him he should apply.'

'Darwin?' I stammer, my heart plunging into my boots. 'Bloody hell.'

'Mmm. Tropical wonderland of the north, gateway to Asia, the final frontier . . . or that's what Google says, anyway. It sounds like a place where I could have lots of new adventures. I reckon it could be fun.'

'So, you'll get work there?'

'Yeah, three days a week would be perfect. I saw an ad on the ADA website for a part-time job at a dental practice called Fannie Bay Dental the other day, so I sent off an application. The plan is to pack up here and head to Rocky after we get back from Dublin.' She is watching me closely as if to monitor my reaction.

'Fannie Bay Dental. That—that's gold,' I stammer, floored at how quickly things seem to be moving and gutted that I'm only hearing about it now.

'I didn't want to tell you about this before,' says Rosie, clearly guessing what I'm thinking. 'You've had a lot going on. And, anyway, I thought if I debated the pros and cons with you I'd never make a move.'

'So you'd leave London for Ben?' I ask, posing the question out loud more as a statement for my consideration than hers.

'Well, not just for Ben. I don't think I'm cut out to deal with this ridiculous feedback thing they've dreamt up at work. Even when I'm totally fine about someone telling me what they think, everyone's so bloody polite and reserved I can't figure out half the time what they're trying to get at! And I know some of them think I'm way too blunt. Can you imagine?' She smiles. 'Besides, I'm working full-time, Luce, and you know how much I love that. I didn't move across the world just to join every other bugger in the nine-to-five rat race.'

I'm about to say that since starting at Scribe I've become a convert to working part-time too, but she's on a roll and I can't get a word in edgewise.

'And I forgot how dark it gets here in winter and how the sky seems so close. I'd even welcome a proper storm instead of this constant drizzle.' She pauses and considers me over her beer. 'I've loved being in London with you, Luce, but sometimes you just have to roll the dice again and go with it, you know?'

'I feel like I'm getting too old to roll the dice again,' I say. 'I'm going to be thirty-three in a couple of months.'

'Thirty-three's not old,' Rosie retorts. 'We're spring chickens!'

I muster a weak smile. 'This chicken's good.'

'Luce!' she says, grinning at my sulky expression.

'What?' I reply, crossing my arms and fixing her with an exaggerated pout.

'Luce! Ha!'

'Bloody hell, Rosie, it's just all a bit of a shock! Man, I'm going to miss you. Maybe I should come to Darwin too. I seem to be making a habit of following you around the globe!'

'Well, I'd love for you to come to Darwin, but you've got to do what's right for *you*,' says Rosie.

I sigh. 'I don't know what's right for me anymore.'

'Yes you do. Underneath it all you do, Luce.'

We both pretend we're not about to cry and then button our jackets and walk towards the Aldgate East Underground. I feel slightly ashamed of my earlier sullenness. Despite Rosie's seemingly laissez-faire approach to life, in some ways she's remarkably more level-headed than me.

'Rosie?' I say after a while.

'Yes?'

'What do you think I should do about Oscar?'

'If you fucking love him, then fucking show him, Luce! For fuck's sake!'

'I really can't understand why your workmates might think you're too blunt,' I reply. 'Maybe I'll develop a new feedback protocol for you too.'

We both laugh and then Rosie tells me that Oscar confided to Ben that I don't seem that interested in leaving London or in him, and that he's resigned himself to putting thoughts of me to bed—a conclusion I find both promising and problematic.

'You need to let him know how you feel, Luce,' she says. 'You've got him at sixes and sevens. You need to be clear.'

'I just don't think he should assume I'll drop everything here and automatically move to Sydney because that's where he lives.'

'But have you really spoken about that with him?' says Rosie. 'He's got that guy working for him now and he's been spending a fair bit of time in Brisbane and Rocky lately. I'm sure he'd be willing to compromise if you talked about it. I think your issue is that you bloody like him and you're scared out of your wits at the thought of being vulnerable again. I mean, holy shit, Luce, he's put himself on the line for you, hasn't he?'

'Yes.'

'—He's come halfway around the world to say he wants to be with you, and you still second-guess him and have doubts. I think you have to look at the bigger picture. Do you want to settle down with someone? Or do you want to meet another guy you're not quite sure about and keep questioning everything?'

I sigh heavily and she rests her red leather glove on my shoulder as we continue along the pavement in silence.

It isn't long before she starts up again. 'Also, I know I'm not exactly a role model for what I'm about to say, but I think you could do with some good sleeps and three weeks off the booze.'

I nod, knowing she's right.

Then, suddenly, she stops dead and grabs my arm. 'Holy fucking shit, Luce!' she exclaims. 'Look at that!' She points at a streetlight ahead of us.

I follow her gaze and see a poster wrapped around the pole, emblazoned with a picture of Cher and listing dates for her upcoming 'Lovers and Others' world tour. We walk up to read it and see the tour is kicking off in London before heading down under.

Wide-eyed, we focus on the date for Sydney—21 January.

'Denise!' says Rosie at the same time as I say, 'Mum!'

∽

Before Rosie leaves for Dublin, I persuade her to chuck a sickie and we spend the day visiting our favourite London haunts. We start the morning with jam duffins and coffee at Bea's of Bloomsbury near the British Museum, then catch the tube to London Bridge and sample our way around the gourmet food stalls of the Borough Market, before strolling along the South Bank promenade, past the Globe Theatre and the Tate Modern, across Westminster Bridge and into

St James's Park. After backtracking for lunch at the Westminster Arms, we catch a bus to Piccadilly Circus and join the queue outside the Prince of Wales Theatre for a matinee performance of *The Book of Mormon*.

Afterwards, we buy some tea for Rosie's mum at Fortnum & Mason, then head to Battersea and walk across beautiful Albert Bridge, before coming to a stop in front of The Ivy on King's Road. I tell Rosie that as her Christmas present, I've booked us in for afternoon tea and we take selfies of us enjoying champagne and courgette frites among the flowers and finery.

Later that evening, on Putney High Street, I hug Rosie goodbye with a heavy heart and head back to my Airbnb bedsit. Preoccupied, I don't spot Oscar on the front steps until I'm about ten metres away.

'You look a fright!' he says, hopping up as I approach.

'A fright?'

He grins. 'I'm trying out a few British phrases.'

'I don't know if that's the right one to use on a girl!' I reply, feeling infinitely brighter for seeing him. 'Still, I suppose you'd better come in.'

'Nice digs,' he says, when we reach my room.

'Ha! It's awful, isn't it?'

He shrugs and walks into the grotty kitchenette, where he inspects the sad-looking excuse for a kettle before filling it up.

We're quiet for a while as the tea brews, then after he empties the last of the milk into my mug and hands it to me he says, 'Tell me everything you're worried about.'

'Well, for starters I'm worried about you Simpson boys'

ability to make tea,' I say, looking down at the three-quarter-filled mug he's given me.

'What?' he asks, puzzled.

'Tide's half out, Oscar!' I say, tilting it towards him.

He laughs and sits beside me. 'Right, go,' he says.

'Huh?'

'Come on, tell me everything you're worried about.'

'Really?' I say.

'Yep.'

'Okay. I need to get my hair cut.'

'Yep.'

'And find somewhere to live.'

'Uh-huh.'

'I'm running out of shower gel.'

'Right.'

'There's no milk left.'

'Good.'

'Not really.'

'Keep going,' he urges and puts his hand on my shoulder.

I take a deep breath. 'I want to have kids. I don't have much money. Sometimes my left knee catches on me and my hip hurts. I often have trouble sleeping.'

He starts rubbing my back and my eyes fill with tears at his kindness. 'I'm worried the Aussie publishers will reject my manuscript,' I say in a shaky voice. 'And it worries me how much I love you.'

Ever so gently he angles my body towards him and wipes away my tears. 'Luce, you are the most ridiculous, gorgeous, confounding person I've ever met! Nothing could be simpler than us.' He wraps his arms around me and pulls me close.

'I love you, you annoying little wandering vagabond. At times you make me want to tear my hair out, but you also make me feel so alive and content. When I'm with you, I don't want to be anywhere else and that's why I've felt so restless back home. I've missed you something chronic. When you're not around I don't laugh half as much and that's what I want to be—laughing through life with someone. I love how you're always dreaming and always surprising, and I want to have kids too, Luce, I—'

'Oscar,' I say, every fibre of my being in love with him, 'I was sort of hoping you'd say you'd get milk.'

We then kiss like those attractive people captured in photographs on New York street corners, and I feel almost all of my worries melt away.

27

My best Christmas present, apart from waking up next to Oscar in the irresistible moose-patterned long johns he bought for five quid from M&S, is Margie's expression when she looks up from chopping potatoes to see Dennis walk into the kitchen. He smiles at her as he puts two bottles of wine on the bench and then leans down to plant a quick kiss on her cheek, and it's all I can do to stop myself from applauding.

Heartened by their sweet exchange, I think of my last Christmas in Australia, sitting with Glenda in the back of Mum's car listening to a CD of Michael Bublé singing carols blaring on the way to visit relatives in Gracemere. Mum and Dad had bickered for a good half-hour about Dad's latest Christmas present offering, a white wire laundry hamper with castors. Ironically, the horror vision of my parents arguing to 'Deck the Halls' makes me yearn to talk to them, so as

Margie's brother and Oscar clink beers on the patio, I duck into Margie's lounge room and call home from the couch.

I've been holding on to the news about Cher's world tour and, having already posted Mum a tin of The Queen's 90th Birthday Luxury Shortbread Biscuits, I decided to wait until Christmas Day to deliver the show-stopper gift.

～ೞ

There's silence on the other end of the phone when I tell Mum that, for one night only, Cher is coming to Sydney.

'Lucy, can you repeat what you just told me?' she says in disbelief.

After I triple-confirm that the Goddess of Pop has decided to don the suspenders once more and turn back time, and that Rosie and I want to go halves in tickets for her and Dad, Mum starts crying tears of joy. '"I keep coming back because I have no place else to go. What else would I do? I love to sing,"' I say, quoting Cher in an attempt to make her laugh.

Mum tries to speak, but her words are punctuated by tiny sobs and I can't understand what she's saying.

'Mum, don't worry, I'll make sure I get the tickets. Pre-sale's soon and even if it means staying up all night I'll just be online until—'

'It's not that, Luce,' says Mum, her voice breaking. 'I had a lump removed from my breast on Monday.'

Suddenly I'm the one who's speechless.

'I felt a lump when I was in Mongolia and had a biopsy as soon as I got home,' says Mum. 'We got on to it early, thank God.'

'What?! But why didn't you tell me before? I would have . . .' My voice fails me as shock gives way to fear.

'Come on, none of that, Luce—I didn't tell you precisely because I don't want you thinking you have to drop everything and come home. And you don't. It's all going to be okay.' Mum has pulled herself together now and her voice is strong and clear. 'The surgeon's confident he got all the margins and he'll have the pathology results back in no time.'

'Oh, Ma,' I say.

'My dear Lucy . . . The last thing I wanted to do is tell you·on Christmas Day, but then you went and blindsided me with Cher, you naughty girl, and that just tipped me over the edge.'

'How big was it?' I ask.

'Between the size of a marble and a ping-pong ball.'

'Oh, Ma,' I repeat. 'Does catching it early mean it won't ever come back?' I ask, seeking the unrealistic reassurance only a parent can give.

'Yes,' she answers emphatically. 'It's gone now, never to return.'

And because it's my mum, my beautiful, crazy, wonderful mother, I try to believe her.

'I tell you, it hasn't stopped word getting around town, though,' she continues. 'I was only in hospital for forty-eight hours and the fridge was stocked from top to bottom with minestrone and lasagne when I got home. Even Ruth dropped off a chicken casserole, although I don't think I'll be going near that.'

'Ma!' I chuckle, and wipe away tears. 'That was nice of Ruth, Mum!'

'Hm,' she sniffs. 'Good way to knock Brian and me off in one fell swoop too!'

'That would be one *fowl* swoop! Ha!'

I feel brighter when Mum laughs at my silly joke and starts grumbling about Ruth like she always does.

'Don't you think it's time you and Ruth made amends?' I say. 'She went out with Dad forty-two *years* ago!'

'I know, but I've got to keep my guard up, Luce. Brian broke her heart, and I think she's had designs on him ever since.'

'Designs? Are you from a Jane Austen novel?!'

Over Glenda's furious barking, I hear the smile in Mum's voice as she tells me how Glenda has been playing nursemaid, dispensing lots of licks and providing steadfast companionship.

'How's Dad been dealing with it all?'

'He's been very good, actually. We were both shocked at first, of course. But you know Dad, ever practical. He's made my recovery into a project, and has me doing CrossFit for the Over-60s videos he's found on YouTube. He read an article about the healing power of antioxidants and the juicer's always going. To be perfectly honest, if he doesn't start heading out to the farm or the Men's Shed again soon, I'll be locking him downstairs in ours! On the upside, Glenda's lost a few kilos now that Brian's not going past Bernie's as much.'

I cry quietly into the phone, desperately sad at the unbearable possibility of not always hearing Mum prattle on about Dad. I wish I could teleport myself home to share Christmas with them, even if it meant listening to Michael Bublé.

'Anyway, Lucy, that's that and we're not going to worry,' Mum says firmly. 'Oh, I'll tell you who else has been my rock . . .'

'Cher,' I say immediately.

'Well, that's a given. Guess again.'

'Ruth,' I say with a giggle.

'Fat chance,' she says dryly.

'Colleen.'

'Like hell. Although she did drop off a lovely vanilla slice, I shouldn't be mean.'

'I know—Trish from the drumming circle!'

'Nup.'

'Give me a hint, Ma,' I say, stumped.

'Next door,' she sings.

'Helen!' I cry, slapping my hand triumphantly on the couch.

'She's been great, but someone else has too,' she says coyly.

Suddenly the answer hits me, and as the colour rushes into my cheeks, I find myself tongue-tied. Mum fills the silence between us with laughter and I realise she knows Oscar's with me.

ॐ

'I can't believe you were hanging out Mum's undies,' I say to Oscar as we lie together later that night in his room at the Cranley Hotel.

'It was more your Dad's saggy Bonds trunks that had me thinking twice,' he replies, and we both laugh.

'So you *are* here because you *want* to be and not because you're on Her Majesty's Service, aren't you?'

'Of course I'm here because I want to be,' he says, leaning over and kissing my forehead. 'Your mum's like Jenny Brockie off *Insight* or something; she wangles everything out of you. One session on her swinging chair and she knew how much I cared about you. And when Ben said Rosie wasn't completely convinced about your feelings for Joe, Denise told me to grow a pair and tell you how I felt.'

'She never let on she knew about Joe!' I say, surprised. 'And I'm sure she wouldn't have used those words exactly.'

'Well, it was more like "Are you strong enough?"' he says with a grin.

'Probably not,' I quip. 'Joking, Oscar, joking!' I yell as he starts to tickle me.

As I catch my breath, his expression turns serious.

'When your mum told me she had cancer it brought everything about Dad back up. That's when I decided to hire someone to help share my workload and have a break. And then, when I was no longer distracting myself with Bev's Buffet, I realised I'd never forgive myself if there was still a chance we could be together.'

'Oh, Oscar,' I say. 'I'm sorry about your dad.'

'I know, Luce.'

I turn on my side and trace a curl of his hair with my fingers.

'You know, your mum doesn't want you to think you have to come home for her,' he says. 'She wants you to make choices independently of how she is.'

'Mmm,' I respond.

'But not independently of me,' he adds quickly.

'Oscar, do you think Mum'll be okay?' I ask.

'Yeah, Luce,' he says, drawing me closer. 'She'll be okay.'

⁓

Despite Oscar's reassurances, and Margie's happy updates about her dalliances with Dennis, I go through my entire month's mobile budget in two days ringing up Mum. And whenever I get a phone call from home I answer with a leap of anxiety in my stomach, and a tightness in my throat, wondering if this will this be the call where Dad tells me the pathology results are back and the cancer is one of the aggressive types.

On several occasions I greet Mum, my heart clanging against my chest, only to have her ask me how to create a Ticketek account.

Thankfully, Dad puts my mind at rest with a morning call saying the pathology's back and the oncologist has given Mum the all-clear. I'm so relieved I start crying.

'How about bloody Cher, hey?' says Dad, trying to cheer me up. 'S'pose we'll have to look at flights to Brissie soon.'

'No, she's only going to Sydney, Dad.'

'What!' he exclaims. 'What about poor old bloody Queensland?'

I tell him Rosie and I are buying tickets to Cher for both of them, but he says not to be silly, and that it'll be a relief to buy Mum a birthday present she'll actually like for once.

I laugh, remembering the time he gave her a stainless-steel shower stool for her sixtieth; she barely spoke to him for the rest of the day.

When I ask how Mum's been travelling emotionally, I find enormous comfort in Dad's inability to beat around the bush.

'She's been up and down like a yo-yo, love, but that's to be expected. Now that she's got the all-clear she'll be right as rain. God, we could do with some of that here too. It's terribly dry. Bloody awful result in the Ashes, wasn't it?'

28

In the end, my deliberations over whether to return home to Australia sooner rather than later are resolved for me at our first post-Christmas staff meeting at Scribe, when the managing director soberly informs us that the owners have accepted a takeover offer from a major bookstore chain. In a classic English understatement, he adds there may be some 'realignment' of staff.

Over the next few days Penny is told her position is safe, but Margie and me and all the other expats will be losing our jobs. After the initial shock, I'm relieved because, as much as I have to play my own hand at life, sometimes it's liberating to have a couple of cards fall in a certain direction.

When Margie and I clock off from the children's section for the last time, we join Penny, Sally and a few of her Aussie nanny mates for a pint at the Cat's Back. After a couple of drinks, Penny is well and truly three sheets to the wind as she laments the loss of my Aussie-accented Storytime sessions and Margie's outbursts of Afrikaans.

Margie announces she's going to stay on in London, joking she's been in England long enough not to mind the weather anymore, though it's clear her burgeoning romance with Dennis is influencing her decision. With a wink, I tell her I'll be rsvp'ing 'yes' to her and Dennis's wedding braai, and assure Penny I intend to keep writing fiction, promising to let her know if I hear back from any of the Australian publishers I've contacted about my manuscript.

Then, as Penny and I hug each other farewell, I tell her how much I love her and how her belief in me has changed my life. She squeezes me tight and says, 'One day, Lucy, I'll be boasting to everyone, "I know her!"'

Oddly, my most poignant farewell is with Sally, who says I was her dose of Queensland in London and the highlight of her week. She then asks me shyly whether I'd mind if she texted Joe to see what he's up to and I assure her that nothing could make me happier.

~ꔫ~

'Gee, I haven't see you at the pool in a while!' says Dominic Cavendish as I squeeze in beside him at the baggage carousel in Rocky's airport. 'Been too cold for ya?'

'No, I've been living in London for seven months, Dom,' I say with a laugh. 'Bit far away to come for a few laps.'

'Oh, right,' he says, picking up his bag. 'See ya.'

'See ya,' I reply.

As I wait for my battered red suitcase to come into view, I recognise several parents of high school friends; the man from behind the counter at Officeworks; the husband-and-wife team from Newcastle who run Gone Bush; and a burly bloke with a grey beard and buttoned-up shirt patterned with pineapples, who barrels past me to retrieve his swag from the conveyor belt.

'Excuse me, love,' he says gruffly, and I glow with the warmth that comes from touching down on home turf and chuckle at the complete disparity between this terminal and Heathrow.

Amid cries of, 'Gee, she's warm!' I roll my suitcase into the mid-January furnace-like heat, and feel steam rise off the bitumen as I cross over to the passenger pick-up zone. 'How hot is it!' I say to the women beside me and we all laugh, because that's what you do when you're sweating profusely.

Dad's rusty old LandCruiser rumbles in, and I'm so over-joyed to see Glenda's little head panting out the passenger window, I run over and give her a kiss even before Dad hops out of the ute and takes my bag.

'Where's Mum?' I ask, just as Dad says, 'Where's Oscar?'

I smile at the thought that every single member of my damn family seems to be having their own separate love affair with this man. 'He's staying in Sydney for a few days to catch up with things. He'll be up here soon.'

'Very good,' says Dad, buckling his seatbelt. 'Mum's busy making pumpkin scones for when you turn up.'

We're silent for a while as I soak in the vivid blue sky, the feeling of warmth on my arm on the windowsill, the air alive with the screech and call of birds and the scent of star jasmine, the ridiculous sense of space.

'Are you happy to be home, Luce?' asks Dad, breaking into my reverie.

'Yeah, Dad,' I reply. And as we pass the bull statue astride the airport entrance roundabout, the sun glistening off its fibreglass rump, I know in my bones that this time I mean what I say, and that I am happy to be back.

⁓

As soon as Dad pulls up in the driveway, I bolt inside with Glenda. I find Mum in the kitchen setting out a plate of Iced VoVos, her damp togs outlined beneath her cotton dress.

'Oh, Ma!' I say, breaking down at the sight of her freshly combed wet hair. 'I don't want you to die, Ma! I want you to know my kids.'

'Well, hurry up and have them then!' she says with a laugh, rubbing my back as we hug. 'Don't be ridiculous, Luce. Your father's got me healthier than ever with his CrossFit programs and nutri-ninja smoothies or whatever they're called. I did thirty laps at the pool this morning! I would actually consider myself to be superbly fit!'

'Jeez, thirty laps is alright!' I say, wiping away my tears. 'I saw Dom at the airport.'

'Ha! I think he fancies me.' Mum gives me a wink and flicks on the kettle.

I burst into laughter; Mum is definitely back to her normal self.

'God no, I'm not going anywhere,' she continues. 'Particularly not now that I've got VIP tickets to Cher!'

'What? VIP tickets!' I exclaim incredulously.

'Yep, your father splashed out big time, darl. After all, how often do you get the opportunity to have champagne and canapés with Cher?'

'But how did he get those tickets? Wouldn't they have been snapped up in minutes?'

'Oh, don't you worry about Brian and me, Luce! You should have seen us Tuesday morning. Dad was on the website at eight-thirty, ready to swoop at nine.'

'Dad? Buying tickets online?' I say as we move to the kitchen table with our tea.

'Yeah, he's enrolled in a computer course for seniors out at the uni, knows all about USB sticks and control-alt-delete and Facebook—and thankfully he was able to navigate the Ticketek site.'

'Ha! That's hilarious.' I grin. 'Don't go joining up to Facebook, Ma,' I add quickly.

'I spoke with Rosie and she's taken care of your ticket,' she says, ignoring me. 'She's been so good about helping me, the sweetheart. No doubt she'll be around soon.'

I nod and watch the spindly arms of brigalow trees wave about outside in the summer breeze, smiling as the kookaburras break into their familiar cackle.

'How's my lovely Oscar?' says Mum over the birds' raucous laughter.

'He's good, Ma,' I say with a big grin. 'Weren't you conniving over here like Mrs Bennet out of *Pride and Prejudice*!'

'Sometimes you young pups need an old, steady hand to help you see what's what,' she says. 'Particularly you with your horse blinkers on in London, eyes down in your book, head in the clouds. Meanwhile, I've got Oscar on my swinging chair, pouring out his heart and pegging up my bras.'

I put my head on her shoulder in embarrassment.

'It was all just too absurd,' giggles Mum, and we laugh and laugh.

29

The sound of my bedroom door opening stirs me from a jetlagged slumber, and I glance across to see Rosie in her bicycle lycra.

'How are you?' she shouts, flicking on the light and striding over to give me a hug. 'Fucking hot outside!'

Immediately energised by her presence, I tear down the covers and stand up in my pyjamas.

'Hello, Rose! Should we go to the pool?'

⁓

As we kick alongside each other in adjacent lanes, Rosie tells me that Ben's been accepted into Charles Darwin University and is now up in Darwin, scoping out a place for them to live. She says they're going to fly up there permanently after Cher's concert.

'He loves Nightcliff and Rapid Creek, says they're right on the ocean and have some cool troppo houses to rent.'

'Wow, sounds awesome,' I say.

'Yeah, he's having a ball in the Top End. Already has a gang of friends and has been to a few wild parties. We might lock it in for a while, I think.'

I tell Rosie about Oscar helping Mum and she nods like it's old news, saying Mum filled her in over multiple cups of tea on the swinging chair.

'Of course she did,' I reply.

After the pool, Rosie and I relax with prosecco on her balcony. We've got so much to say to each other, that we say nothing, and instead watch clouds of bushfire smoke swirl around the Berserkers, cloaking the town below us in a blanket of thick, soupy air that stings your eyes, catches in your throat and seeps into your clothes.

It's among these mountainside flashes of flames, the dim twinkle of city lights and soundtrack of insects and birds that I finally realise I'm home, and I rest my feet on Rosie's railing and look over at her.

'I can't believe how many lines my hands have all of a sudden,' I say, examining my wrists. 'I just don't know how they got like this.'

'Ha!' says Rosie absently.

'I always quite fancied my hands. Remember Daisy Geraghty from uni? She told me once I could be a hand model.'

'Did she?' Rosie touches her throat. 'I'm worried about my neck. I think it's going to go next.'

'Tell me about it—I turn thirty-three in a fortnight!'

'I know! I'll have to buy you some heavy-duty wrinkle cream . . . Actually, wasn't there a range in the latest Home-Hints catalogue?'

'Yeah, I titled it: *Firm Solutions for Thirty-Somethings*!'

When our giggles have subsided, I propose a toast to Rosie and her impending move to Darwin, and she proposes a toast to me and my move to the cockroach capital.

⁕

'Are you sure Oscar and Helen don't want any, love?' Mum asks casually a few nights later as Rosie and I arrive home with takeaway Chinese.

'No, Mum, he's been over here almost as much as he's been there,' I reply. 'Helen will want some time with him.'

'Not sure what that means!' Mum says archly, meeting my eyebrow raise with one of her own.

'So tell us about Darwin, Rosie,' says Dad, peering at her over his reading glasses. 'When do you leave? They sink a lot of piss up there, you know,' he adds.

Rosie, who is fetching bowls from the cupboard, ignores this observation. 'Ben and I head up next week from Sydney, after Cher.'

'Cher! Bloody hell!' says Dad, sitting up in his chair. 'While I've got you both here, we need to talk strategy.'

Rosie looks at me, bemused, and I shrug my shoulders.

'Oh yes!' Mum cries. 'Now, hang on, let me get my list, Brian.' She bustles off and returns with a clipboard.

'Right, first of all, timing. The concert's at seven, but of course you and I have got champagne and canapés with Cher first, Brian.' She gives him a fond smile. 'That's at six.'

'Right, six. So, let's work back—we have to get from our hotel to the concert, avoid traffic, allow for any hiccups or delays ...' He pauses, thinking. 'We'll have to get there by two.'

'Two!' I exclaim. 'Dad!'

'Oh, Lucy, they're all half mad down there,' Dad explains. 'Even two could be pushing it fine.'

'Your father's right,' says Mum, nodding. 'You know, you start off in Sydney and you think you've got all the time in the world, and before you know it, your taxi's taken a wrong turn and suddenly you're in bumper-to-bumper traffic going in the opposite direction. No thank you! Not when you've got a date with Cher! Oh, I'm almost in a cold sweat at the thought of missing it.'

Rosie and I look at each other again and our shoulders shake with laughter.

'Well, you and Dad are the chosen ones, you can go along at the crack of dawn,' I say, still chuckling as I snap the lids off our Chinese. 'I'll Uber in with Rosie.'

30

'There's nothing wrong with your face,' says the agent, looking across at me from her computer screen. 'How old are you?'

'Thirty-two.'

'Okay, still got a couple of years left,' she says, glancing at me momentarily. 'Can you sing or dance?'

'No.'

'Mmm. Could be a problem.'

I watch her massively long fake nails strike away at the keyboard and wonder whether she's even hitting the right letters.

'Now, about the way you sound . . .'

'Yes?'

'Would you consider going to voice classes?'

'No.'

'I see. Okay; well, lovely to meet you, Lucy.'

'Yes, you too, Jessica,' I say, and shake her outstretched hand. Then, because I can't resist, and know that I'll never see her again, I call out, 'Hooray!' in my broadest Aussie accent as I leave.

I step out of the A1 Talent Agency office into Darlinghurst's busy Oxford Street feeling flatter than a red-bellied black snake. I'd arrived in Sydney a few days earlier than the others to hang out with Oscar and start looking for work. He planned to return to Rocky with me after Cher's concert to help me pack up, and then we would both drive down to Sydney in my car. I still hadn't heard back from the Aussie publishers, and so I resolved to meet Sydney's flashy lights with my plan B: get represented as a TV presenter and land a sweet role hosting documentaries about the unusual wildlife on exotic islands. The problem was that neither Jessica Moore from the A1 Talent Agency nor the several other production companies I met with had any interest in acquiring my services.

Now, as I walk along the pavement, the weight of this unfamiliar city lying heavily upon my shoulders, I permit myself to engage in a fully fledged pity party.

Sydney is too big! Yes, I know Oscar's here, but I have no history in this town. These streets could swallow me up and no-one would know. Nobody loves me here, besides Oscar. I don't know which side of the street to stand on to catch the bus I'm meant to take. I don't even know which direction I should be heading. It takes too much effort to learn all of these things again. I've moved around too much. I'm too tired.

I then look up and see the bus I'm supposed to catch arrive, and when I ask the driver if I'm heading in the right direction for Paddington, he says yes. I grin and take my seat, thinking how beautiful Sydney looks in the afternoon light.

ⲟⲉⲟ

Later that evening, as I force Oscar to watch an episode of *The Secret Life of Babies*, my mobile pings with an email. I recognise the address as being from one of the Aussie publishers. I immediately hide my phone under a cushion and bury my head in Oscar's lap.

'I can't face it,' I say. 'I can't.'

'What's happened?' he asks and presses pause on his laptop.

'One of the publishers has replied,' I say, my voice muffled against his jeans.

'Well, let's see what they said.' He reaches beneath the cushion for my phone and I slap his wrist and take my mobile into the kitchen.

'Alright,' I say to myself and take a deep breath. 'Just get it over with.'

I open the email from Alice Callaghan at Judge & James and quickly scan it.

Then I place the phone on the bench and my hands on my head as tears of relief spring to my eyes.

'She wants to read it!' I call to Oscar. 'My manuscript! She wants me to send the entire manuscript! There's no "all the best!" There's "hope to hear from you soon!"'

Oscar is by my side in an instant. 'Fucking brilliant! I'm so proud of you, Luce!'

Almost immediately, my jubilation is replaced by anxiety. 'Oh man, what if she doesn't like it?' I say.

'Nup, cut it out,' he says, putting his arms around me. 'She's going to love it. She's going to fucking love it.'

⤜⟀⤛

Three days after sending Alice Callaghan my manuscript, I receive an email from her saying that she really enjoyed reading *Diamonds in the Dust* and hopes that we can work together and turn it into an amazing novel. She says she thinks I have the talent to do so. I almost fall off my chair, then read that she's free for about half an hour in two days' time, and would I like to meet her for a coffee near their publishing house in Surry Hills?

Oh my god, I think. A real-life publisher likes my manuscript and wants to meet me! I then google her and discover she's a highly respected trailblazer in the publishing world, and has fostered the careers of many Australian writers. I read her email again and again, then print it out and stick it on the fridge, just to make sure that it exists.

⤜⟀⤛

'But what does it all really mean?' asks Dad, when I call home after returning from a celebratory dinner with Oscar.

'I don't know, Dad. I don't know. But it has to be good that she's written back to me.'

'For Christ's sake, have that coffee with her before she leaves! She mightn't even be in that job next week!'

'Don't worry, Dad,' I say. 'I think Alice is genuine. I think she's actually going to help me.'

'Well, we'll see,' he mutters. 'Keep us posted.'

⤜⟀⤛

Alice greets me with a hug and her warm manner immediately puts me at ease. She asks me about the setting for *Diamonds in the Dust* and I tell her how I first became fascinated with the gemfields during a school trip in grade seven. She smiles and says she grew up around Bendigo and was impressed with my research and evocative characters.

'You make us care about them all,' she says. 'And that's not an easy thing to do.' She then tells me that she thinks the manuscript is wonderful and she'd like to offer me a publishing deal.

When we leave the café a little while later, I am proud of the dignified way in which I've handled the meeting; I didn't get carried away and promise her my firstborn or even gush too much. As I hold out my hand to say goodbye, Alice hugs me instead, saying with a laugh that she's never met anyone more subdued on being offered a contract.

That does it. 'You're the best person ever, Alice!' I gush. 'I think you're the absolute best!'

ꞩℯↄ

A key part of Mum's Cher strategy involves us all having a good breakfast the morning of the concert, and so Rosie and I now sit elbow to elbow with Mum and Dad around a table in the Westfield food court.

'I wonder what she'll be wearing?' muses Rosie.

'Hardly anything would be my guess!' I reply.

'See that bloke over there?' says Dad, gesturing not so subtly at a young man in a suit waiting for coffee. 'He'd only have an apple in his briefcase. They're all pretenders.'

'What are you going to say to her, Denise?'

'I will just be my sparkling self, Rosie,' replies Mum with a grin.

'Oh, come on, Ma. I know you've rehearsed what you'll say to Cher.'

'Yes, you're right. You know me too well, Lucy. I will simply say, "Cher—you're an inspiration. Because of you, I often ask myself, *Am I strong enough?*, and because of you I can answer every time, *Yes, Denise, you are.*'

'That's beautiful, love,' says Dad, patting her wrist.

'Well,' says Rosie, pushing aside her plate, 'I'd just like to say, how bloody lucky are we? We're sitting in the best fucking food court in Australia—sorry, Denise,' she adds quickly. 'Lucy's just realised her lifelong dream and is going to be a published author, Ben and I are moving to paradise tomorrow and Denise is going to meet her pop idol tonight.'

'What about me?' asks Dad.

'You, Brian, are a legend—for shouting us breakfast.'

'Thank you, Rosie,' says Mum. 'That was lovely. Alright, Brian. Let's get some nuts for the road. Plenty of water. How much cash have you got on you?'

'God, it sounds like you're heading off on safari!' laughs Rosie.

'Oh Ma, you should quote a Cher quote back to Cher!' I say suddenly, snapping back into the conversation.

'Which one?' asks Rosie.

'What about—"A girl can wait for the right man to come along but in the meantime that still doesn't mean she can't have a wonderful time with all the wrong ones!"'

'What are the brothers up to today?' asks Mum, ignoring me.

'Oscar's in at Bev's Buffet HQ.'

'Then he's helping Ben move out of his unit,' adds Rosie. 'Boring!'

ঙ৶

After recommending I change out of my tight jeans and into my tighter ones, Rosie orders an Uber and we head to Allianz Stadium to join the thousands of Cher worshippers filing into their seats.

'This is actually really exciting!' I say, my hand on Rosie's wrist.

'You have no fucking idea how excited I am, Luce,' she replies.

'I can't believe that at this very moment, Mum and Dad are having champers with Cher!'

Rosie laughs. 'Your dad with Cher—classic! Your parents have become pretty tight again after Denise's scare, hey?'

'Yeah, really tight.' I nod, feeling a rush of gratitude— that Mum is okay, that she and Dad are closer than ever, that we are all here, now.

On the dot of eight-thirty, the stadium descends into darkness and the only sound to be heard is the beating of a lone drum. Then the drumming picks up in pace and intensity, whipping the crowd into a frenzy of expectation, until Cher suddenly appears from above—suspended in sequined suspenders, floating on a cloud of crystals.

Of course we're all completely beside ourselves, crying and cheering and whistling, and as Cher welcomes everyone to her world tour and breaks into 'Believe', I can only imagine the state Mum's in.

Soon after, Cher does a costume change into Pocahontas Cher and has us all dancing in our seats to 'Gypsies, Tramps and Thieves', then belting out the words to 'Just Like Jesse James' while she straddles a flaming rocket ship onstage, before being launched ten feet in the air and donutting above the crowd.

I feel my phone buzz in my pocket, and when I manage to tear my gaze away from Cher's feathered headpiece to look at the screen, I see that it's Dad. I answer just as the latest round of applause dies down.

'Lucy!' he says urgently. 'You've got to come quickly—it's Mum.'

My heart leaps in my chest. 'Mum? What's the matter?'

'Just come now, we're right down the front, Row AA.'

'I've got to go,' I say to Rosie. 'There's something wrong with Mum.'

She squeezes my hand and I race down one of the centre aisles, the crowd going wild as Cher sings the first lines of 'I Got You Babe'.

Has it all been too much for Mum? I wonder, my stomach churning. Has she had a heart attack or something? Has the cancer recurred and they were waiting until tonight to tell me?

'She's backstage,' says Dad sombrely when I finally reach him standing at the end of the row.

'Backstage?' I echo, but before I can say anything else, Dad pushes me towards a security guard, who takes me by the hand and leads me out a side door, up some stairs and into one of the wings of the main stage. In a daze, I then turn to see Mum off to one side, grinning at me with a microphone in her hand.

'Mum,' I begin, dumbfounded, 'what—?' But before I can manage to finish my sentence, a crew member pins a lapel microphone to my t-shirt, and in the next second Cher alights from her rocket ship and says, 'Ladies and gentlemen, I'd like to take a little pause now and introduce one very special lady. She is a survivor, a lioness and a warrior for every goddamn gorgeous woman in this stadium tonight. She's on a mission here in Sydney. She is . . . Denise Crighton!'

Mum then steps from the shadows into the spotlight and, as the crowd roars, takes a bow onstage.

'Thank you, Cher,' she says, as I attempt to pick my jaw up from the floor. 'Does anyone out there have a lighter? It's time to put your lighters up, people.'

The crowd erupt in delighted laughter and immediately obey Mum's command, illuminating the stadium with thousands of flickering flames.

'Oh, isn't that stunning, Cher,' remarks Mum, then continues, 'Look, Cher, you're a busy woman and the show must go on, so I'll make this quick.' In a stern voice she says, 'Lucy, come out here, please.' Then, when I don't move, she adds, 'Now!'

Sheepishly, I step onto the stage and blink into the floodlights.

'Oh,' gasps Cher, 'she's beautiful!'

I then realise, over thunderous applause and wolf-whistles, that I'm being projected onto a thirty-metre-high screen to forty-five thousand people.

'Um, hello, Cher,' I say. 'I like your quotes.' I look at my feet, embarrassed to hear my every word amplified.

'See!' Mum appeals to the crowd. 'See what we're dealing with?'

The stadium is filled with fits of laughter, and it occurs to me that I don't know what's more ridiculous—the fact that I'm standing on stage at a Cher concert, or that Mum's working the room.

'Mum, what are you doing up here?' I ask, foolishly thinking that by whispering I won't be heard.

'Moral support!' she yells, addressing not me but her adoring audience, and receiving an appreciative ovation in return. 'Cher, quite frankly, this daughter of mine might be a journalist, but sometimes she can't communicate!'

'Can't you, babe?' asks Cher, who has surreptitiously changed into Catwoman Cher and now slinks across the stage to join me and Mum. 'What's the matter?' she asks playfully as I look at her, stupefied. 'Cat got your tongue?'

There is a chorus of hysterical laughter, and I grin hopelessly at Cher's glossy leather torso, realising I could soon be subject to Australia's greatest-ever heckling.

'She's fucking unreal!' I then hear Rosie yell from the crowd, and I break into a big smile.

'That's more like it, honey,' says Cher, giving my backside a friendly flick with her whip. 'Could we have a spotlight on Mr Simpson?'

Oh, fuck me! I think as Oscar's face suddenly fills the screen.

'Whoo!' exclaims Cher, fanning herself. 'I've already won an Oscar, but I wouldn't mind getting my hands on that one!'

I watch Oscar's cheeks redden, and recognise a corner of Ben's head as he tries to get in the frame.

I stare at Mum in horror, as all the pennies drop, fully aware now of what she's up to, and plead with her silently to make it stop.

Mum, though, appears to be picking up steam, calling on the crowd to be quiet.

I look out at the ocean of darkness, which has now become so deathly silent that you could hear a pin drop, and watch as the giant screen splits in two, revealing live pictures of both Oscar and me.

'Lucy,' he says, 'I know there are things about me which annoy you. I sleep with the fan on, even when it's cold, because I like the noise. I go for Manly, and I don't agree it's normal that you spoon your kelpie. But I love you, and if you can put up with me, Lucy Crighton, will you marry me?'

The atmosphere is electric with tension, and I briefly consider bolting, but then Cher sashays closer to me and says softly, so that only I can hear, 'Until you're ready to look foolish, you'll never have the possibility of being great.' She then adds, with a wink, 'Think carefully, babe—words are like weapons, they wound sometimes.'

I smile and, feeling enormously empowered by this seventy-one-year-old feline demi-god, take a deep breath and say, 'Mum and Rosie and all my self-help books told me that no-one was just going to turn up on my doorstep— but you did, Oscar. And I fell in love with you as soon as I saw you.'

The crowd now tear the house down with riotous cheering, and as I raise my voice to speak over them, and see Oscar's face smiling down at me from the huge screen, it feels strangely like I'm talking just to him.

'I am by no means perfect either, and if you can bear my complete lack of direction, and the fact that sometimes my head is so far up in the clouds that I may as well be hanging out with the Care Bears, and that our children will go for Queensland in the State of Origin, then I'd love to marry you, Oscar! Of course! Yes!'

31

On my twenty-first birthday, Dad presented me with a novelty-sized syringe, telling me to get a big dose of reality. Twelve years later, as we sit around the kitchen table and I blow out the candles on a strawberry jam and cream sponge, he bestows on me another gift.

'Luce, this is very special,' he says gruffly, placing a thin rectangular box in my hands. 'Treasure it, please.'

I look across at Oscar and catch his grin, before opening the box to reveal a beautifully handcrafted timber pen.

'That won first prize in the Men's Shed woodturning comp, you know! It's all Burdekin plum, from the farm,' he says proudly as I hold up the pen. 'Got old Gordon down in the mall to engrave it for me.' He takes the pen from me and inspects it closely. 'He did a good job too,' he remarks.

'Give it back to her, Brian!' exclaims Mum. 'She hasn't read it yet!'

'Oh, shit—here you go,' says Dad, returning the pen.

'Read it out, Luce,' says Oscar.

'*Lucy Crighton—Author.*'

'That's for autographing copies of *Devils on Horseback*, love,' says Dad.

'No, Brian—it's *Sapphires in the Sky*!' cries Mum.

'You're both wrong—it's *Diamonds in the Dust*!' says Oscar, and I grin at him fondly, touched that he always remembers the things that are important to me.

'Oh, I've got something for you two, actually,' I say, hopping up. 'I'll be back in a sec.'

I stride into the hallway but then stop abruptly, realising it was about twelve months ago that I was last lingering by these walls, listening to Mum and Rosie exchange whispers of worry.

Now, I'm delighted to observe that I've completely vanished from the agenda, and that the topic of my welfare has been replaced by an animated discussion about the best time of year to go whale watching.

Unlike the Lucy who was skulking around this doorway a year ago, I'm no longer feeling sorry for myself and, best of all, I have renewed confidence in my ability to love again. And now that I am in love, the questions in my mind have also become Oscar's questions, and the anxieties I entertain can be shut down with his decisive words and pragmatic acts of kindness.

'Here you go!' I return from my bedroom with a large rectangular gift and place it in front of Mum on the kitchen table. She tears off the wrapping to reveal a wooden plaque engraved with the words: *Where there's tea, there's hope.*

'Oh, Lucy,' she says, standing up to hug me. 'Isn't that gorgeous. I love it! Where will it go?' Her eyes flit around the room before settling on mine, and in her meaningful look, I know the answer.

Oscar and Dad and I trail behind Mum into the lounge room, and stop in front of the framed photo of Cher.

'Are you sure about this, Denise?' asks Dad gravely as we look up at the picture.

'Yes,' she says firmly. 'She got Lucy and Oscar together and that's all I'd asked for. It's time.'

'What will you do with her?' asks Oscar quietly, putting his arm around me.

'Well, it's a limited edition print—from her first concert back in '84. It would be worth quite a lot, I suspect.' She turns to face Dad. 'Brian, you can have her for the Black Dog Ball you've got coming up. Auction her off and raise some money for the Men's Shed.' She turns back to address the poster. 'Thank you, Cher—you've been good to me.'

As Mum speaks, I watch Dad's expression soften.

'That's a lovely gesture, Denise,' he says, his voice distinctly unsteady. 'Very thoughtful of you.'

I look from him to Mum and decide I'd better break this show up.

'Come on, Dad,' I say, and pull across a chair from the dining room table. 'Let's get it up there.'

With great care, he passes Cher down into Mum's out-stretched arms and replaces her with my plaque. We then all step back and silently admire it.

∽

'Should we send out a twitter about this? Or we could all update our status!' says Dad excitedly the next morning, clearly trying out the new terminology he's learnt from his computer course on Oscar, me and Mum as we walk with Glenda beside the Fitzroy. He's become so proud of himself, the Rocky chapter of the Men's Shed have appointed him their social media person.

'You don't really tweet about moving from one town to another, Dad,' I reply.

'Yes you do!' cries Oscar. 'I tweeted this morning about you moving to Sydney!'

'Oh,' I say and grin at him. 'Okay then.'

When I look back at the path, I see Ruth charging towards us, her headphones in and her eyes down, not noticing that Mum and Dad have stopped in their tracks. Oscar takes my hand as we step aside and watch the three of them now staring at each other, facing off like cowboys in some spaghetti western.

'Ruth,' says Mum eventually.

'Denise,' she replies.

'Ruth,' says Dad politely.

'Brian.'

'Look, Ruth, I know you and I haven't seen eye to eye for the past forty-two years . . .' says Mum. She swallows hard. 'But I do appreciate you dropping off that chicken casserole a few weeks ago. It was delicious.'

Oscar and I swivel to look at Ruth as she sucks in air through her teeth.

'Denise, first of all, let's get one thing clear: I'm not in love with Brian. To be honest, I never was, and the day you took him off my hands was actually one of the best days of my life.'

'Steady on, Ruth,' says Dad.

'But you seemed hell-bent on making me your nemesis, Denise, and I kind of enjoy playing that role, so I went with it. But the fact is your cancer scare gave me a real shake-up, and that's why I've bought these bloody sandshoes and am pounding the pavement. I saw how you bounced back and, to be frank, you're an inspiration to me and Colleen.' She scuffs at the gravel with her shiny white sneaker. 'I'm willing to call a truce, Denise. However, if you'd like to continue being my arch rival, I'd be happy with that too.' She nods at Mum and Dad, then replaces her headphones and turns on her heel.

'Ruth!' yells Mum. She starts to jog after her. 'Wait!'

Ruth turns around and she and Mum hug to our awkward applause—and I find myself supremely relieved that, unlike the time I broke down in the lounge room eight months ago, we are not clapping me.

⌒e⌒

'Hey, before we start packing the car, do you mind if I go for a drive?' I say to Oscar. 'There's a few people I want to say goodbye to.'

'Yeah, sure,' he says. 'I'll be at Mum's. I promised her I'd fix the clothesline—it's still giving her trouble.'

We grin, remembering that first night we got to know each other in Helen's backyard.

'See you soon, Luce,' he says.

Glenda jumps in the passenger seat and we reverse out of Mum and Dad's oh-so-familiar driveway. I turn left out of their street and head up the range, the blue silhouette of the Berserkers dwarfing the north-side of town below.

Now that I'm leaving, Rocky suddenly seem delightful. The towering gums and mango trees that line the road, standing so starkly against the blue sky that they could be cut-outs, now strike me as old friends. I see everything with an open heart—the wide streets; the screeching parrots and cockatoos wheeling across the sky; the butterflies flitting past; the beautiful timber Queenslanders; and the roundabouts dotted with statues of bulls. Rockhampton will always be home—but it's time for me to move on and make a new start with Oscar.

And so I wind down my window as I drive down the range, yelling out, 'Goodbye, Bernie's pie van! Goodbye, my old school friends pushing your little babes in prams! Goodbye, bull statues, and utes with dogs in the back, and trains that appear out of nowhere! Goodbye, Colleen at Bits 'n' Pizzas and Video Ezy and Romancing the Rock and the Bottle O! Goodbye, Ruth and your one-woman carwash on the corner of Fitzroy and Albert!'

I look wistfully at the cattle trucks on Gladstone Road; at the drivers who beep and wave to me at the traffic lights; at the splashes of bougainvillea that colour the streets. I say goodbye to life in the country, and as I drive around and sing out my farewells, I recognise a shift in my perspective. All of these sights don't suffocate me anymore. They just are what they are—signs of life in the small, sunny town where I grew up.

I save my final farewell for Rosie's place. Pulling up opposite her unit, I find it strange to see her bike missing from the balcony, and a For Sale sign in the yard.

'Goodbye, my mate,' I say with a shaky smile. 'See you sometime in Darwin.' My eyes cloud with tears as I look at her railing and grin, remembering my crazy best friend and me in Rocky, and the courage she gave me to commit. 'Goodbye!'

Epilogue
One year later ...

Glenda nestles her head in my lap and sighs before closing her eyes. I smile and pat the damp fur between her ears, then reach behind me for the sunscreen and dab some on the pink patch of skin at the tip of her snout. She's so tired from bounding up and down in the waves, chasing after the jumping baitfish, that she doesn't flinch for a second as I rub in the cream.

'Hello little Rhonda,' I say, as our staffie, who Oscar adopted from a shelter in Sydney, runs over and licks my feet with a sandy tongue. 'Are you back from your trip with the boys? What did you think of Dad's new fence?'

I turn around to see Dad, Oscar and Ben walk through the gate that leads onto the beach, and then glance across at Rosie, sunbaking on a towel beside me, the latest Home-Hints catalogue shading her face.

'You've got some devoted girls there, don't you?' says Mum as she walks up the beach towards us, wringing wet and wearing the same faded coral seahorse swimmers she'd loaned Rosie the last time we were all together at Dad's farm, about twelve months ago.

'Ma, I'm seriously shouting you some new togs when my book comes out,' I say.

'It is all actually happening, Luce, isn't it?' asks Dad, bending down to rummage around in his picnic basket.

'Yes, Dad, I can assure you one hundred percent it's happening. I just spoke with Alice yesterday and we're on track for a June launch.'

'So, about six months,' says Mum, then pulls at the elastic straps on her shoulders. 'I could probably get another six months out of these.'

'How's the new fence looking, Dad?' I ask.

'Bloody beautiful,' he says, pouring water from his thermos into enamel mugs. 'The boys thought it was just marvellous.'

I smile at Oscar when Rhonda jumps up and claws at his board shorts and he takes hold of her paws and pretends to dance.

'Aren't you tired after your big adventure?' he says, lowering his face to hers. She barks at him excitedly before sprinting down to the water's edge, where Helen is standing, calling her name.

Oscar squints into the distance as she streaks across the sand, then shakes his head at me. 'I think I rescued Australia's most energetic staffie.'

'Help me, Rhonda!' I grin.

'Right, enough of that,' says Rosie, flinging the catalogue from her face and sitting up straight. 'I'm gonna be red as a lobster if I keep lying there.'

'You're already a bit sun-kissed,' says Ben, leaning down and kissing her.

'Why don't you ever kiss me like that, Brian?' asks Mum.

'What's that, you want a fishing line?' replies Dad, jiggling teabags across several cups.

Rosie and I look at each other and laugh and Mum shakes her head in dismay. 'He's becoming deaf as a post, that man.'

'Well, who wants a tea?' says Dad.

'I will, Dad,' I call out.

'Sounds good,' says Oscar, and he walks over to retrieve two cups for us.

'Tea!' exclaims Rosie. 'Only if it's a Long Island iced tea! Ben, can you crack open those Peronis while you're up?'

'Watch out, Glenda,' I say as Oscar hands a tea down to me and I spot Rhonda racing towards us, with Helen trailing behind. 'Think I'll just get up.' I take hold of Oscar's outstretched arm and shake the sand from my dress.

'Here you go, Luce,' says Ben, offering me a beer.

'Nah—I'm right, thanks, Ben.'

'Phew!' says Helen, wiping her brow as she nears us. 'A cold drink would be lovely, thank you, Ben.' She takes the beer from his hand.

'Doesn't anyone want a bloody tea?' says Dad. 'I've made eight cups here!'

'There's not even eight of us in total, Brian,' says Mum, walking over to him. 'But I'll have a tea. Thank you, darling!'

'So, what did you settle on for the book title in the end, Luce?' asks Dad shooing Glenda and Rhonda off the picnic blanket and sitting down.

'I haven't settled on anything, but I need to come up with something by the end of the week or I'm in big strife!'

'Why didn't Alice like your original bloody title? What was it—*Heroine of the Highlands*?

'*Diamonds in the Dust* was already taken, Dad, so we need another title.'

'Alright, well, let's see . . . It's about horses, isn't it?'

'No, it's got nothing to do with horses!' I laugh as Rosie giggles too.

'It's a sweeping multi-generational family saga set on the gemfields,' Oscar inserts helpfully.

'Alright, well, how about *Strike It Rich!* or *Find A Fortune!*' says Dad.

'They sound like game shows hosted by Warren Buffett,' I reply.

'I'd watch it too if he did a gameshow,' says Dad. 'Well, what have you buggers come up with?'

'I thought of *How it All Pans Out*—you know, like panning for gold? Or, for a bit of humour, *The Family Jewels*!' Helen chortles.

'Mmm,' says Oscar doubtfully.

'I quite like *Fields of Gold*,' says Mum.

'But Sting's all over that,' Ben points out.

'I can't seem to get past Kanye with "Gold Digger",' Oscar says, chuckling. Then, as I glare at him, he adds quickly, 'But I'm always thinking about it.'

'Well, maybe something will come when we're not thinking about it,' says Rosie, draining the last of her beer and standing. 'Let's play touch. And sorry, Luce, but there's no question you two are New South Wales. You can't move to Sydney and expect there to be no consequences.'

'Oh, I might sit it out, Rosie,' I say, glancing across at Oscar and knowing I'm about to smile. 'I'm feeling a bit tired.'

'Hang on,' she says, narrowing her eyes at me. 'Lucy Crighton never turns down a game of touch footy—or a beer, for that matter . . .'

As the others turn to look at me I grin. 'Yep, she's on to us—I'm pregnant!'

'Oh, Lucy!' says Mum, running over to give me a hug. 'Congratulations, darling! That's wonderful news.'

'Yes, congratulations, Luce,' says Dad, kissing me as Helen hugs Oscar. 'We'll have to buy some mini enamel teacups, hey?'

'Well done, big fella,' says Ben, slapping Oscar's back.

Helen and I embrace, then I step into Rosie's hug, my eyes filling with tears as we silently hold on to each other.

'When are you due?' asks Ben.

'Twelfth of June,' replies Oscar.

'Yeah,' I say, 'would you believe the due date is a couple of days before my book's launched? They're both coming out in the same week!'

'Is that right?' says Mum. 'Brian, as soon as we get home, let's look at flights.' Mum's eyes are flashing with purpose. 'You'll need to call Lenny and Max, Luce. They'll be thrilled.'

'I know.' I smile. 'I'll ring them tonight.'

'So now we've got to think of a name for the book *and* the baby!' says Oscar with a grin.

'Just call them both Rosie,' says Rosie, flipping open the esky lid and passing me a soda water, then handing stubbies to everyone else.

'Here's cheers to Lucy and Oscar, soon to be a mum and dad!' she says, and we all clink our bottles together, sending Rhonda into a renewed state of excited barking.

⁊ℯↄ

'Where'd you get those cool sunnies?' I ask Rosie after lunch as we bob about in the ocean.

'Online—UNIQLO. That's the only thing about Darwin,' she adds. 'Costs a fair bit to get stuff posted there.'

'But otherwise you're loving it, hey?'

'Yeah, it's bloody awesome! It's just like no other place in Australia. A totally different feel up there.'

'How much longer has Ben got to go?'

'About eighteen months. He loves the course. And Fannie Bay Dental's good. No formal fucking feedback procedure, which is a relief.'

I laugh and say, 'Ah, London.'

As we float on our backs and watch the seagulls swoop and dive for the occasional jumping fish, I ask Rosie, 'Do you and Ben ever hear from Joe?'

'No, not really. Sometimes he likes Ben's posts on Facebook. I did see a picture of him with Sally the other day,' she says, looking across at me. 'Think they've hooked up.'

'That's good,' I say. 'That's great! They're both lovely.'

'Yeah,' she says. 'Hey, in your book, there's two daughters in the family on the gemfields, isn't there? And one of them's a bit wild?'

'Yep,' I reply.

'How about *Two Birds, One's Stoned*?'

'Ha! I like it. Maybe that can be the name for our joint memoir one day?'

'Hey!' She grins across at me as we both stand. 'I cut all that out last week!'

I laugh and put my arm around her. 'You know I wouldn't be where I am now if it wasn't for you.'

'Yes you would,' she says, smiling. 'You just might not have had as much fun along the way.'

'Not half as much fun!' I exclaim. 'Rosie, I love y—'

'I know, mate!' she says, splashing me with water. 'I know you love me.'

'I love UNIQLO,' I say, laughing. 'I was going to say I love UNIQLO.'

Acknowledgements

It's been quite the journey for me in writing this book and there are a few people I'd like to thank for helping me along the way.

Firstly to my parents Janny and Wayne. Thank you for all the love and laughter and the ability to appreciate the ridiculous and silly moments of life. The hilarious chaos growing up and the confidence to laugh at ourselves was one of the greatest gifts you gave us.

Thank you also to my extended family, including my 102-year-old grandfather Dave, and siblings Nick, Carl, Sam and Sally who were very excited for me to become a published author and have always been proud of my creative pursuits. I know that my grandmas, Eileen and Mary, would also have been thrilled. Thanks to my sister-in-law Betina for coming up with the title, and a particular thanks to my little sis Sal, who never failed to respond to my novel-related texts, even when they were at midnight and asking, 'Should the girls buy Calippos or Golden Gaytimes from Red Rooster?'

For all my friends, who've been so happy for me to get where I hoped to be with *Girl In Between*, you are superstars and I'm lucky to have you. A particular thanks to Brooke Carrigan, Alice Harriott, Kelly Evans and Camille Banks who sometimes acted as silent editors and never tired of hearing me update them on my word count! Thank you to Suz Lambert and Kath Crocker in the UK, and to Shannon Byrne and the Irish gang who helped me meet some major deadlines in between the *craic*.

Thanks to *The Project*, ABC Radio, Saxton Speakers Bureau, Brisbane Writers Festival, my former high school The Cathedral College, Duchesne College and QUT for supporting my ambitions over the past years. I grew up in Rocky, and I'd like to thank the community there. My book is for you and everyone in regional Australia who has a big dream in a small town.

I benefited from the advice of fellow writers and would like to thank Suzanne Leal, Rebecca Sparrow, Benjamin Law, Rohan Wilson, Kirsty Brooks, Christine Retschlag, Sam Carmody, Paula Ellery, Don Reiman and the Queensland Writers Centre. Thanks also to UK comedian John Bishop for the chats and encouragement.

I first began writing my manuscript, originally titled *Rocky Road*, in 2013, and I would not be writing these acknowledgements four years later if it weren't for *The Australian*/Vogel's Literary Award, for which I was shortlisted in 2016. I will never forget your phone call, Annette Barlow! A massive thanks to you and your fellow judges for opening up a new world of opportunity to me, and to Allen & Unwin for taking me on and supporting me on this writing journey. I'm thrilled to tell people that I'm with you! A particular thanks to editor Ali Lavau for your brilliant feedback and suggestions; Genevieve Buzo and Sarina Rowell for your expert editorial eyes, and Henrietta Ashton, whose wondrous emails set this whole ball rolling.

Finally, it's hard to find the right words to convey just how thankful I am to Louise Thurtell. I first met Louise on a fortuitous Sydney evening at the Vogel's Award party atop the Allen & Unwin Terrace, and I will remember it as one of the best nights ever!

Louise had faith in me and my writing from the get-go, and never once doubted my ability to transform *Girl in Between* from a novella of 38,000 words to a manuscript of over 80,000 words—something I never thought I could do.

Louise, thank you for everything—for championing me as a debut author, for cheering me from the sidelines when I was developing the story and for guiding *Girl in Between* in the right direction. I've had the time of my life working with you (and many laughs!) and it's an honour to call you my publisher, editor and friend.